Fair Game

Damon did not avert his eyes as Katy Snow descended the bookroom ladder, her derrière wiggling as seductively as any man could wish. Why should he? His mother might be fooled, but the girl was a homeless waif who should not have risen higher in the household than parlor maid. Yet now she stood before him proudly, hands primly folded in front of a gown that was as fine as any lady's.

She was shockingly lovely. Wisps of pale gold curls framed an oval face marked by a patrician nose above a pink and inviting mouth. In short, a picture to warm a man's dreams.

And his bed.

That was it, of course—the reason he must banish her from the library. He was being noble, eschewing temptation. For his sake, as well as hers.

But what the devil was he thinking? The chit was a servant, and so he would treat her. Katy, the girl the cat dragged in, that's what she was.

Fair game for the caged lion.

She had insisted on entering the cage, had she not?

Ever so slowly, Colonel Damon Farr's lips stretched into a thin smile.

SIGNET

REGENCY ROMANCE

COMING IN AUGUST 2005

Lady Whilton's Wedding and
An Enchanted Affair
by Barbara Metzger

Two novels of intrigue and romance from "the queen if the Regency romp" (*Romance Reviews Today*) together for the first time in one volume.

0-451-21618-0

The Abducted Bride
by Dorothy Mack

All Amy wants is some freedom, but her chaperon won't leave her side. When she finally escapes, Amy runs into a man who believes she is his beloved Desiree. The next thing Amy knows, she is at his estate, waking from a drugged sleep—and falling for this enigmatic stranger.

0-451-21619-9

Twin Peril
by Susannah Carleton

The Duke of Fairfax is looking for a wife who will love him—not his money. Lady Deborah fits the description, but her twin has some tricks to keep the lovers apart—and keep the Duke for herself.

0-451-21588-5

Available wherever books are sold or at
penguin.com

Lady Silence

Blair Bancroft

A SIGNET BOOK

SIGNET
Published by New American Library, a division of
Penguin Group (USA) Inc., 375 Hudson Street,
New York, New York 10014, USA
Penguin Group (Canada), 10 Alcorn Avenue, Toronto,
Ontario M4V 3B2, Canada (a division of Pearson Penguin Canada Inc.)
Penguin Books Ltd., 80 Strand, London WC2R 0RL, England
Penguin Ireland, 25 St. Stephen's Green, Dublin 2,
Ireland (a division of Penguin Books Ltd.)
Penguin Group (Australia), 250 Camberwell Road, Camberwell, Victoria 3124,
Australia (a division of Pearson Australia Group Pty. Ltd.)
Penguin Books India Pvt. Ltd., 11 Community Centre, Panchsheel Park,
New Dehli - 110 017, India
Penguin Group (NZ), cnr Airborne and Rosedale Roads, Albany,
Auckland 1310, New Zealand (a division of Pearson New Zealand Ltd.)
Penguin Books (South Africa) (Pty.) Ltd., 24 Sturdee Avenue,
Rosebank, Johannesburg 2196, South Africa

Penguin Books Ltd, Registered Offices:
80 Strand, London WC2R 0RL, England

First published by Signet, an imprint of New American Library,
a division of Penguin Group (USA) Inc.

First Printing, July 2005
10 9 8 7 6 5 4 3 2 1

Printed in the United States of America

To Riley,
the newest prospective booklover in the family

Prologue

Wiltshire, February 1809

She did not think of herself as a child, for she was all of twelve, and the last four months had been harsh and bitter, aging her from credulous schoolgirl to shrewd, calculating survivor. But tonight, caught in the early dark of winter, with snow beginning to fall, she feared the end was near. Exhausted, hungry, and ever so cold, she could do little more than put one foot before the other and pray for a light—any glimmer that might signal a cottage, a farm, a wayside inn. A hovel or barn would do.

Her half boots were worn through from walking; she could feel the freezing dampness seeping through to her equally worn woolen stockings. Her stomach growled. She shivered and clamped her teeth together to keep them from chattering. Then opened her mouth again to catch a snowflake on her tongue, licking it greedily. Her throat was parched and her lips dry from walking, walking, walking, searching for a kind face, a slice of bread, a few moments' warmth by a kitchen fire.

She must have taken a wrong fork after being shooed out of the last village, for the road had dwindled to little more than a cart track and, now, to a mere footpath. She trudged on. If she'd had a tear left in her, now would have been the time to shed it. But she'd cried them out—for the parents she wished she might have known, for the grandmother she barely remembered, and for her beloved grandfather who was all that was good and kind and true. She'd cried for being sent to unwelcoming strangers. For venomous words. For bruises that turned her fair skin every shade of blue, black, purple, and later, green.

What was cold and hunger compared to what she had escaped?

Yet somehow the freedom to die on a lonely road to nowhere was not such a fine freedom after all.

The girl gasped, rocked to an abrupt halt, her once fine cloak swirling around her. Too frightened to move, she pulled the cloak tight about her shoulders and simply stared. She seemed to be on top of one of the many low rolling hills in the area, for below her was spread out the wondrous glow of a tidy estate. An impressively large house and stables. Perhaps a party was in progress, for the house was ablaze with lights, and torches lined the carriageway.

Her knees buckled. Clenching her fists even as she offered a swift prayer of thanks, the girl who had given up childhood vowed that this time things would be different. Below her was not only shelter, but home. She would make it so.

Chapter One

"Mad as a hatter, the master," Cook declared. "Goin' off to fight the Frenchies when he could stay snug as a bug right here. Don't need money nor glory, not him. Got all a man needs right 'ere at Farr Park."

"Indeed—if he feels so strong about king and country, he could buy a commission for some local lad without a feather to fly with," declared Humphrey Mapes, butler to Mr. Damon Farr. "Or get up his own militia. Many of the gents are doing that, I hear."

"Shame to you both!" cried Millicent Tyner, Mr. Farr's housekeeper. "The Frenchies came that close to wiping out our army at Corunna, and you expect a lad of his courage to stay at home and read of the war with his morning beefsteak?"

"But his uncle, the nabob, left him all that money," wailed Betty Huggins, the cook. "Why should he go and get himself killed?"

"Because he's two and twenty, too young for sense," Mapes grumbled.

"Courageous," said Mrs. Tyner proudly.

"Foolish," Cook sniffed.

"Did you hear something?" Mapes asked.

"A scratching," the housekeeper agreed, "but couldn't be someone at the door on a night like this. Perhaps it's time to put out poison for the mice again."

"There!" said Cook. "'Twas the door, not mice."

All three stared at the rear kitchen door as if they expected a ghost to walk through. No one would be foolish enough to be out on a night like this.

"A groom sent to fetch a pint or two to warm their gullets at the stables," Mapes pronounced, and all three faces of Mr. Damon Farr's primary staff smoothed with relief at this reasonable explanation. The butler strode to the door with his usual confident step, unbarred it, and inched it open. Snow swirled in, instantly melting on flagstones warmed by the kitchen's great fireplace.

"Merciful heavens," said Cook.

Humphrey Mapes stared, even as he opened the door wide enough to accommodate the slim width of the child outside.

"Not a mouse," declared Mrs. Tyner, "but she surely looks like something the cat dragged in."

She also looked wet, cold, hungry, utterly exhausted, and very young. Not even the hardest heart could have turned the girl away on a dark night in the midst of a snowstorm. So while Mr. Damon Farr enjoyed the company of a few friends chosen to join him in a last riotous evening before he left for a commission in the cavalry, a lost child gobbled food belowstairs. Her fingers might shake, her teeth might continue to chatter, but her determination was hardening into Damascus steel. She had finally found good kind people. Here she would stay. Somehow.

"Well, child," said Mrs. Tyner when the lost waif's plate was polished clean and not a drop of milk was left in her mug, "what's your name, and how came you to be out alone on a night such as this?"

The girl raised a pair of stunningly lovely, long-lashed green eyes to the housekeeper, who was standing over her, black bombazine gown bristling with the authority of her office. The child's eyes widened; her entire body radiated distress.

"Well?" Mrs. Tyner snapped. "Cat got your tongue?"

Solemnly, the girl nodded.

Mapes and Mrs. Tyner exchanged incredulous looks. Cook shook her head.

"You can't talk?" the butler demanded, none too gently. Again, the child nodded.

"Everyone knows mutes don't hear either," said Mrs. Tyner, "yet you—"

"Are you reading lips, girl?" Mapes snapped.

The waif shook her head.

"So you can hear me?" At an affirmative nod, the butler forgot himself enough to whistle through his teeth. "Well, what's to be done with you I'm sure I don't know." He looked at the two women and shrugged.

"Ain't you the one, Mr. Mapes," chided Betty, the cook. "Think we're goin' to solve your problem for you?"

"With the master going off to war, we don't need extra help," Mrs. Tyner mused. "She can find a warm corner for the night, but in the morning she'll have to be on her way. Oh, for goodness sake, don't shake your head, child. What else am I to do with you? Stop that! You'll shake yourself to pieces."

But the child had dropped to her knees, clutching the housekeeper's stiff gown as if she would never let go. And all the time her head kept shaking *No, no, no, no, no!*

"Good God," Mapes muttered. "Stop that at once!" He sighed. The child went still as a statue, still clinging to Mrs. Tyner's bombazine skirt. "Do you have any skills, girl? Do you know how to serve in a gentleman's household?"

Slowly, with effort, the girl pushed herself to her feet. The green eyes took on shadowed depths; her lower lip thrust slightly forward. She gave a sharp, decisive nod.

Mapes glared at the girl who stood before him. A waif, a ragamuffin . . . yet her clothing had once been quality. Her eyes pleaded, even as they shot defiance. Proud as a peacock, she was. No second parlormaid, this one. With the Frenchies causing trouble again, few houses were hiring staff. If Farr Park turned her out, it was the workhouse. Or worse. Mapes took another look at those eyes, rich as emeralds, proud as Lucifer. No . . . as yet he judged her an innocent. A bud not yet plucked by the raw cruelties that could befall a lost child.

Mapes pursed his lips, heaved a resigned sigh. There were,

after all, limits to how hard-hearted even a butler could be. Looking down his nose at the bedraggled but defiant child, he announced, "In the morning I will discuss the matter with the master."

With almost regal bearing, the girl inclined her head in a nod of gracious acceptance. Almost, by God, Mapes thought, almost as if she were granting Farr Park the privilege of her presence.

Desperate. She'd been so desperate she'd gone on her knees. To a housekeeper! Let her eyes beg favor of a butler.

Fool! She'd found shelter, a possible home; yet after all she had suffered, pride still rankled, threatening her safety. When would she learn she had lost all claim to rank and privilege when she had run from the shelter provided for her? When would she learn to be humble, to fit into the world belowstairs?

Now. Now was the moment! Her wandering days were done.

Meekly, with a smile of unfeigned gratitude, the girl allowed herself to be led away to the attics. Warm and dry and tucked up in a voluminous cotton nightdress, she settled into a warm featherbed and bid pride good-bye. Whatever it took, she would stay in this place. The unknown Mr. Farr must have a kind heart. She willed it so.

Surely that wasn't asking too much.

But before she could dwell on her morning encounter with Mr. Farr, the child—safe, warm, and belly full—fell fast asleep.

Damon Farr charged down the massive staircase at Farr Park, then instantly regretted it. Halfway along, he staggered, clutching the banister for support before proceeding at a far more decorous pace. He should never have had a party the night before his departure. A full day to recover would have been eminently sensible, but what his friends called his mad idea had come on so suddenly there had been no time for proper planning. The nightmare of Corunna had reverberated across the country—half Britain's army lost, the rest escaped by the skin of their teeth, thanks to evacuation by one of the greatest armadas since the Spaniards tried to conquer good Queen Bess.

Of course he had to go. Britain's honor was at stake. The army had to return to the Peninsula, and he was going to be one of them. But if he was to go off to war, he'd have to develop a harder head. Devil it, but it was going to be a nasty carriage ride to London.

With considerable relief, Mr. Farr stepped down onto the marble tiles of his entry hall, leaving the jarring demands of the staircase behind. *Feet. Legs. Livery. Skirts.* He forced himself to look up, struggled to summon a smile. Of course his staff was waiting to say good-bye. He stood stiffly before them, not daring to nod, resigned and vaguely pleased that Mapes was undoubtedly about to launch into a formal farewell.

Instead, the butler cleared his throat and said, "Before you go, Mr. Farr, there's a matter needs to be set to rights." He reached behind him, hauling forward a child Damon Farr had never seen before. A girl child, dressed in a brown horror of a gown obviously made for someone else. A child who held her disheveled blond head high and whose eyes stared straight back at him, equal to equal.

"And what have we here, Mapes?" Damon asked.

"A stray, sir. Came to the door last night in the snow. We—Mrs. Tyner and I—wondered if you might have a place for her, sir."

A domestic crisis, that's all he needed, with his head splitting open and what little wits he had left firmly fixed on his new life in the cavalry.

"You, girl," Damon barked, "what's your name and where are you from?"

"Sir, she doesn't talk," Mrs. Tyner interjected.

"Nonsense! Well, girl, answer me!" The green eyes went wide, the frail shoulders firmed. Chin high, she stared right back at him. Flaunting her defiance, by God.

Truthfully, Damon had seen such a sorry sight only when his carriage passed through the teeming stews of London. Someone had made certain the girl had clean face and hands, but her hair was a tangled mass of dirty blond curls, and the gown that fit her like a flour sack must have come straight from the rag bag. Clearly, it was unfit even for the poor box.

Well, what was a man to do? The parish took care of its own, but this child was a stranger, of that he was nearly certain. Undoubtedly, her fate was to be chased from parish to parish until she was snapped up by some girl-nabber and added to a London brothel. *Hell and the devil!* Damon's head ached, his stomach churned.

"She doesn't look like she eats much," he pronounced, settling the waif's fate. "Doubtless you'll find something for her to do."

"Indeed, Mr. Farr. Thank you, sir." Mapes shooed the girl back into the crowd of servants. Once again, Mr. Farr turned toward the door. Mapes cleared his throat. Damon halted, swaying slightly as his devoted butler finally delivered the expected speech of farewell, to the accompaniment of an occasional sniff and one outright sob from a parlormaid, earning her a glare of reproof from Mrs. Tyner.

Mr. Farr managed the proper responses. *Noblesse oblige.* And only then could he descend the front steps and enter his waiting carriage. Where he suffered a perfectly abominable journey to London, his only consolation thoughts of the grand new life awaiting him as an officer in one of His Majesty's cavalry regiments. No thoughts of the blond child adopted into the confines of Farr Park so much as entered his head. In fact, the girl was of such small significance that he barely recalled her existence through his five years on the Peninsula, his months as an aide-de-camp at the Congress of Vienna, and certainly not during that final great battle in Belgium.

He was, however, all too frequently forced to think of his sister-in-law, Drucilla, wife of his elder brother Ashby, Earl of Moretaine. For every time he received a letter from his mother, the young countess's name was prominently mentioned—at first, with long-suffering, then indignation, and finally outrage. The dower house was not, it seemed, sufficiently removed from

Castle Moretaine to make coexistence possible between the dowager and her daughter-in-law.

Therefore, shortly after Talavera, when Captain Farr was laid up with a nasty saber slash in his thigh and had ample time to reflect on his mother's plight, he offered her use of Farr Park during his absence. This seemed to serve quite well, as the dowager's letters turned positively cheerful, if frequently dotted with references to a Katy. He did not recollect anyone of that name among his staff, so decided she must be some impecunious family connection employed by his mother as a companion.

When, after six and a half years of war, Damon—now Lieutenant Colonel—Farr headed home, he was a far different man from the young fire-eater who had gone off to war expecting to lick the Frenchies in a year or two. His thoughts were all of Farr Park, of his mother and elder brother Ashby. Of English soil, English villages, the English language echoing around him like some litany of joy.

Home. He was going home.

To Farr Park, a cocoon of peace waiting to welcome him. At twenty-eight, he was an old man, longing for serenity. No guns, no blood, no mud. No blistering heat on the plains or shocking cold in the mountains. No smoky-eyed señoritas. Or mass graves. No bugle sounding the call to arms. No pounding hooves and gleaming sabers. No letters to write to grieving relatives.

Farr Park. Serenity. A box into which he could plunge and pull down the lid.

Not all wounds of war ran red.

Chapter Two

On the last few miles of his long trip home, Colonel Farr's thoughts turned to his welcome at Farr Park. He groaned. Mapes would turn them all out again, standing stiff as boards in the hall or—*devil take it!*—perhaps lined up along the front drive like soldiers on parade. He wasn't his brother the earl, all pomp and circumstance, pontificating in the House of Lords. He was just a country gentleman, who, like a fox just escaped from being torn to bits by a hunt pack, wished only to withdraw into his den and lick his wounds.

But this time his mother would be among the crowd of servants. Or perhaps not. Would she choose to stay in the drawing room, asserting her right to a private reunion with her younger son? Her son, the stranger, who was nothing like the eager young man who had charged off to war with dreams of glory obliterating even the slightest hint of reality.

The colonel swore, rather colorfully, in a combination of Spanish, Portuguese, and French. He would endure his welcome back to Farr Park, this last hurdle before freedom, as he had the war. And then he would draw his home and his land around him like a cloak of invisibility and retire from the world.

At least for a while. Until he felt fit for the society of those who had not seen what he had seen, nor done, even in their wildest nightmares, what he had done. Would his coming days at Farr Park be like the fantasy of the peace conference at Vienna—starched and pristine uniforms, glittering gowns, royalty and nobility from a dozen countries greedily dividing up

Europe by day and dancing away the nights—dreamlike months sandwiched between the Peninsula and Waterloo? Or would the horror finally begin to fade? Would he once again be able to touch and be touched in something other than desperation?

Jarred out of his none too sanguine thoughts by the post chaise's sudden turn to the left, Damon leaned forward to drink in the sight of the curving drive leading to Farr Park. He was home. By God, he was home!

Farr Park was a fine eighteenth-century structure of mellowed red brick with a well-scythed park ornamented by the exotic shapes of several Cedars of Lebanon and the colorful glow of numerous copper beeches. His mother had written that the gardens behind the house still thrived. His steward vouched for his stables, his crops, and his sheep.

A shiver shook the colonel's lanky frame. How was he coming home to all this when so many others had died?

Damon Farr uttered a word usually reserved for his troopers. For there was his staff, every last one of them, poised under the heat of the August sun on either side of the front entry. Mapes, standing at the forefront, looked surprisingly like a sergeant-major in spite of his conservative tailoring. He was still a beanpole of a man, Damon noted, with an angular jaw and a bit of gray beginning to show. Beside him was Mrs. Tyner, plump-faced and heavier by a stone or so, her beaming face looking as if she'd never had a serious thought—when, truth be told, he'd often wished he'd had someone with her efficient organizational skills with him on the Peninsula.

And there, running down the steps like the veriest schoolgirl, was his mama, Serena, Dowager Countess of Moretaine. He would have sworn he had no tender emotions left, but his feet insisted on running to meet her. When he recovered enough to put her from him for a good look, Damon discovered she had changed very little. The countess had always been slim and was now perhaps even more so. And yes her hair showed more gray than brown, but her eyes were filled with pride and joy. He made a silent vow not to disillusion her. His mama's gown, the colonel noted, was in the first style of elegance, not unlike the day gowns of the highborn ladies in Vienna and Brussels. Obviously, living in the wilds of Wiltshire had not cut his mother off from the world of fashion.

Colonel Farr endured the formal welcome of his staff with far more aplomb than he had tolerated his long-ago farewell, for Wellington's officers had had to put on a good front no matter how they felt, no matter what conditions they faced. And then, finally, he was alone, staring at the walls of his room as if he had never seen them before. On the Peninsula, Old Hooky and his entire staff would have considered themselves blessed to share a suite of rooms the size of his personal apartment. And now, it was all his. As was Farr Park, an inheritance from his uncle Bertram for which he had never been more grateful.

Supper was a quiet affair, exactly as he wished. Damon paid little attention to his mother's apologies for the absence of her companion, the oft-cited Katy, until Lady Moretaine added that she feared the dear girl did not wish to intrude. Nonsense, of course. Dear Katy would never be encroaching.

Dear girl? He must have misheard. For years he had pictured Katy as an elderly cousin or maiden aunt. No matter. He'd find out soon enough. For the moment, he was content to eat Mrs. Huggins's welcome-home feast, which included a compilation of his favorites, including pea soup with bacon and fresh herbs, dressed crab, asparagus in white wine and cream, minted lamb, and a Florentine of oranges and apples—grandly topped off, after his mama left him in solitary splendor, by a generous sampling of the port he had had shipped home from Portugal.

With each sip Colonel Farr's foreshortened world seemed to take on a more rosy hue. At Farr Park, the problems of the world beyond Wiltshire would not intrude. In the morning his new life awaited him. And tonight he need only fob off his mama with some of his more humorous tales. Strangely enough, there were more than a few. Somehow—yes, somehow—he would manage to get on until the shadows went away.

During the weeks after Waterloo, with his duties down to

seeing that his wounded were tended, letters written to the families of the dead, and his able troopers sheltered and reequipped, Damon had had time to select a method for the exorcism of the shadows—the ghosts, if you will—that haunted him. Some men, he knew, could put the war behind them as if dropping the handle of a pump, shutting off the rush of water on the instant. He envied them, but he could not emulate them. He would, therefore, make an effort to record his experiences. Not that anyone would ever read what he wrote, but if a man were going to crawl into a box and pull down the lid, he must have some occupation, must he not? Concentrating on the memoirs of Colonel Damon Farr should do the trick.

Or should he, perhaps, compare Wellington's maneuvers to great commanders of the past? Actually write something someone might want to read? Not just military officers and trainees, but the many Englishmen who had sense enough to be grateful to those who had rid the world of the overly ambitious Little Emperor?

After spending the morning with his long-suffering steward, Elijah Palmer, Damon sat at his mahogany kneehole desk, frowning at the blank paper centered in front of him. He glanced at the quill sitting in its standish, then back to the paper. His frown deepened. He raised his eyes to the tall windows to his right, and felt a slight amelioration of his gloom as he noted that the gardens did indeed still flourish. He reached for the quill . . . hesitated . . . then, barking one of the worst of his acquired foreign profanities, buried his head in his hands. How could a man write if he couldn't make up his mind what he wanted to write about?

A small thump. Damon opened his eyes to a silver tray on which reposed a steaming cup of tea, fragrant with spice, and a matching china plate with macaroons and two biscuits, one that looked like ginger, the other vanilla or lemon frosted with sugar. His mouth watered.

But how . . . ? For nearly seven years his life had depended on being alert, yet he had not heard anyone enter the room.

He looked up. Straight into the face of an angel.

She was young. She was beautiful. Blond and green-eyed, with a figure that would have inspired whole regiments to duel for her favor. Her gown, sprigged in blue, was modest for a gentlewoman, decidedly out of place on a maid. No matter. She was far more mouthwatering than the biscuits.

The girl bobbed a curtsy, turned to leave.

"No, wait!" Colonel Farr, catching the frantic note in his first words, lowered his voice. "Who are you?" he asked.

Merciful heavens! Yesterday, her view of the returning hero had been obscured by misty eyes and a sudden attack of shyness that had kept her lurking behind Jesse, the tallest footman. Still fixed in her mind was the half-drunken boy who had stumbled down the stairs on his way to war. Not this whipcord-thin, dark-haired, broad-shouldered, lantern-jawed, *imposing* adult with lines radiating from the corners of eyes as dark as his hair, deep-cut slashes from nose to chin, cheekbones that formed lines of their own, and a mouth that looked as if it never smiled.

Yesterday, she had been afraid to put herself forward, afraid to join the homecoming celebration for fear that when Colonel Damon Farr remembered how she came there—when he recalled the careless largess that had resulted in her elevation so far above the waif rescued from a cold winter night—he would have her dismissed on the instant. In the light of a fine August day, she had gathered her courage and had decided to brave the lion in the privacy of his den. And all she was gaining was the knowledge that her savior, whom she had worshipped through all these years, was far harder and more implacable than she had ever dreamed.

"Who are you?" he repeated. Far more ominously.

If you think I'm going to tell you, you are quite mistaken!

The blasted girl stuck up her chin and stared straight back at him. Blond . . . green eyes. A memory flickered to life. A child with matted hair and a borrowed gown. Something odd about her . . . ah, yes, he'd been told she didn't talk. "Ring the bell," he ordered. Silently, she glided across the thick Persian carpet and did as she was told. "Stay!" he added sharply as the girl continued on toward the door. She skidded to a halt, folded her hands demurely in front of her. She stayed.

"Mapes," the colonel demanded as the butler entered the room, "tell me about her."

"Ah . . ." The butler cleared his throat. "You may recall, sir, the little miss we took in the night before you left, the one that came to the kitchen door during a snowstorm?"

"I recall a waif, Mapes, one not even fit to be a tweeny."

"You said we could keep her, sir."

"Yes . . . and I wasn't myself at the time, as I recollect."

"A bit askew, as I recall, Mr. Farr, Colonel, sir, but you never was one to turn a child out into the snow."

Damon drummed his fingers on the mahogany desktop. "And what would you say we have now, Mapes?" He waved a hand toward the girl who was standing regally straight, taking it all in. "Who, pray tell, is this? Lady Silence?"

"'Tis Katy Snow, sir," the butler declared, happy to have a solid fact to grasp. "You see, Mrs. Tyner said she looked like something the cat dragged in, so we decided to call her Kate or Katy. And since she came to us in the snow . . ." Mapes allowed his voice to trail off, casting a hopeful look at his master, who used to be such a gay, charming, and generous lad.

"And she still doesn't talk," said the colonel flatly.

"No, sir, not a single word."

"Yet, if I am not mistaken—and pray, do not fail to enlighten me if I am wrong—this is Katy, the companion my mother has frequently mentioned in her letters?"

"It is, sir."

"I see." Though he certainly did not. "And how is it possible for a girl who cannot talk to be anyone's companion, let alone companion to the Dowager Countess of Moretaine?"

Out of the corner of his eye, Damon saw the girl bristle. Interesting. The chit was quivering with rage when *she* was the jumped-up scullery maid or orphan or whatever the hell she was. She ought to be quivering because she was shaking with fright, but he had dealt with too many young men her age not to be able to tell the difference between fright and rage.

"She fetches and carries, Colonel. Runs errands to the village. She helps the countess with her embroidery, arranges flowers a real treat." Mapes broke off, coughing behind his hand at this digression from his customary stately presentation. "You see, Colonel," he added, "it did not take long for us to see she could not tell a feather duster from a carpet beater. Didn't even know the proper way to wash a dish or hang up laundry. Not that she didn't try—she surely did—but 'twas clear she'd had no training in service, sir. When Lady Moretaine came to us, she took to Katy right off, and it was a blessing to see the child blossom when she was put to chores she understood."

"Good God!" the colonel growled as the implications began to dawn, for he had not become a colonel solely because of his ability to purchase his exalted rank.

While his mind wandered over a problem that might be more serious than anyone had thought, he continued his conversation with Mapes. "Are companions not supposed to read to their employers?" he inquired with more than a touch of sarcasm.

Mapes straightened his shoulders, stretched his considerable height half an inch taller. With eyes fixed somewhere over his employer's shoulder, he replied, "Fortunately, Colonel, Lady Moretaine seems to enjoy reading to Katy."

"Indeed. How odd of me not to think of that."

"She takes baskets to the sick and infirm, Colonel, and helped make lint bandages during the war, and—"

"Enough!" the colonel roared. "But she never talks?" he added more softly. "Not even a squeak at sight of a mouse?"

"Never, Mr. Farr. Not once."

"You may go, both of you. But, ah—Katy . . . do not think you have heard the last of this. I shall have much more to say on this subject after I have spoken with my mother."

When the door closed behind his two employees, Colonel Farr ran a hand through his dark brown hair, clutching a handful and tugging till it hurt. *Damn and blast!* Home not yet a full day, and he had a mystery on his hands. Either he was giving houseroom to a shockingly adept adventuress or else he was harboring a sprig of the *ton,* an underage runaway for whose disappearance he could be charged with kidnapping.

Not to mention the fact that the girl aroused feelings he could only term lust. If he had ever had the capacity for love, it had died long since. He lusted. She was a girl of no background, no family protection. Although honor forbade her seduction, he rather thought he'd left that on the battlefield as well.

Katy Snow. A common name for a most uncommon girl.

Katy Snow. Who did not talk.

Katy Snow, who was likely a brass-faced hussy, who had honed herself a place at Farr Park through the soft hearts of his staff and his mama's gullibility.

His body was dazzled. His mind had taken her in dislike.

And she dared be furious with *him.* Yes, she was, he knew it.

Who did she think she was? Ah, but that was the problem, was it not? She, and only she, knew the answer. And did not tell. For years she had made fools of them all. But he was home now. And nobody made a fool of Colonel Damon Farr.

Chapter Three

Katy, whose attic room had long since given way to a fine chamber not far from the countess's own, slipped down from her high bed and settled on a seat beneath an open window. A soft night breeze wafted the scent of the garden from two stories below. A three-quarter moon cast a pale glow over the irregular shapes of hedges, flower borders, fountains, and winding paths. A fantasy garden in silver, as fleeting, as ephemeral, as her life.

She'd been so happy at Farr Park. The months, the years of her growing up, had drifted from one day to the next on a haze of contentment. Of course there had been a few moments. . . . Katy's lips curled softly in remembrance of broken plates, unstarched shirts, Mrs. Tyner's frown as she found dust where Katy had never thought to run a duster, Mapes's haughty and terrifying scowl when he had found her charging down the front *family* stairs at what he later described as "full tilt." But they had all been kind, even as they threw up their hands and wondered whatever would they do with Katy Snow.

And then Lady Moretaine had arrived. And ever so gradually, the youngest member of Farr Park's staff—the not-quite-child with patrician features and proud bearing—had become, if not a lady, then certainly a gentlewoman. Her ability to read had been revealed even before the dowager countess came to Farr Park, when any search for the rescued waif always ended in the library. So perhaps it should not have been such a surprise to discover Katy could not only sort silks, but was capable of setting as neat an embroidery stitch as Lady Moretaine herself. The mystery child wrote in a flowing, well-formed script. She could arrange flowers, as if to the manor born. She could drive a pony cart, ride a horse. And on one well-remembered day the entire household had come to halt when notes were heard from behind the closed door of the music room. The pianoforte. Someone was playing the pianoforte.

Katy Snow.

Katy supposed she should not have been so bold. Yet pride was a terrible thing. Combined with childish bravado, it was lethal. When Lady Moretaine decided to set her to stitching a sampler, she had stayed up half the night decorating the small piece of cloth with every embroidery stitch she knew. The dowager had blinked, exclaimed, rung for Mrs. Tyner, who had echoed Lady Moretaine's surprise and praise. And after that, Katy had succumbed to the temptation of revealing the skills of a young lady of quality. So many disasters that first year, so many scolds—surely it would have been inhuman to continue to keep her light under a bushel.

And now, at eighteen, she was a respected member of the household, a well-known figure in the village, the only wrinkle in her smooth path the occasional necessity of demonstrating to overeager males that her inability to talk did not mean they could do as they would with her. But today she had looked into Colonel Damon Farr's eyes and seen doubt, suspicion, and something far worse. For years now, the household at Farr Park had awaited his letters with bated breath, poured over every word, sought his name in the military despatches printed in the newspapers. He was a hero, their darling, the wonder of his mama's life. The object of Katy Snow's devotion. She had filled her head with daydreams of the tousle-haired drunken boy staggering off to war, with thoughts of soothing his brow, satisfying his every whim, as she did for his mother.

But there her dreams had stopped, for her mind would

allow her to go no further. Not from naïvete but from horror, for Katy Snow well knew that men were not always what they seemed. And what she had seen in the eyes of Colonel Damon Farr was not only suspicion, but lust. *Why, why, why,* when she had been so happy?

No . . . she had been content. Comfortable, well-fed, accustomed to her routine. But happy? Perhaps not. She was eighteen, an age to be wed. Yet before her stretched only endless years of fetching and carrying. No husband, no children, no home of her own. By chance, augmented by her own wits, she had found shelter, a place to grow up. But now she could almost see the walls beginning to crumble around her. She recalled the carelessness with which the boy had allowed her to stay, recognized his generosity for the indifferent exercise of *noblesse oblige* that it was. She had mistakenly idolized a man who, instead of a hero, had become a solemn, sharp-eyed, sour old man who was going to toss her out of her fine nest. Or worse yet, begin to make inquiries.

What to do, what to do, what to do?

To Lady Moretaine, she was almost like a daughter. To her son, she was a nobody, a possession. Someone to be used as he chose. She had read of men and wars in the books of the vast library compiled by Damon Farr's uncle. And of the fate of women at the hands of soldiers. No, she did not at all like the flare of appreciation in the colonel's eyes, no more than the scorn and anger that swiftly followed.

Perhaps it was time . . .

Impossible! She'd guarded her secret too long to give it up now. In the twinkling of an eye she'd find herself back in the nest of vipers she had successfully eluded.

Slowly, sadly, Katy returned to her bed. For the first time since she was twelve years old, she dreaded what tomorrow would bring.

On the following morning Colonel Farr, not yet adjusted to a nonmilitary life, almost made the disastrous error of sending for his mother. He had already barked out Mapes's name when he recalled that he might be at his own desk in his own bookroom, but no gentleman would summon his mama to him as if she were a naughty schoolgirl—particularly a mama who was not only Dowager Countess of Moretaine but daughter of a duke.

But when he found his mother reclining on a rose brocade chaise longue in a sunny room on the east side of the house, she was not alone. She was holding up a book, reading aloud to a young woman whose gaze was fixed on the countess in what appeared to be breathless anticipation.

"Snow," the colonel snapped, "you may leave us."

Katy jumped to her feet, stood poised like a small animal mesmerized by a poacher's lantern, then bolted from the room so fast he could swear he felt the breeze as she passed by.

The silence lengthened as Damon seated himself across from his mother, noting that the countess was now gripping her book as if she longed to throw it at him. He leaned forward, attempting to force his countenance into something less stern than the face he had seen in the mirror that morning. This was his mother, and truth be told, he loved her dearly. Enough to give her shelter when his brother Ashby would not, or could not, protect her from that witch of a woman he had been foolish enough to marry.

"Mama," Damon pronounced with care, "it would seem you have made a pet of a girl about whom nothing is known. She could be . . ." He struggled for a word not too shocking, settling on a weak "*anything*."

His mother merely proffered a serenely superior smile. "She is Katy Snow. She has lived here for well over six years. We took a lost child, discovered her talents, and raised her accordingly. Do not, I pray you, force us to look for a flaw in our budding rose."

"Mama," said the colonel a bit more sharply, "her noble features likely come from the wrong side of the blanket. The chit is some noble's bastard escaped from wherever she was farmed out for care."

"Bastards are not usually taught a lady's skills," his mother replied with cool composure.

"Then she is an adventuress, carefully trained to ingratiate herself into a fine house. Something at which she has been most successful, I might add!"

The countess considered the matter. "I grant if she had been older when she came here—sixteen or more—we might have wondered, but not our Katy. And would an adventuress have waited so long to make off with the silver? Do not be absurd, my dear. That is the trouble with wars, I fear. They take our young men and turn their noble minds inside out and upside down."

"Mama!" To the colonel's indignant protest, his mother returned only the blandest look. He glowered. "The final possibility is worst of all. If we have been giving shelter to a runaway, we could be taken up for kidnapping. Whether she is a merchant's brat or daughter of a duke, she is under age, and somewhere she has a father, brother, uncle, or guardian looking for her."

"She could simply be an orphan. A lost child in need of a home."

"A lost child with the skills of a lady," the colonel riposted drily. "I fear it is all a take-in, Mama. The child aped her betters, giving herself airs and graces as false as her lost voice. No doubt if she once opened her mouth, you'd hear Seven Dials or Shoreditch. Indeed," said the colonel, accustomed to quick decisions, "she's bamboozled you long enough. I'll send her off today. You may, if you wish," he added grandly, "write her a character. I shall see she has a mite to live on until she can find another position."

Lady Moretaine, shocked into silence by her son's speech, finally found her voice. "This is Katy's home," she cried. "You cannot throw her out!"

"Oh, can I not?" said Colonel Damon Farr. "I will not tolerate a guttersnipe masquerading as a lady."

The Countess of Moretaine sat up, clutching the book between white-knuckled fingers. "Then we will leave, Katy and

I. It is time, after all, for the child to know more of the world." She nodded decisively. "Yes, indeed, we shall go to Bath."

"You will do nothing of the kind," the colonel roared.

"But, indeed, it is the very thing," declared the countess. "Bath will do nicely for us. Perhaps we shall even find Katy a beau."

Blast the chit! Did his mama's life revolve around that encroaching little minx? Yet . . . somehow the reality of losing the angel who had brought him tea and biscuits held little appeal, no matter how sensible the plan might be. Damon suddenly found himself tempering his blusterings. "Mama, I have just come home. Surely you will remain for the rest of the summer. You cannot wish to leave the country when Bath and London are so thin of company. Unless, of course"—the colonel raised his dark brows—"you fancy joining the prince's fast set in Brighton?"

"Nonsense!" the countess gasped. "As if I would ever—" She broke off. "Naughty boy, you are funning, of course. Very well, we shall stay awhile, if you are certain you would not dislike it."

Though not best pleased by his mother's use of *we,* the colonel assured her he would be delighted to have her company.

"In that case," said Lady Moretaine with rather more care than her usual forthright manner, "perhaps I should mention that Katy is accustomed to spending several hours each morning in the bookroom. I am an indolent creature, you may remember, rarely abroad before noon, so Katy's mornings are free to do as she likes. And even above riding, her preference is books."

All signs of Colonel Farr's brief slip into affability disappeared on the instant. His dark brows narrowed over his angular nose as he scowled at his mother. "I am sure I regret discommoding your companion, Mama, but the bookroom is mine. I expect to spend the better part of my time there. I do not care to share it with some . . . *foundling.*"

"Damon . . . dearest boy, I understand it is difficult, coming home after so many years of war. But truly, there are no enemies lurking here. Katy is a good girl, bright and true. Indeed, when you have become more accustomed to her ways, I believe you will find her a great help in the bookroom."

"Never!"

"But, my dear, she has spent half her time here in the bookroom. Ask anyone. She has a remarkable thirst for knowledge. I doubt she has mastered Greek, but I have seen her reading Latin with my very own eyes. Gave me quite a start, I can tell you."

"You're mad. *I beg your pardon!*"

"As well you should," said his mother.

"You are saying the girl *reads*?" Damon inquired carefully.

"Well, of course she reads. You are the only one among us who believes her born in a hovel."

"And writes?"

"A fine hand—better than my own. I have her pen all my invitations."

Hell and the devil, their goose was cooked. Better an adventuress than the girl should have strayed from some noble house. The reasons a girl of twelve might flee the comforts of a wealthy home were enough to turn his stomach sour. In truth, if he had not gone to war, they might never have occurred to him. No . . . more likely she was the by-blow of a married noblewoman who had left the girl to the not-so-tender mercies of professional child raisers. Many a country cottage was full of children their mothers dared not claim.

An obscure country cottage where she was taught to embroider, arrange flowers, ride a horse, and play the pianoforte? Damon winced.

After taking punctilious leave of his mama, Colonel Farr sought the shelter of his bookroom. Here, at least, he could be comfortable, shutting away all thoughts of the female irritant who was disrupting his dream of peace and quiet. He strode through the door the footman opened—how easily one fell back into the routine of luxury!—and settled at his desk with a long-drawn sigh.

A slight rustle. The soldier, ever ready, found the source immediately. A slender girl, blond and enticing, perched atop the bookroom ladder. "*You,*" he groaned. Summoning his most clipped parade-ground tone, he barked, "You, there, come down at once!"

Chapter Four

Damon did not avert his eyes as Katy Snow descended the ladder, her derrière wiggling as seductively as any man could wish. Why should he? His mother might be fooled, but the girl was a homeless waif who should not have risen higher in the household than parlormaid.

Yet now she stood before him proudly, hands primly folded in front of a gown that was tucked and trimmed as fine as any lady's. *Lady Silence.* He should never have called her that, even in mockery, for the name stuck in his mind, rankling. The girl was nothing but an adventuress, clever and conniving. She had feathered her nest at Farr Park with the softest down, and now she stood before him, head high, emerald eyes looking straight into his own as if they were equals—memory stirred—as she had looked that long-ago day when he had left for the war.

Equals, hah! The bold-faced baggage didn't see him on his feet, did she? She was standing, he was sitting. To the devil with treating her as if she were well and truly a gentlewoman.

"Pay close attention, girl." Damon enunciated each word with biting clarity. "I will be spending most of my time in my bookroom. I want no distractions. You, therefore, will not enter this room while I am in it. Is that clear?"

The green eyes flared, her luscious pink mouth thinned into a line. Obviously horrified, she gaped at him as if she could not believe her ears. Slowly, she shook her head. *No, no, no!*

"This is *my* room," Damon declared. *My sanctuary. A cage for the lion still roaring within.* "I require privacy for a book I plan to write." And why the devil had he told her that? Colonels did not explain themselves.

To his astonishment, the arrogant jumped-up brat melted away, leaving a lovely young creature suddenly intent on making him understand what she wanted to say. She placed her fingertips in front of her mouth, reminding him she was always silent. She made mincing mice feet on the carpet, her slender fingers curled in front of her. Fathomless green eyes pleaded.

Damon scowled at her ploy, even as he interpreted her gestures. She was telling him she would move about as quiet as a mouse. In short, she was begging not to be exiled from his library.

When, fascinated by the uniqueness of the exchange, he did not respond, she tried again, holding her palms in front of her face, pantomiming the reading of a book. Again the great green eyes, peeping over her fingertips, pleaded for his understanding.

"I have no objection to your reading," he pronounced, "but you must select your books when I am not here and you must read them elsewhere."

The girl drew a deep breath, her whole body taking on a pugnacious stance. Her right hand flayed the air, sketching agitated lines.

He almost laughed out loud. The minx! And when was the last time he had felt like laughing? He forced his wavering features back into a frown. "From what Mapes and Mrs. Tyner have told me, you don't know one end of a feather duster from the other, so kindly do not try to fool me into thinking you are needed to keep my library clean."

She was shockingly lovely, he thought as he waited for whatever argument she would think of next. Wisps of pale gold curls, escaped from the mass tied schoolgirl-fashion at the base of her neck, framed an oval face marked by a patrician nose above a pink and inviting mouth. The emerald eyes were flawless, intelligent and penetrating, and her skin was classic English perfection. In short, a picture to warm a man's dreams.

And his bed.

That was it, of course—the reason he was banishing her from the library. He was being noble, eschewing temptation. For his sake, as well as hers. Seducing the servants, most particularly his mama's companion, was scarcely the act of an officer and a gentleman.

There was a blur of movement, and there she was beside his chair. On her knees, blond head bent, shoulders shaking. She seized his hand. Damon froze. He *hated* tears. Had, in fact, abandoned all emotion. Caring, loving, feeling anything at all was far too painful. His homecoming had, for a short time, broken his resolve, but Lady Silence would not. Indeed not.

The colonel shoved back his chair and stood. Grabbing the supplicant by her forearms, he settled her, none too gently, in his place at the desk. He picked up the quill, shoved it toward her hand. "I am told you can write," he said, "so write down your name and where you come from. And why no one has asked you long since," he added under his breath, "I cannot even imagine."

What! By God, the chit was crossing her arms over her enticingly ample breasts. Once again, her lips had become a straight line. She was *refusing* to write? Refusing a direct order? "I fear Lady Moretaine must have been mistaken," he told her. "I see you do not know how to write."

The girl's swanlike neck stretched taller. With superb disdain she took the quill and wrote on the paper he had thumped down before her: "You are a beast and a bully!"

Spoiled, by God! Only an overly indulged daughter of the house would dare speak so. The girl was in sad want of a few sharp lessons in conduct. Which he wouldn't mind administering.

Time enough to think of that later. "If I am a beast and a bully," he informed her with scarcely veiled triumph, "then you understand why you must stay out of my bookroom."

Her lips quivered. This time he feared the tears might be real. Or were they simply temper? The little baggage did not care to lose.

"How old are you?" Damon demanded.

That she was willing to answer, penning a clear, precise "18."

And suddenly, his belligerence drained away. He was Damon Farr, country gentleman, heir to his brother, the Earl of Moretaine. He was currently engaged in bullying a young woman ten years his junior, who also happened to be a member of his household staff. He might pay her wages and have the right to order her about, but he did not have the right to stand over her, glowering, demanding that she tell him her life story.

Well, perhaps he did. But his temper had flown, and he was ashamed. His mockery of a name for her—Lady Silence—seemed far too close to the truth. If the chit was shamming her noble bearing, she was remarkably good at it.

Delightful. He had in his employ an underage runaway of good family. He could expect a visit from Bow Street at any moment.

After six and a half years? If she were truly someone of importance, she would have been found by now.

Damon stepped away from the desk, sketched a quick gesture to indicate the girl could get up. She faced him warily, poised to run. Afraid? Was she actually afraid of him? *Damnation!* He *had* grabbed her, thrust her into his chair, come close to stabbing her hand with his quill. No wonder she looked at him so. Beneath his breath the colonel muttered a few succulent Spanish oaths, adding a resounding, if silent, *Merde!* for good measure. He supposed, in Katy Snow's eyes, he was usurping *her* bookroom.

Perhaps his eyes *could* use an occasional rest from his quill and foolscap, from all those rows and rows of leather-bound volumes. And she smelled good, standing there so close in front of him, the top of her head barely reaching his shoulder. Lavender? He wasn't sure. But the scent was light, evoking memories of England, not of the heavier perfumes worn by the dark-eyed ladies of Iberia.

Regarding her as quellingly as he had his newest recruits, Damon announced, "Mapes clumps over the carpet like a cart horse over cobbles, yet you enter a room as stealthily as you have entered our lives." *Ah . . . that caused her to blink.* "Therefore, I assume you can continue to deliver tea and biscuits without disturbing my work." As hope dawned, light flickered in her eyes, the nicely rounded body settled into a waiting stance.

"You know how to sharpen quills?" A vigorous nod. "You are perhaps acquainted with the location of most of the books in this library?" Another eager nod. *Devil it,* her whole face was beginning to glow. He had designs on her virtue. What little gentleman was left within did not care to see her so eager to plunge to her doom.

"And I suppose you write a fine hand, good enough for a fair copy of my scribbles?" Yet another nod. She was smiling now. Foolish, foolish girl. Did she not understand he was dangerous?

"And when I do not need you," he added sternly, "you will sit in that wingchair over in the corner and not make a sound, is that understood?"

She seized his hand and kissed it, eyes shining with joy. Her lips burned straight down to his black soul. Damon stifled a groan and shooed her off. "You will report to me in the morning at nine," he told her sternly. "A female secretary is a most exceptional concept, but it is possible you may be useful. We shall see."

A brief flash of green before she dropped her eyes and bobbed a curtsy, exiting the room with a decided bounce to her step.

What the devil was he thinking? He had just condoned the chit's crime, undoubtedly aiding and abetting a runaway's escape from her guardian. He was as soft as all the others in his household. Colonel Damon Farr heaved a sigh. If only that were true. Perhaps in years to come the layers of armor laid on for the war might gradually peel away, leaving him a ordinary man, a man capable of loving and being loved.

Odd that a female the likes of Lady Silence should trigger such maudlin thoughts. *Lady Silence, hah!* The chit was a servant, as far from a lady as the barmaid at the Hound and Hart.

And so he would treat her. Katy, the girl the cat dragged in, that's what she was.

Fair game for the caged lion.

She had insisted on entering the cage, had she not?

Ever so slowly, Colonel Damon Farr's lips stretched into a thin smile.

"Katy!" hissed a voice that carried down the empty corridor outside Lady Moretaine's bedchamber. "Katy—this way!"

Katy, who had taken her leave of the countess at the sound of the bell signaling it was time to dress for dinner, looked swiftly around, then followed the whisper around a turn in the corridor. A hand beckoned from an unused bedchamber. Having no doubt to whom the hand belonged, Katy entered the room and closed the door behind her.

The hand, and the body attached to it, had retreated to the far side of the room with the exaggerated stealth of a conspirator in the pantomime the servants had been allowed to view last Twelfth Night. Beaming at Katy, finger to her lips, was Clover Stiles, an upstairs chambermaid so bent on becoming a dresser for a fine London lady that she did not even walk out with the footmen or the young men from the village. She had ambition, did Clover Stiles. A fifteen-year-old scullery maid when Katy had come in from the snow, Clover had taken the waif under her wing, and not even Katy's continued silence nor her rapid rise in status had curbed a friendship born so long ago.

The two girls were a striking contrast—Katy, delicate and blond; Clover, a big-boned, dark-haired farmer's daughter, seemingly born to nurture the weak and wounded around her. "Well?" Clover demanded. "You were in the bookroom, alone with him for an age, my girl. Did he behave himself?"

Katy blinked, appearing genuinely startled. She nodded. Decisively.

"Well, let me warn you," Clover said. "The master used to be a great one for slap and tickle. Not that he did more, I grant—many's the time I've heard Mrs. Tyner boast that Damon Farr knew better than to muddy his own pond—but he cut a swath outside these walls, from tavern wenches to a widow near twice his age."

Satisfied by Katy's wide-eyed stare, Clover gasped for breath and plunged on. "And now he's come home a sour old crab, aglowerin' at everyone, even his ma. Not too big a surprise, I say, to find he left his better self back in that far place where they was fighting. So y've got to remember he's a man, and you're naught but a rare morsel, fit for pluckin'. With you not even able to say yay or nay nor scream for help, he's like to snap you up and spit you out afore you knows what's happenin'."

Slowly, Katy backed away from her friend. *No. No, he wasn't like that.* Even though she had ample reason to know that men tended to think with something other than the brains God gave them, she found herself shaking her head. Damon Farr was an honorable man. Crotchety. Narrow-minded . . . but not more so than the rest of his class. He was . . . a man wounded in war. And, even as she fought him, her heart went out to him. The lines on his face called to her to soothe them.

"Katy, are you listening to me? I heard Mapes and Tyner talking. They said you might be going to help the colonel in the bookroom. Is that true?"

Katy laid her hands, palms together, up to one ear, pantomiming her question.

"Well, of course Mapes was listening at the door," Clover declared, well accustomed to Katy's sign language. "Butlers have to know what's going on, now, don't they?"

Katy plumped herself down on a ladderback chair, frowning mightily. Propping her chin on her hands, she glared at the Turkey carpet.

"Forgive me, love," Clover cried, dropping to her knees beside Katy's chair. "'Tis just I'm that worried about you. The countess's pet you may be, but to the colonel you're fair game. Miss Nobody from Nowhere. Just be careful is all I'm saying. For all he looks twenty years older and as sour as billy be damned, he's a man. And with you twitchin' your tail right there in front—"

Eyes sparking green fire, Katy shot to her feet, quivering with rage, fists clenched at her sides.

"Well, indeed I'm sorry, love, but there's the wood with no bark on it. He's a man, you're a woman. You'll need eyes in the back of your head. And knitting needles in with your hairpins mightn't be amiss."

Knowing full well that Clover was right did not mean Katy could accept her words with grace. But Clover was a friend. Katy took a deep breath, forcing her anger to drain away. Was that not what she always did? Only true ladies, cosseted and well-dowered, could afford to lose their tempers. She proffered a smile, albeit wan. Pantomiming her need to dress for dinner, Katy Snow, waif, left Clover standing in the bedchamber, her brow still wrinkled in concern.

Chapter Five

Dinner was a remarkably awkward affair, for Katy had lost a spirited, if silent, argument with Lady Moretaine, in which my lady's companion had clearly indicated she once again wished to abandon her customary place at the countess's table. A decided "Nonsense!" was all the reply Katy received. That, and a violent shooing motion as the countess sent her back to her room to dress.

And now, here they sat, the three of them, one lady on each side of the master of the house, Lady Moretaine talking nineteen to the dozen, the colonel adding an occasional glum nod, and even glummer looks at Katy's décolletage, which seemed to be what had turned him so twitty in the first place. One glance at the neckline of the pale pink lustring gown the countess had insisted was all the crack in London, and the colonel had turned positively purple. Not once had he spoken to her, but he'd sneaked more than a few peeks. *Blast the man!*

As soon as the two ladies left the colonel to his port, Katy fetched the countess's shawl, draped it over her shoulders, then pleaded to be excused. Lady Moretaine, not unaware she was about to suffer a tedious session with the son who seemed to have turned into an ogre, waved the girl upstairs. If only she had had a premonition, some inkling of how Damon would react to Katy Snow's elevation . . . No, she would not have changed a thing. The child was most certainly a gentlewoman, if not a lady. Worthy of her trust. She had not made a mistake.

"So, Mama," said the colonel as he strode into the drawing

room after perhaps more port than was wise, "just what were you thinking when you dressed mutton as lamb? Or is it, perhaps, appropriate to expose a guttersnipe as if she were Harriette Wilson? Shouldn't the gown have been red, instead of pink?"

"Sit down!" his mother snapped. "And mind your manners." When the colonel had slumped onto the opposite end of the sofa on which she was sitting, the countess said, "I am happiest with beautiful things around me, Damon. It is a fault I freely acknowledge. Furniture, paintings, carpets, Oriental vases, ormolu clocks, marble sculpture, gardens . . . beautiful people. I do not wish to have my companion in drab, looking like a cloud about to pour down rain. It pleases me to see her shine. As I have told you, if you cannot like it, we shall remove to Bath."

Damon dropped his head into his hands. "My apologies, Mama. I fear I have come home, but have not left the crudities of war behind." He drew a ragged breath, finding he could not let the subject go. "Mama, I cannot understand why you did not try to locate her people. She can write. Why did you not ask her who she was?"

His mother shook her head. "My dear, can you truly think we did not? But she refused to answer. Just sat there with her hands folded in her lap, head bowed, as if she knew we were going to toss her down the front steps if she did not tell, yet she would not do it. Nothing would move her. I promise you, we tried."

"Of course you did," the colonel murmured, thoroughly ashamed of the confused and angry thoughts chasing through his head. Had he himself not recognized the same stubborn desperation in the chit when he had attempted to discover her history. "She's a baggage, mama. I know it. I do not believe she cannot talk."

Silence hovered between them, as Lady Moretaine's brow wrinkled in thought. "But why?" she inquired at last. "And surely she could not have maintained such a masquerade for so long?"

"What sets us apart from our servants, Mama?" Damon

asked. "From the common soldiers on the march, the women trailing in the dust of the baggage train? 'Tis easy enough to clothe an urchin in silk, but the way we talk is bred in us. The upper class speaks in accents all its own, carefully polished by parents and tutors until it is perfection. For everyone else the way we talk depends on where we live. From broad Yorkshire to the almost unintelligible mutterings heard in the London gutters. Clearly, your Lady Silence is hiding her origins."

"You know, my dear," said the countess mildly, "you have come home with a remarkably nasty mind."

"Yes, Mama, I know."

"Damon?" Lady Moretaine paused, uncharacteristically uncertain. "Perhaps I should not have suggested Katy assist you in the library. But she loves books, and I thought she might be useful. Yet now I realize I, too, have been guilty of placing Katy in an anomalous position. Neither fish nor fowl nor rare roast beef. If I truly knew her to be a young woman of good family, I would not have thought of offering her to you—" The countess broke off, crying, "Merciful heavens, Damon, what have I said?"

"The truth," he replied, reaching out to lay his hand over hers. "Only the truth."

"Shall I ask the vicar if he knows a young man who might serve as your secretary?" Lady Moretaine asked in a small voice.

Damon was surprised by the depth of his revulsion. Was he actually looking forward to dueling with the devilish little minx? And watching her roaming about the bookroom, wiggling her—

Brightening his day.

"No, Mama, thank you, but that will not be necessary. We will see how the girl goes on. Though, I beg of you, do not tell all and sundry that I have acquired a female for a secretary."

With her head low over her chestnut mare's neck, Katy galloped across the meadow as if escaping the hounds of hell. Away from Farr Park. Away from Colonel Damon Farr. Away from emotions so tumultuous they terrified her. Men were to be ignored. Shunned. Evaded when necessary. Fought, if nothing else would do. Escaped, when all else failed.

But now it was she who was being ignored. She'd swear the colonel hadn't raised his eyes to her during so much as one of his curt commands, yet many a time this past week she'd felt his gaze burning into her back. *Devil!*

Yesterday, her hands had shaken so badly, she'd slopped tea into his saucer. Appalled, she'd dashed to the kitchen, where everyone had gathered round, urging her to tell them what was wrong. Had the colonel misbehaved? Lady Moretaine must be told immediately. Katy, thoroughly mortified, had just kept shaking her head. *No, no, no, no!* She was fine. An accident, nothing more.

And then the miserable man, when accepting his second cup of tea, had actually looked at her—and smiled. "Not so solemn, child," he'd told her. "The world won't end over a few drops of tea in a saucer."

More like a sea of tea. But at sight of that smile as rare as hen's teeth, her treacherous heart had done a jig in her chest, leaving her breathless. She had loved him blindly, and he had betrayed her. Clearly, he thought her an adventuress. If he had so much as an inkling of the havoc he was wreaking on her feelings, how easily he could—

As she approached a line of trees, Katy slowed her mare, Mehitabel, to a walk, remembering, as she entered a winding ride through sun-dappled woods, the year her figure had suddenly blossomed into womanhood. When even the well-trained Farr Park footmen followed her with their eyes as she crossed a room. The men working in the fields or in the village had been less subtle. Gestures, whispers, appreciative grunts and whistles marked her path. She was naught but a servant. Easy prey.

Just when she thought she had found sanctuary.

Millicent Tyner, a sharp-eyed woman as a housekeeper must be, had sat her down for a good long talk. Katy listened attentively, making no attempt to indicate she was already well aware of the vicissitudes of men. In fact, she paid little attention until the housekeeper, in her usual frank style, warned her that it was she, Katy Snow, who could well precipitate her own downfall. If she did not hold her heart close, she would be ruined. "Men are not for women like us," Mrs. Tyner told her. "You cannot hope to marry higher than a farmer or an innkeeper. Best keep what you've got to yourself and rise to housekeeper in a fine home. Goodness knows you've got the wits for it. But give rein to your feelings, child, and you're lost. Lie with a man, and he'll soon be gone, leaving you fit for nothing but Haymarket ware." At the question in Katy's eyes, she added, "That's a whore, child. Cyprian, courtesan, filly o' joy, share-amy—whatever strange words they use—'tis all the same. A girl's ruined. Useless to any decent man or to serve in any decent household. Your friend Clover listened to me, a good girl is Clover. Keeps to herself, with her eye on being dresser to a titled London lady. And she'll do it, she will, as long as she keeps her legs tight scissored and her head out of the clouds."

Head out of the clouds. And so Katy had—until now. The few hours she spent each day in the bookroom—sorting the household mail, finding long-unused volumes of history on high shelves, making notes from the colonel's dictation, sharpening quills, refilling the inkwell, and serving tea—were treasured moments. For the most part, the colonel remained glum and irascible, but once having decided on the course of his writing—a comparison of battles of historic significance—he had set to work with an intensity bordering on obsession. She might be young and inexperienced, but Katy could not help but wonder if the colonel was attempting to exorcise his years of war by finding refuge in someone else's battles.

And there she was, feeling sorry for him! Which made her poor heart grow more tender, even when she knew that on her own particular battlefront *he* was the enemy. It was nothing but propinquity, of course. Shut a single man into the same room with a single woman, particularly when both were young in age, if not in spirit, and the result was almost inevitable. So why had her dear Lady Moretaine suggested such a remarkable arrangement? Was Katy the bait to tempt the colonel out of his sullens?

A sacrifice to her son's baser needs?

The countess couldn't . . . she wouldn't . . .

Katy found her mare had come to a halt in a clearing and was happily cropping a lush stand of grass. *Propinquity*. No wonder young ladies of good families were guarded almost as closely as the crown jewels. Propinquity was lethal. Even now she could feel his eyes on her, her heart beginning to beat like a drummer sounding Charge. Her mare lifted her head, whinnied.

Oh, dear God! Not a fantasy. He's here!

"Good morning, Katy," said the colonel from atop his black stallion, Volcán, who had survived the war, as miraculously as his rider, with scarcely a scratch.

His thighs were quite beautiful. Far better displayed on horseback than in the library. Katy tried not to stare, but here in this lonely place, she knew better than to look her employer in the eye. She nodded her head in regal greeting.

"Do you always ride alone?"

And how else would she ride? With a retinue of grooms, as if she were the lady of the house?

"Of course," the colonel murmured. "How foolish of me. Lady Moretaine's remarkable notions have addled my wits. I forgot you are merely a servant. A servant out for a morning ride on one of my finest mares."

Almost—but not quite—a sound escaped her lips. Katy swallowed her shock. *Bastard!* It was the worst word she knew. How could he attack her so? She was his helper, his secretary. And what right had he to tromp on the flutterings of her heart, no matter how misguided she was discovering them to be?

Unable to defend herself, Katy sat slumped in the saddle, head bowed, demonstrating her dejection as graphically as she could.

"You think me harsh?" A tiny nod of assent. "Come, child, do you think I attained my rank by coddling my men and blowing kisses to the enemy?"

Katy pressed hands and reins over her mouth, stifling a laugh. *The devil! How dare he make her laugh?* Peeping at him over her fingers, she noted that he was once again looking grim. The clearing was small, their horses nearly nose to nose. His dark eyes were deep haunted pools into which she could so easily tumble.

"You will recall," he told her, "that I do not want any distractions from my work. Therefore, I find it easier to think of you as one of the young men under my command. This is not," he conceded, looking even more morose, "always effective. When I find you wandering in the woods, all alone"—his already disconcerting dark eyes ranged over the tight fit of her forest green riding habit—"I am forcibly reminded that you are female."

Ignoring the flush she could feel staining her cheeks, Katy took her reins in one hand, waved the other in a broad circle, then pointed her index finger at her employer's chest.

"Yes, yes," the colonel responded impatiently, "I understand you stay on my land, but nonetheless, I fear for your safety. You are not exactly . . . that is . . . you, ah, tend to attract attention, Katy Snow. You are not easy to ignore."

Was she not? Katy's traitorous heart soared. *Fool! That way lies disaster.*

"If I assign a groom to ride with you," Colonel Farr said into the awkward pool of silence that had formed after his last remark, "I will elevate your status beyond what is comfortable for either of us. Yet I am reluctant to curtail your riding, as it is a privilege granted by Lady Moretaine. One you enjoy?"

Yes, oh, yes! Katy nodded vigorously.

"Then I shall merely ask you to stay on my land and keep a cautious eye out for strangers. If you see anyone not known to you, ride the other way."

As if it were only strangers she had to fear!

"You may go, Snow." The colonel waved her on. As she carefully guided her mare by him, he added, "And find my copy of the *Iliad*. Now there's a war that lasted even longer than ours on the Peninsula."

Wars! Is that all the man thought of? When love was so much more satisfying. As she knew quite well from all the years she had held his youthful image in her heart. For Damon Farr, her savior, difficult as he now was, she would do anything—

Haymarket ware, Katy, my girl. Haymarket ware.

Chapter Six

Damon sat, chin in hand, ostensibly studying the few paragraphs he had written the day before. In truth, his mind was filled with a pert young face kissed by a green ostrich plume that curled against her cheek, and an exceptionally fine figure straining so hard against a jacket of green twill that he had thought a button might pop. It would appear his young secretary was still growing.

At the moment, she was on the library ladder again, and he was making a furious effort not to look. The Farr Park bookroom—a central feature of his uncle Bertram's life—was two stories in height and ringed by a high gallery on all but the outer wall. Although the upper story of books could be accessed by a circular staircase, the top shelves beneath it could only be reached by a ladder that moved on wheels.

There was something about Katy on a ladder. . . .

She was his employee, his mama's companion, an innocent child entrusted to his care. Yet the more he attempted to ignore her—the more sternly he reminded himself of duty and honor—the more intriguing and enticing she became. Lately, she was taking on a glow—he was quite certain it was not all his imagination. She was softer, not so wary. A bud begging to be plucked.

She trusted him! Her willingness to be alone with him, day after day, was proof enough of that. Colonel Farr closed his eyes, swearing silently. He had come home to Farr Park for peace and quiet, not to endure daily torture!

A decided thump not far from his nose snapped his eyes open. For a moment he stared blankly at the book Katy had just delivered. He opened the leather binding, flipped a page. "And what," he asked of the girl standing demurely before him, "is this?"

She raised her brows, eyes wide and innocent.

Damon's lips twitched. Blast the girl! She refused to leave him to his sullens. "I shall answer for you," he said. "From what little I remember of my schoolboy days, this is the first volume of Homer's *Iliad*, is it not?" The little minx, still wide-eyed, nodded. "In the original Greek." An infinitesimal nod of agreement. "And you think this soldier, ten long years after seeing his last Greek letter, might care to do research with this particular tome?"

The emerald eyes turned accusing.

"Yes, yes, I know I asked for the *Iliad*, but it never occurred to me you were capable of recognizing the title of the book in Greek."

Arms akimbo, she glared at him.

Katy Snow . . . scholar? Absurd. Since the age of twelve, she had had no education other than access to his library. Therefore, how could she possibly . . . ? Seven Dials and Shoreditch suddenly seemed impossibly distant. As much as he hated to admit it, his mama's notions of Katy Snow's origins were likely more accurate than his own.

And now the chit's gaze had turned mischievous. From behind her back she produced a second thick leather volume. The Dryden translation, by God. And then the books before him faded as he succumbed to temptation and took a good look at his bookroom assistant. Damon leaned back in his chair and stared, cursing silently as the ruthless, hardened soldier sprang to life, threatening to escape the bonds of civilization.

It would appear someone—Katy, his mama, his female staff?—had decided that Katy Snow's elevation to the post of secretary required a new look. Her masses of blond curls were now twisted on top of her head, secured not only by hairpins and combs, but by what looked remarkably like some sort of lethal instrument. Protecting their precious nestling, were they? She needed it, for the difference was astonishing. In the twinkling of an eye the hint of the woman seen on horseback that morning had been transformed into a siren in his bookroom. A siren with wisps of gold framing a marvelously mobile and expressive face that, with the language of her body, was her primary means of communication. And an immensely satisfying change it was from his recollections of the bored ladies of the *ton* whose faces more closely resembled marble statues incapable of displaying—or perhaps feeling—any emotions whatsoever.

Damon swallowed, gulped for air. "Thank you," he said. Ducking his head, he opened the book. The words swam before his eyes. *Devil it,* but the girl was a menace. At this rate his book would take as long to write as Agamemnon had taken to lay waste to Troy.

A scrap of paper descended onto the page he was pretending to read. In Katy Snow's precise hand, three words and a question mark: "Pope and Chapman?"

She couldn't possibly . . . "What about them?" Damon growled. Katy pointed to a top shelf at the far end of the room, just beneath the gallery. "I own them?" he asked, incredulous. Katy shrugged, and with a heart-quickening flutter of her lovely long lashes, regarded him expectantly. "By all means," he said, "let us look at all the translations available."

His gaze followed hungrily as she walked toward the towering bookroom ladder. The tethers of honor, best intentions, and common sense disappeared as if at the wave of a magician's wand. Nothing could hold him to his chair. As silent as Katy herself, Damon followed her across the room. He stood at the foot of the ladder as she climbed, entranced by a flash of lace from the hem of her petticoat, the glimpse of neatly turned ankles above the leather slippers on her astonishingly small feet. He closed his eyes, desire and conscience locked in battle. When he opened them again, Damon gulped, discovering he was eye level with Katy's delightful derrière, as, oblivious to his presence, she had found the books she wanted and was descending the ladder straight into his arms.

What was a man to do? He seized her, books and all, turned her neatly to face him, and swooped in for a kiss.

Positioned as they were, Katy's knee did not have far to go. Colonel Farr gasped, stumbled backwards, swore with heartfelt vehemence as he doubled over in worse agony than suffered with either of the wounds he'd taken on the Peninsula. Only later, as he sat with his head in his hands, cursing jumped-up chambermaids, the war, the army, and even his mother, did he wonder how he could have been so woefully stupid, so pitifully weak that he had strayed from *noblesse oblige* straight into *droit de seigneur*.

Katy Snow's fault, of course. Tempting little morsel that she was. And who among the fine officers and gentlemen he knew would even think of resisting such a succulent plum when it was dangled before their noses?

Would she come back? He doubted it.

He could order her to serve him. He paid her salary, not his mother; he had checked the household accounts to be sure. Katy's fine clothes came out of his mother's jointure, but the girl's wages came from Farr Park funds. She was his, to do with as he pleased. *Droit de seigneur*. Right of the master. And in medieval times that right had included taking the place of the groom on the wedding nights of the fairest maidens. *Ah, yes!*

He was an officer and a gentleman. Far above such things. Or should be.

Perhaps he'd wring her neck, instead.

Colonel Farr picked up the heavy volume of Homer in the original Greek and shied it across the room, where it made a most satisfactory thump against the black fireplace grate. Staggering to his feet, he limped across the room to retrieve the precious volume, his head awhirl with contradictory thoughts. Behind him, the translations of the *Iliad* by Pope and Chapman lay where they had fallen at the foot of the bookroom ladder.

* * *

Supper that night was as much of an agony as Colonel Farr anticipated. Katy stalked into the dining room behind his mother, radiating belligerence and animosity. How the blasted girl managed to convey her feelings so clearly was astonishing. And she'd tucked some kind of scarf into her décolletage, but it did little good. His imagination, the colonel discovered grimly, was quite capable of stripping her bare.

"Damon! Woolgathering at table? Surely your book does not occupy your thoughts every moment of the day and night?"

"I beg pardon, Mama. Would you kindly repeat your question."

"Not a question, dearest. I merely said that I have had a letter from Ashby. He wonders that you have not visited him."

Guilt. How could he possibly tell her that not only did he wish to be alone, but he did not want to face his too perfect, ever infallible elder brother because Ashby thought him a hero. *A hero, by God!*

"'Tis true, the two of you are as different as chalk and cheese, but you always dealt well together. At least . . . so I thought?" The countess's voice trailed off into a question.

Ashby, the noble. Pattern card of an English lord. Possessor of every virtue—except, evidently, the sense to choose a wife who would suit his mama.

As if she read his thoughts, the countess interjected a familiar theme into her plea for a visit to her eldest child, the Earl of Moretaine. "Even if the poor boy was foolish enough to marry that horrid creature, he is still your brother; you, his heir."

"That 'poor boy' is four and thirty, Mama."

"And still childless. It begins to seem likely your son will be Moretaine."

The colonel swore, begged pardon. "I assure you Ashby is more likely to have sons before I," he stated grimly. "I have no thought to marry."

"Has it occurred to you," said the dowager countess with some care, "that Ashby may, by now, be aware that he ruined his life when he married that woman? That he may be in need of support from his only brother?"

With some deliberation, Colonel Farr laid his fork onto his plate. For some reason—force of habit?—he glanced at Katy Snow. Their confrontation seemingly forgotten for the moment, she was staring at him, her beautiful green eyes full of concern—offering encouragement.

"Very well, Mama. I will write to Ashby today, asking him to set a convenient time for a visit. You will come, too, will you not?"

"I must, of course," the dowager sighed. "Fortunately, I see Ashby in town during the Season." The countess offered her younger son a loving smile. "And thanks to your generosity, my dear, I have not had to live next or nigh the witch these many years."

Damon raised his napkin to his lips, hiding a smile. His mother had a more than ample jointure and lifetime use of the dower house on the grounds of Castle Moretaine, yet she had snapped up his offer of a home at Farr Park. She was fond of him, he knew, but he suspected that, when escaping Drucilla Moretaine, witch of Castle Moretaine, his mother had rather enjoyed the notion that she was practicing the economies of widowhood. And now she was spending the funds she had saved on Katy Snow instead of a fine townhouse in Bath!

With relief, Colonel Farr watched his mother lead his nubile and distracting secretary from the room. He reached for the port.

"It ain't right," declared Jesse Wiggs, glowering at the other members of the Farr Park staff as they gathered round a long pine table for their evening meal. "It just ain't right." Jesse was a tall, broad-shouldered young man as a footman should be, his honest, indignant blue eyes making a fine contrast to the white of his wig.

"What ain't right?" Jedadiah, the second footman asked, picking up his cue.

Knowing full well he should keep his tongue between his teeth, Jesse Wiggs threw a belligerent glance at Humphrey Mapes at the head of the table before stating, "Our Katy shut up every morning with the colonel, that's what. Her nothing but a babe, and him come back from doing God knows what in heathen lands."

"The Spanish are Catholic, not heathen," said Mapes sternly.

"Don't make no never mind. He's a good man, the colonel, but my daddy was a soldier, and many's the time he's told me men forget themselves in a war. Learn things they oughtn't to know. Don't think the colonel should be in there, all alone, with our Katy. Enough to tempt a saint, she is. And our Mr. Farr was never that."

"He is your employer," Betty Huggins, the cook, burst out. "An officer and a gentleman. You'll keep a civil tongue in your head, Jesse Wiggs, else you'll find yourself on your backside in the dust with not so much as a character."

"Perhaps a stint in the army would do you good," Mapes suggested blandly. "For don't think I haven't seen you staring your eyes out at our Katy. I daresay the green-eyed monster has you in its grip."

"She's not for the likes of you," Mrs. Tyner, the housekeeper, declared indignantly, joining the conversation for the first time as guilt had kept her silent. She, too, had been wondering about the propriety of Katy Snow spending hours alone with Colonel Farr for as much as six days a week.

"Ain't for the likes of the colonel either," returned Jesse Wiggs, scowling fiercely.

"I think maybe," Clover Stiles ventured, "Lady Moretaine wants to put her in the master's way—"

"That's enough, Stiles," Mrs. Tyner snapped.

"You don't think there's any hope of a m—?"

"Hold your tongue, girl!" Mapes barked.

With soft sounds of resignation, the Farr Park servants applied themselves to their food. After several minutes of silence, near bursting with unspoken speculations, Mapes raised his voice to reach the housekeeper at the far end of the table. "Mrs. Tyner, perhaps you might be good enough to speak with our Katy . . . ah, make sure all is well with her."

"Of course, Mr. Mapes." As if she hadn't planned on doing that very thing!

With a collective sigh of relief, general conversation broke out around the table, although mostly in whispers, with the various servants darting quick glances at Jesse Wiggs and Clover Stiles. Katy was one of theirs. They might sometimes envy her rise, but mostly they only recalled she had come to Farr Park with nothing, not even a voice, and had become the darling of the house. She was Katy Snow, their Katy, and nothing and no one would be allowed to harm her.

The dowager arranged her indigo silk gown over an elegant settee upholstered in leaf green damask, then waved her young companion into a matching armchair close by. "Katy," she declared, "what has happened? If one could make a meal of tension, we might have dined in splendor this evening. Katy?"

Avoiding Lady Moretaine's penetrating gaze, Katy hung her head. Her hands were clasped tight in her lap.

"He has snapped at you," the dowager declared. "Treated you as a tweeny."

Katy shook her head.

Lady Moretaine frowned. "He has made unreasonable demands. Expects more than you are trained to do." The only response was a sharp shake of Katy's head. What pride the child had! Any insinuation that she was unable to be of help to her son was rejected with scorn.

Katy hunched her shoulders, drawing farther into herself.

The countess did not care for what she was beginning to suspect. *Dear God, surely not.* She should have thought, should have considered . . .

Oh, but she had. She had known quite well what she was doing when she thrust the child in her son's path. A man so long at war. A girl in the full perfection of youth and beauty. But she had not thought far enough. She had allowed herself to forget Katy's origins. By treating the child as a family connection rather than a lost waif rescued from a snowstorm, she had come to believe the fabrication—even to the extent of vague dreams of a more close alliance. Something she should have examined with more care, recognizing it for the absurdity it was.

Men of noble birth did not marry the Katy Snows of this world, no matter how fine their manners, how beautiful their embroidery and flower arrangements, nor how exquisitely they played the piano. Even a governess might occasionally dare to hope for such an exalted alliance, but not a girl of no name and no family. A foundling who did not talk.

The Dowager Countess of Moretaine clasped her hands together as tightly as Katy's own. "My dear," she began softly, "it would seem I may have made a dreadful mistake. Has my son attempted to molest you?"

An infinitesimal shrug.

"Katy! That is not a proper response. Tell me at once—did my son touch you, attempt to kiss you?"

Katy's lower lip jutted out. The toe of her slipper traced a flower on the thick Axminster carpet.

"Very well," said Lady Moretaine, looking grim, "since you do not attempt to deny it, I shall assume it is true." For a moment, the countess seemed to study the fire that had been lit in the white and gold marble fireplace to take the chill off the September night. "My dear, I believe we must remove to Bath. You would like that, I am sure. You would have an opportunity—"

But Katy had sprung to her feet, her lovely face contorted with horror. Her blond head was shaking so hard a long strand of gold came loose, tumbling over one ear.

Lady Moretaine's eyes widened. "Sit down," she commanded in a tone of voice she had not used to Katy Snow in many a year. Reluctantly, Katy resumed her seat. "Although I am loathe to lose you to marriage," said the countess, "I have come to look upon you as a member of my own family. I am obliged to do what is right for you, even though that may not be what either of us wishes. Do you understand me, child? In Bath, you may meet eligible young men. You cannot aspire to a great house or a fine title, but you should find some young man willing to accept you for what you are."

Katy returned to examining the deep colors in the carpet.

"My son is heir to an earldom," declared the countess baldly. "He is not for you."

Even after Lady Moretaine's long acquaintance with Katy Snow, she found the sudden lift of the girl's head, the lightning flash of those green eyes, startling. There was defiance, fury, outright rejection of her warning.

"Child," the countess gasped, "you cannot think to have him. It is quite impossible, I assure you."

Fists clenched, Katy bounced to her feet, stalking toward a tall, unshuttered window to gaze out at the lingering twilight.

Their impasse was interrupted by the colonel's entrance. Katy turned—and was caught in a dizzying maelstrom of yearning and repulsion. Colonel Farr's burgundy jacket lent warmth to skin tanned by weather and lined by cares. His dark hair gleamed in the lamplight; his lean soldier's body was silhouetted in ramrod stiffness as his gaze moved from his mother to Katy Snow and back again. He opened his mouth, snapped it closed.

Until this moment, Damon had refused to address his mother's companion as anything but "Katy" or "Snow." She was a servant, by God, and that's the way it would be. But after the morning's disaster, either he gave her the sack or he mended his fences. Or his mama was going to reiterate her intention of leaving Farr Park.

There was, of course, only one acceptable course of action.

Damon cleared his throat, pursed his lips, fidgeted—more like a schoolboy than a proper colonel. Inwardly, he winced. "Miss Snow," he said through gritted teeth, "shall I expect you in the bookroom at the usual time in the morning?"

Katy bobbed a curtsy so slight it was more a regal incline of her head.

Lady Moretaine drew a gasping breath. Katy, willing herself not to tremble, stood staring over her employer's shoulder, her chin so high she could see nothing but a Canaletto scene of Venice surrounded by its ornate gilt frame.

With an abrupt nod, Colonel Farr thrust his hands behind his back and exited the room, adding a curt good-night only as he passed beneath the lintel.

Behind him, Katy sank down into the damask-upholstered armchair. Serena, Lady Moretaine, steepled her hands before her face and wondered how she could possibly have been so foolish.

Chapter Seven

He'd wanted to kiss her! Katy, curled up on the chintz-covered window seat in her bedchamber, hugged herself as she stared blankly at the darkness outside. Damon Farr—scowling, taciturn master of Farr Park—had come within a hair's breadth of pressing his lips to hers.

And she'd done what Clover had taught her. And done it well.

Death was preferable to the agony of remembrance! Well, perhaps not. But if the moment could be taken back, she'd gladly do it a thousand times over. What she had actually done was run from the bookroom in panic, but not before she caught a glimpse of her employer's distress. Clover had not warned her that a knee to that portion of a gentleman's anatomy was so painful. Too late, Katy grasped the point.

She sniffed. A tear slid down one cheek, then the other. Glum and irascible as the man was, he was still Farr Park's hero. Her hero. Even with a face seamed by the horrors and hardships of war, she thought Damon Farr quite the most attractive man she had ever seen. Including Jesse Wiggs, the second footman, Elijah Palmer, the steward, and Mr. William Rowley, the local doctor, all of whom had shown considerable interest in her since she had blossomed from child to woman. Mr. Rowley, in fact, seized every opportunity to study what he called her affliction, although, as Clover had once remarked, the saucy bloke seemed more interested in examining Katy's bosom than in looking down her throat.

If she tried very hard to be objective, Katy supposed, all three men were more handsome than Damon Farr. Certainly they were better-natured, yet . . . Why, oh, why, had she not let him kiss her? It would have been a moment to treasure for the rest of her dull life.

More likely it would have led to utter disaster. Disgrace. Dismissal.

But what if . . . what if the opposite were true? What if he were captivated, charmed out of his sullens? What if he fell in love, fulfilling all her fantasies? What if . . . ?

Oo-oh! Katy winced and clenched her teeth. Silently, of course. What if she had inflicted permanent damage? With Clover Stiles as a friend, Katy was not as ignorant as most young gentlewomen. Dire thought chased dire thought. What if he could not . . . ?

Katy clasped her hands before her face and bowed her head. She prayed for the colonel's good health, for wisdom beyond her years. For some way out of the coil she had fastened round herself. For the future she should have had, instead of the path, lonely and forlorn, that stretched endlessly before her.

Unless . . .

Katy heaved a shuddering sigh—and prayed harder.

The following morning, an hour before he must of necessity make his apologies to Katy Snow, Colonel Farr sat across from the highly competent Elijah Palmer and attempted to understand what the steward was telling him. The fact of the matter was, after Palmer's eight years at Farr Park—most of them in sole charge of everything but the running of the household—any conference the steward might have with his employer was in the nature of tutor to pupil. Damon gave the man his due. He just wished Palmer weren't quite so . . . ah, well-made. Above medium height, blond, blue-eyed, single, and still well short of forty. Was it because of Palmer that Katy Snow had had to learn how to defend herself?

With a wave of his hand, Damon indicated his acceptance of the steward's report. In truth, he had not understood one word in ten. He'd have to have Katy find some books on agriculture and agrarian reform. Beyond the concept of crop rotation, he was lost.

"Tell me about Katy Snow," said the colonel.

"Sir?" A slow blush spread over Elijah Palmer's even features.

Good God! At his age a man should have left blushes behind long since.

"A fine young lady, colonel," declared Mr. Palmer. "Devoted to Lady Moretaine."

"And attractive."

Mr. Palmer squirmed in his chair before evidently concluding that honesty was best. "Indeed, sir, an eyeful she is. Brightens the day for all of us, she does."

"And you in particular?"

Elijah Palmer reached out, carefully closing the account books he had laid before his employer. "Well, Colonel, I'll not deny I had thoughts in that direction. If she weren't a foundling, I'd never get a chance at such a lady."

Damn the man! Palmer looked so expectant, as if the girl were about to be delivered up to him on a silver platter, tied with a bow. "My mother is inordinately fond of the chit," Damon said as if he cared not a whit what his steward thought of his secretary. "Are there any other potential suitors I should be aware of?"

"Rowley, Colonel. The doctor. Says he's determined to discover what caused her problem and find a way to cure her, but no one believes a word. Likes to touch her, he does. Peer down her bosom. Enough to make a man sick, watchin' him watchin' her!"

It was the colonel's turn to squirm, as he recalled the number of times he himself had peered at Katy's fine bosom, even after she had taken to wearing those flimsy things the ladies called a fichu. After all, a man would have to be dead not to—

"Anyone else?" Damon asked, not bothering to hide either his annoyance or his sarcasm.

Mr. Palmer nodded. "Jesse, the second footman. I swear that

boy can keep his face straight front while his eyes roam three hundred degrees. Doctor ought to study *him,* he should! Swivel eyes, that's what he's got. And focused on Katy Snow every chance he gets."

Only long years of strict discipline kept Colonel Farr's temper in place. The girl was a veritable houri with a swarm of swains panting at her skirts. Disgusting!

That he should be one of them, even more so.

He opened his mouth to express his satisfaction that the girl would not go wanting for a husband. What came out was something else entirely. "I find her useful," he told Elijah Palmer, "so do not expect that I will give her up anytime soon." Colonel Farr picked up the stack of estate records and handed them to his steward, effectively ending their interview.

Damon looked up to find Katy Snow standing five feet from his mahogany desk, looking vastly pleased with herself and flashing a smile at Palmer as if he were her dearest friend.

Blasted female. He'd choke before he apologized to the little minx for discussing her with his steward, let alone for his attempt on her person.

Hell and damnation, he'd just been caught telling his steward he found her useful. He might as well have groveled at her feet. The chit was a menace. She'd bamboozled the men around her as handily as she had his mother. Damon just wanted to get his hands on her—although whether to wring her neck or kiss her senseless, he wasn't quite certain.

"Bring me the Chapman," he snapped without so much as a *good morning.* "We might as well begin where we left off." *He could not have said that!* "I beg your pardon," Damon gasped. And promptly proved that Elijah Palmer was not the only grown man who could blush.

He expected her to dash from the room as she had the day before. Instead, Katy was holding both hands over her mouth, shoulders shaking. She was *laughing*?

She was.

In that case, perhaps they *should* begin where they left off. The colonel's spirits soared.

But Katy, ever elusive, straightened her face and marched across the room to the table on which Mapes had placed the books he had found at the foot of the ladder. But, as she stacked the Chapman translation in front of him, Damon could swear her lips were twitching.

Which meant their odd relationship had not been shattered beyond repair. No matter she was the object of the affections of at least three men with seemingly honorable intentions, *droit de seigneur* was looking more appealing by the moment.

"Colonel Farr?" Mapes cleared his throat, tried again when his employer did not look up from the Chapman, which Damon found genuinely fascinating, for all its seventeenth century language. "Colonel, sir? Mr. Rowley, the doctor, is here."

"Is someone ill?" The words were so quiet and blandly spoken that only Katy Snow, tucked up in a wingchair in a far corner of the room, caught the menace in them.

"No, indeed, Colonel. Mr. Rowley—Mr. William Rowley—is a frequent visitor. He is making what he calls a study of our Katy. He plans to tell her story in some fancy doctoring journal."

Hidden in the wingchair, Katy made a face that Mrs. Tyner had once described as "sure to curdle milk."

"Mr. Rowley is also attempting to help our Katy find her voice," Mapes added with what sounded suspiciously like the hope and pride of a fond parent.

"Very well, send him in." Damon's quick survey of the bookroom revealed not a sign of Katy Snow, but he knew quite well she was lurking somewhere about.

Devil it! Damon had pictured a leering roué of forty-odd years, perhaps a widower. The young man before him could not be a day over twenty-five or -six. As tall as he, if a bit gangly. A confident gaze looked out from eyes that closely matched his warm brown hair, fashionably cut in one of London's latest styles. His clothing was equally well cut. *A dandy, by God.*

A dandy who could not keep his hands off Katy Snow!

His Katy. Blast the girl—she was capturing him as handily

as she had all the others. Far from an innocent child, she had to be an adventuress, pulling the wool over everyone's eyes, assuring her continuance in her snug little nest.

Damon asked the doctor to be seated. After exchanging the customary greetings to be expected between a wealthy landowner and a lowly local doctor—which reminded the colonel strongly of exchanges between himself and fresh-faced officers just out from England, exuding the confidence of their ancient lineages—he said, "I understand you have an interest in Katy Snow."

"A unique case," declared William Rowley with considerable enthusiasm. Far too much, Damon thought sourly. "Most unique to find a mute who can hear. I have decided to write a paper about her."

Damon leaned back in his chair, raised his voice to be sure it carried to wherever Katy had hidden herself. "Has it ever occurred to you, Rowley, that Katy Snow might not be a mute?"

Surprisingly, the doctor's enthusiasm brightened still more. "Ah, then you are aware of the power of hysteria, Colonel? No doubt from your experiences on the Peninsula?"

That was not at all what he had in mind, but Damon would never admit it. "Hysteria, Rowley? I suppose that *is* a common female complaint," he pronounced. At any moment, he expected a book to come flying at him, well aimed by Katy Snow's allegedly hysterical hand.

"That is exactly what I was going to propose in my paper, Colonel," declared the doctor. "There are a number of cases in which a perfectly normal child has been frightened into silence by some disastrous event."

Damon inclined his head. "Perhaps. But I fear that was not my meaning." He watched William Rowley intently as the young man finally comprehended the colonel's remark.

"Impossible! She was twelve when she came to Farr Park. She's past eighteen now. No one could manage such a masquerade for that length of time. Nor would she. Miss Snow is a sweet, charming young lady. How frequently have I heard Lady Moretaine call her a treasure—which she undoubtedly is," the doctor added, regaining his customary confidence in the superiority of his judgment.

The colonel proffered a tight smile that was more chilling than his frown. "I believe we must agree to disagree," he murmured. "Did you wish to see the girl today, Rowley?"

"Indeed," replied the doctor cooly. "I am attempting to stimulate her voice by applying pressure to the muscles in her neck—"

"I beg your pardon."

"I apply pressure here . . . and here," said Mr. Rowley, raising his fingers to his own throat and demonstrating his technique.

"You massage Katy's neck?" said Colonel Farr, most ominously.

"Ah, yes . . . I believe you might call it that."

"Katy!" Damon bawled. His recent condescension to addressing her as Miss Snow had completely slipped his mind.

She appeared from behind him and stood to his right, keeping the width of the desk between herself and William Rowley. Damon did not think it was by accident.

"Katy, Mr. Rowley wishes you to go with him for one of his treatments."

She planted her feet hard against the carpet, as if a tree of ancient root. She crossed her arms over her chest; her head shook a tiny but decisive *No.*

"Miss Snow"—*at last he remembered!*—"now acts as my secretary," said the colonel. "I am certain that as a fellow author you can appreciate how much work is involved in that chore. I believe—no, I am sure—I cannot spare her. Your efforts on her behalf are much appreciated, Rowley, but I think such treatments must cease. If you will send a reckoning to my steward, you will receive your fee promptly."

Masterful! Katy chortled. She could kiss every last line in the colonel's face, particularly that small jagged scar at the corner of his mouth. When the door shut firmly behind Mr. William Rowley, Katy fell to her knees beside the colonel's chair. She grabbed his hand and kissed it.

"I take it," said the colonel in strangled tones, "that the good doctor's hands did not always stay on your throat? Oh, blast it, child, don't cry all over me!"

How had he known? How had he guessed that of all the men in her new life, she feared Rowley the most? But Lady Moretaine, Mapes, and Mrs. Tyner thought the world of William Rowley—and the man undoubtedly knew his craft. It was only with her he strayed. And never quite enough for her to be a talebearer, upsetting the household. But Colonel Farr had instantly taken the doctor's measure. He was her savior—again. Well and truly her hero.

With his free hand, the colonel touched the mound of curls piled high on top of her head. Katy gulped, tried to gather her wandering wits. And failed.

"I'm not a magician, child," he said, as if reading her thoughts. "Palmer gave me a hint. He has a fondness for you, I believe. Not a bad match for a girl of no background. I doubt you could do better."

He was twining his fingers through her hair and suggesting she wed his steward! *Beast!* Didn't he realize he was supposed to be a hero? The romantic do-no-evil fantasy of her girlish heart? Ruthlessly, Katy kept her head down, eyes tight shut, hiding her fierce rush of anger.

He'd been too long without, Damon thought, his face twisting in disgust as he took in what his fingers were doing. He'd clung too fervently to his fierce desire to be left alone. No wonder he lusted after the first pretty face. . . .

His employee.

His mama's companion.

A *virgin,* by God—or maybe not.

Hair so soft, like waves of golden grain. Struggling against frustration, Damon groped for a defensive strategy, some means of cutting through the thrall that was threatening to bind him.

She was an encroaching baggage, Katy Snow. A child of mysterious, and surely lowly, origin. He was quite right when he had called her an adventuress. He had to fight the insidious power of her beauty, the fascination of the mystery from which she'd sprung, the strange allure of a female who did not talk. Surely any man who had survived the Peninsular campaign and Waterloo could manage one small girl.

"Tell me, Katy Snow," he drawled, "are you an hysterical mute, as the esteemed Mr. Rowley argues, or are you the conniving little minx I think you are?"

Katy shot to her feet, fists clenched, green eyes smoldering.

Did she have the slightest idea how close to the brink she teetered? How much he wanted to scoop her up and . . .

Ostentatiously, she lifted the pendant watch dangling about her neck, perusing it with all the fascination of one who has never seen a timepiece before. A small secret smile tugged at her lips.

In the few weeks they had been together Damon had learned to read her quite well. The answer to his first question was: *That's for me to know and never tell.* The answers to the questions he had asked himself were less visible. Did she recognize her power to attract? Did she sense how little control he had left? He greatly feared she did.

The dastardly little chit dropped an exaggerated curtsy and stalked from the room. Time for Lady Moretaine's portion of Katy Snow's day.

Hell and damnation, and the devil fly away with all women.

Chapter Eight

"Mama," said the colonel a few days later as they dipped their spoons into a light clear soup liberally sprinkled with fresh dill, "I have had a brief note from Drucilla, informing me that Moretaine has gone shooting in Scotland. She has sent on my post but does not know when it may reach him."

"Clearly, she did not accompany him." The dowager's tone was a condemnation.

"A shooting party is scarcely the place for a female."

"Activities are arranged for the wives," his mother responded repressively. "*I* always accompanied your father when he decided to reduce the population of partridge, pheasants, grouse, and woodcock. And possibly ptarmigan and a hare or two," she added to demonstrate her acquaintance with Scotland's fine variety of wildlife.

"I should have remembered," Lady Moretaine continued. "Ashby goes to Wishart each year at this time. I doubt he will return before October." She sighed. "I believe you must simply tell that woman we will visit as soon as he is in residence at Castle Moretaine."

"*I* must?" Damon said, a spark that might have been humor kindling in his usually solemn dark eyes.

"Indeed," his mama retorted. "I do not correspond with that . . . with the other Lady Moretaine."

Whatever had occurred between the two countesses of Moretaine, Damon thought, it must have been momentous. Or was it all a tempest in a teapot, female bickerings over little or nothing? Women were such strange creatures.

Shame struck him. He was echoing nearly forgotten mutterings of men over brandy at their clubs. The mutterings of soldiers had been more charitable—a wistful, even worshipful, longing for the women they left behind—sometimes even as they fondled the dark-eyed doxies at their side. Not that Wellington had ever complained of the absence of his wife, of course. But he'd always had the pick of the Peninsular crop, had he not? And little sentiment for poor Kitty, left cooling her heels at home.

Damon supposed that, to women, men were strange creatures. In truth, how dull the world would be if the good Lord had not made the thoughts and actions of one sex incomprehensible to the other. Even his mama was frequently a mystery. And the women who followed the drum had to have been as mad as they were gallant. And Katy Snow? Katy was a most strange creature, he could not deny it. Yet her singularity added to her appeal.

As he did so often at table, Damon glanced at her out of the corner of his eye. There she sat in a gown the color of light jade. The gauzy fabric she wore tucked into her bosom was woven with silver thread. Candlelight reflected off her porcelain skin, her rosy lips, the wispy blond curls escaping her upswept coiffure. The green eyes were hidden, however, demurely lowered to her soup.

The dowager interrupted the colonel's vicarious enjoyment of his table companion. "We must have some new gowns made for you, Katy, before we visit Moretaine."

Katy choked on her soup, coughing and vehemently shaking her head at the same time.

"Indeed, yes," declared the dowager, after Colonel Farr rose to the occasion by springing up to pat his secretary on the back.

Katy's coughs eased, but she sat there with tears still dripping down her face, shaking her head as hard as her breathlessness would allow.

The colonel produced a handkerchief and gently dried her

tears. Ignoring him, Katy thrust out her hand, index finger jabbing downward with considerable force. The emerald eyes, as belligerent as he had ever seen them, shot fire.

"You will *not* eat in the kitchen," Lady Moretaine stated firmly. "Nor do you need to look at me so, Damon. I am not proposing to adorn the child in silks and satin. In fact, I concede the necessity of clothing her as a proper companion while at Castle Moretaine. The new gowns I speak of will be drab—though not wholly without appeal," she added as Katy stared at her in dismay. "Believe me, child, I am far too fond of you to expose you to my daughter-in-law's wrath. We shall make every effort to have you disappear into the woodwork."

Colonel Farr's snort of derision was enough to set the candles in the center of the table to fluttering. But all he said was, "She needs a new riding habit as well. And no need to dip into your purse, Mama. I shall stand the nonsense. Without an owner roistering his way through society these near seven years, the estate has done very well. Palmer's a good man. Have the reckonings sent to me."

"That is generous, my dear. Thank you." Lady Moretaine and her son avoided Katy Snow's indignant gaze by turning their attention to the trout sprinkled with chives just placed before them.

Castle Moretaine was in Gloucestershire, not far north of Bath. Castle Moretaine was not at all where Katy Snow wished to go.

Castle Moretaine was close by Oxley Hall, an ugly four-square manor house without a hint of architectural style, except for its construction in what was commonly known as Bath stone. Its walls might be lighter than the soot-drenched houses in Bath itself, but the heart of Oxley Hall was black as a moonless night. Dark as the people inside it.

She would never go back. *Never!*

Farr Park was her sanctuary, yet there was no way she could beg to stay at home while Lady Moretaine braved her daughter-in-law's uncertain temper. For most of the years Katy had attended the dowager countess, she had been young enough to easily avoid the dreaded Drucilla's notice. The younger Lady Moretaine paid only a single duty call on her mother-in-law each Season in London. The remainder of their enforced meetings were at routs, balls, and other *ton* events that Katy Snow did not attend. This past Season, however, had been more difficult, for the earl's wife had finally noticed the delicate beauty of the elder countess's companion. She had asked questions, demanded answers. Drucilla had not been pleased by the encroaching little chit's origins, her all-too-charming person, nor by her mama-in-law's obvious preference for what the younger countess referred to as the Upstart Tart.

Worse yet, it was likely Lady Oxley was on calling terms with the younger Countess of Moretaine. The thought was nearly paralyzing. A variety of disguises flitted through Katy's mind. A wig? Penciled lines of aging? Hunched shoulders? But disguise was impossible without an explanation to the countess. And the colonel. And that, of course, was wholly impossible.

Yet the alternative—discovery—was too terrible to contemplate. For, legally, she was underage and had no rights. She was chattel. She could be disposed of, like a sacrificial pawn on a chessboard, at the whim of her guardian. She could be screamed at, shouted at, beaten. Used as a "convenient." She had no rights. No one to whom she could complain. Not even the vicar had been willing to interfere between a recalcitrant child and her guardian.

So she had run away.

And now she would be going back.

"Katy, Katy, my dear, what is wrong? You look quite pale."

Katy Snow looked down at the uneaten trout on her plate and, of course, said nothing at all.

Katy sat tall in the saddle of her dainty bay mare and gazed down at Farr Park. From here—from this very spot—she had first seen the solid rectangle of the house, the drive lit by torches, the sturdy stables off to one side beyond the gardens. With snow stinging her face, hunger in her belly, and despair in her heart, she had stumbled to the top of this hill—and found paradise. Warmth, food, kindness. A lightening of her soul.

A home.

And now she must risk it all on a visit to Castle Moretaine. For no excuse was sufficient to explain a refusal to accompany Lady Moretaine. When forced to live in close confines with the Dreadful Drucilla, the countess needed her support. Yet for both the dowager and herself, Katy feared the results. There was something ominous afoot, as if a storm cloud were moving in—now just a wisp of gray here and there, but presaging a great mass of shadows yet to come.

Surely not. Her childhood fears were rearing their heads, expanding into monsters. . . .

No, indeed. The fears of those last months of her childhood *were* monsters. Else she would not have run away. Would not be here, gazing down so longingly, so lovingly, at her refuge.

But with Damon Farr in residence, was it still a refuge? Surely the most diabolical mind could not have devised a more clever trap. And she, fancying herself the most clever of mice, was attempting to spring the trap and seize the cheese without damage to her person. Katy slumped in the saddle, glowering at the corner of the great house that housed the bookroom. Colonel Damon Farr thought her an adventuress. Lower than a servant. A convenience to be used and discarded at will. They might have agreed to a truce, but it was tenuous at best. She'd caught the assessing glances, the speculation, the flashes of disgust when he realized what he was doing.

Undoubtedly, the colonel had been raised with all the tenets of honor, duty, and gentility, but Katy suspected a good deal of his better nature had been stripped away in the crucible of war. The Damon Farr of the present was quite capable of making use of her skills and contemplating other, more intimate, services, even as he thought her a scheming adventuress.

Perhaps *because* he thought her an adventuress.

The saddest part was, he would not be far from wrong.

"You have become a statue, Snow."

She had heard him coming, had known he would stop and

speak to her. Had felt her heartbeat quicken, her breath shorten, even as she kept her eyes fixed on Farr Park below.

"A lovely sight."

A double entendre? Did she want him to be looking at her as he said it, not at Farr Park? *Haymarket,* whispered the breeze. *Ha-aymarket.*

"Look at me, dammit!"

Katy's hands jerked, her mare caracoling close to the edge of the steep drop-off. The colonel, grabbing the bridle, towed Katy's horse back from the brink. "Idiot female," he roared, "you shouldn't ride if you can't control your horse. I've a good mind to forbid it."

She was an idiot? When he had gone from caress to bark in the space of seconds, startling her no end. The man was impossible, with no way to tell what he would do next. She patted her mare's mane, attempting to coax a calm in her mount she could not feel herself. Katy squared her shoulders, looked her nemesis straight in the eye. *See . . . my head is up, my pride intact.*

"We will be leaving for Castle Moretaine sooner than expected," he told her, still frowning. "I have had a letter from my brother's steward informing me that Moretaine has cut short his shooting trip. It seems he took a chill in the confounded Scottish weather, and rather than staying by the fire to recover, he wishes to return home. He should, in fact, be in residence by the time we arrive. Naturally, my mother is anxious to attend him. As a child, Ashby was ever subject to inflammations of the lungs."

Even as Katy nodded her understanding, she was urging her mare forward. Her mistress, not trusting the Dreadful Drucilla to attend her son, would be frantic with worry.

The colonel grabbed her bridle. Katy rocked in the saddle. Glared.

"You will listen to me carefully, Snow," said the colonel, towering over her on his black stallion. "You will efface yourself at Castle Moretaine, be no more than a dark wraith trailing in my mother's wake. No stylish gowns, no winsome smiles, no putting yourself forward. You will remember that you are nothing, a product of the gutter raised to the astonishing heights of upper servant solely by my mother's generosity."

Katy stared at him, trying not to blink. Attempting to appear stoic when her face threatened to crumple under his onslaught. When she wanted to open her mouth and howl, say it wasn't so.

"According to my mother, my brother's wife does not associate with servants. She does not wish to see you, hear you, or acknowledge your existence. You are dust beneath her feet. Is that clear?"

Katy's anger faded just a trifle, for most certainly she did not wish to be seen. Greatly daring, she raised cupped palms before her face, pantomiming the reading of a book.

The colonel appeared thoughtful. "If our stay is a lengthy one," he ventured, "I will wish to work on my book. You may assist me. And if you are asking if you may read, I see no reason why you may not," he added magnanimously. "Though you are warned not to do so in front of Lady Moretaine. The younger countess," he clarified, as Katy's brow wrinkled in a puzzled frown.

She patted her mare's withers, raised her brows.

"As for riding . . . I suppose it may be arranged—if I make the request directly to Moretaine. He's an obliging fellow, for all his poor taste in women."

Ashby. Damon tried to picture the older brother he had not seen since he'd left for the Peninsula. Ashby had been about the age he himself was now. A young man-about-town. An earl. A great prize on the marriage mart. Always a bit too thin, too solitary, serious to the point of pomposity. Although he performed his duties as earl with punctilious attention, he had had to be pushed into the London social scene by his mama and, later, by his brother, who had been as outgoing as the earl was reserved. When Damon was on the Peninsula, however, his mama had written of Ashby's transformation after his marriage to the most sparkling diamond of the Season of 1812. Quite the man-about-town, she had declared, pleased that her eldest had blossomed at last.

For a while. Poor Ashby had been ripe for the plucking. Damon heaved a sigh.

Born seven years apart, they had never been close, particularly when Damon grew old enough to best Ashby in footraces, wrestling, shooting—even horse and curricle races. Although he'd seldom felt a twinge of desire to stand in his brother's shoes, competition had been fierce, until one day Ashby had shaken his head and declared, "Enough." Damon had felt a rush of triumph, followed closely by shame for wanting so badly to best his elder brother. Had he wanted to demonstrate his skill because younger brothers were forever competitive, or had he wished to flaunt his superiority to the Earl of Moretaine? His country's call to arms had come none too soon. The farther away he and Ashby were from each other, the better.

And now look at us, Damon thought in disgust. *Moretaine is disillusioned, haring off to Scotland to flee the Dreadful Drucilla, and I have become a worse recluse than my brother ever thought of being. A fine pair, we are.*

Time, and past, for a reconciliation.

Damon came back to the hilltop with reluctance. She was still there, Katy Snow, regarding him with anxious eyes. Such a tasty little morsel. Drucilla would snap her up in a single mouthful. A pity his mother would defend the little baggage as fiercely as a bear guards its cub. Life without Katy Snow would be so much more . . . peaceful.

"Be sure your dressmaker delivers your new gowns immediately," he snapped. "You have only today and tomorrow to pack."

After acknowledging his order with a curt nod, Katy turned her mare and rode off down the winding path that led to Farr Park. Damon watched until she disappeared from sight into a small copse at the base of the grassy hill. A puzzle . . . an irritant . . . an intrigue. That was Katy Snow.

Chapter Nine

Katy laid the last of her four new gowns on her bed, then stepped back, examining them with critical intensity. Two dirt brown, a gray that was nearly charcoal, and a dark blue. High in the neck, long in the sleeve. She scowled.

"They ain't—aren't—so bad," said Clover Stiles. "Quality cloth, and, see, there's a bit of trim on each. Piping, tucks, a dab of lace on the blue."

Katy heaved a sigh, shoulders and bosom heaving, though not a sound escaped her lips. Reluctantly, she nodded. It wasn't as if she wished the occupants of Castle Moretaine to notice her. These gowns were perfect for her purposes. But . . . she was eighteen, and if what she felt for the difficult colonel was not love, it was as close to that emotion as made no difference. She was young, her mirror told her she was lovely, and she had given up hiding her light under a bushel long since. And now she was expected to efface herself, fade into the paneling as if she did not exist. Well, these gowns would certainly do it. The Dreadful Drucilla was not the only person for whom she wished to be invisible.

"Oo-oo, I knew it!" Clover exclaimed. "It ain't all vanity, is it, my girl? You're thinking you won't cut such a dash before the master. Well, let me tell you, Katy Snow, it's grateful you should be, for like I've told you time and again, no good can come of him noticing you're beautiful. Men like that sample the wares and move on. The very best you can get is a few months in a rose-covered cottage before he tires of you and passes you on to one of his friends. Or maybe leaves you flat to fend for yourself. Or with a bun in the oven and no place to go but the workhouse. And you can stop glaring at me, 'cuz that's just what'll happen if you don't take off the blinders and see life as it is. You can't have him, and there's an end to it. Though the way he is now," Clover added a shade less brusquely, "'tis hard to understand why you'd want him."

Agreed. If she had not known what it was to suffer, she might be repulsed by the colonel's glowering ways. Instead . . .

Katy turned her head away from Clover's astute gaze, idly fingering the narrow white lace at the cuff of the dark blue dress. The maids' uniforms at Farr Park had more trimming than this, the least drab of her new gowns. She hated them. She welcomed them. For now was the time to put away her fantasies—to find a way to be in a room, yet not part of it. To be so dull and inconsequential that no one noticed her.

She had guarded her virtue well through the years, aided by Lady Moretaine and Farr Park's staff, but reputation was the least of her worries at the moment. There might be those who put virtue above survival, but Katy was quite certain that those who whispered of a fate worse than death had never had to survive the slightest buffet of ill fortune. Katy knew better. Death was forever. There were fates worse than loss of virtue. If all else failed . . .

So she would wear these ugly gowns and sit in the shadows because the alternative was discovery. Pain, humiliation, suffering in mind and body.

But never enough to prefer death. She was a survivor. She was Katy Snow.

No, she wasn't. It was a lie. Her whole life at Farr Park, a lie.

"Should have ordered more while we was in town, sir," said Benjamin Briggs, the colonel's valet, shaking his head over the few garments laid out for packing. Briggs—yet another indication that his employer's heart did not match his hardened exterior—was an ex-soldier fallen on hard times whom Damon had somehow acquired between Dover and Farr Park, his former man having long since procured a place elsewhere. "You was a boy when you left home, Colonel. There's nothing from the old days as fits exceptin' your cravats. Mayhap your dress uniform?"

"No!"

Briggs, a burly man of medium height with both face and temperament of a bulldog, persisted. "From what I hears in the kitchen, Colonel, that there lady, your brother's wife, is right partic'lar about how folks look. Her husband being an earl an' all. Maybe you should have the little miss write to that Weston—"

"If I desire new clothes, Briggs, I am quite capable of ordering them myself." Damon scowled at the fashionable wrinkle he'd been attempting to put into his cravat before descending for dinner. He used to know how to tie the demmed things—had, in fact, thought he recalled the skill quite competently—until he had looked at himself through the critical eye of Drucilla, Countess of Moretaine.

Briggs snapped to attention. "Yes, sir, o' course, sir." Eyes straight front, he added, "Just thought what with you going to a castle and all . . ."

Damon swore, raised his chin, and while peering down his nose at the mirror, gave his cravat one last disgusted tweak. As if it actually mattered what the Dreadful Drucilla thought. Then again, perhaps Briggs was right. What could it hurt to trot out his uniform for dinner each night? One less thing for the witch to complain about. *Hell and the devil,* what was wrong with him? He hadn't even met the woman. His entire opinion of Drucilla Moretaine was based on what his mama had told him. Ashby's wife could be a charming young woman who simply could not abide to live in the powerful shadow of her mother-in-law.

No . . . that dog wouldn't fight. Over the years he had received letters from Ashby as well as from his mama. Letters distinguished by what they did not say. Letters full of politics, social gatherings, and sporting events; yet, except for the first halcyon days of the earl's marriage, they had been letters devoid of the slightest hint of connubial bliss.

"Pack the uniform," Damon ordered. "And Briggs . . . kindly do not refer to my mother's companion as 'the little miss.' She gives herself enough airs as it is. I suspect her encroaching ways are far more likely to upset our hostess than my lack of wardrobe."

"Ah, but she's a taking little thing, sir. Seems quite like one of the family."

"Enough!" the colonel roared. "Pack everything fit for an earl's country seat. We leave at nine in the morning." If he could roust his mama out of bed. Which he very much doubted.

Colonel Farr's fears proved justified. In spite of the dowager countess's concern for her elder son, their cavalcade did not depart until half ten. Damon, knowing good manners would have him sitting with his back to the horses, avoided an intimate all-day tangling of his long legs with those of the diminutive Katy Snow by choosing to ride beside the carriage. From the eagerness of his stallion's gait, he could tell that Volcán was pleased to be on the road again, moving out into territory unknown to the Arabian-bred horse. Blasted animal was probably already sniffing for the smell of gunpowder, pricking his ears for the roar of cannons and the crack of rifle fire.

Well, *he* was not. Though, in truth, the thought of a confrontation with his brother was far more daunting than going off to fight the French. At least that little baggage Katy Snow looked more the thing. Odd, but sight of the plain brown gown she was wearing today had brought back a flash of the long-ago child in the ugly dress gazing at him defiantly, equal to equal. It was not, he realized, his mama's indulgence that had given the girl notions above her station. Pride, even arrogance, had always been there. His mother's patronage had only given the minx the office to display it.

Strange. He should have remembered that before. Not that it mattered, for Katy Snow was of no importance. She was a mere convenience to his mama, to himself. They could, of course, manage quite well without her. He was on his way to Castle Moretaine to reconcile with his brother—to attempt to turn a relationship marked more by duty than by love back to what it had been when Ashby taught him to play jackstraws, draughts, and later, chess. A time when Ashby cheered his first efforts in the saddle and helped him lift his first shotgun.

Yes, it was time he went back to the home of his childhood. To the great, sprawling country seat of the Earl of Moretaine. To the great, sprawling, *inconvenient* pile of stone that was Castle Moretaine. A pity the lords of Moretaine had always been politically adept, keeping the right face to both monarch and Parliament, their home never suffering the fate of being demolished, as had so many of England's castles. But eventually, the stones of the massive curtain wall had been used to fill in the moat and add to the village, a mile away. The living area had been expanded with each generation, until the bailey—in a final burst of construction in the mid-seventeenth century—had become nothing more than a modest courtyard. Damon sighed as he looked at the results. A hodgepodge of architecture it might be, but it was the home of his childhood, the principal seat of the family Farr.

Damon patted Volcán's neck to indicate his appreciation of the horse keeping to a steady trot even though his rider's mind was obviously wandering. A great campaigner, Volcán. Damon glanced back, making certain that the two coaches—one with his mother and Katy, the other with Briggs, the countess's maid Archer, and the remainder of the luggage—were still following sedately behind.

They were. Colonel Farr sighed. The incongruity of a veteran of nearly seven years of war, atop his charger, leading a cavalcade composed of women and servants through the serenity of the Cotswolds struck him with force. This was what he wanted, was it not? No challenges, no responsibilities, no—

Damon spurred Volcán into a gallop. John Coachman knew the way. In the peaceful green hills of Gloucestershire lieutenant colonels were superfluous. As he tore down the road, *ventre à terre*, Damon Farr reached for his saber.

But, of course, it wasn't there.

The sun was nearing the western horizon when they approached the great wrought-iron gates that barred the long drive leading to Castle Moretaine. Dusk flirted with the trees as the gatekeeper rushed out, stumbling over his own feet in his eagerness to welcome home the prodigal mama and son. Ah, but he'd not pay for drinks at the Golden Lion for a month or more! Fancy that young scamp a colonel, and looking like his face would crack if he smiled. But the dowager, now there was a one. Not a day older than when she left, not a day. And the young miss with her, a real looker, she was. Going to set the tomcats on the prowl, yes, indeed. And that grand lady up there in the castle wasn't going to like it, not one bit.

The gatekeeper followed the progress of the coach until it disappeared around a curve in the heavily forested park. Damon Farr and the dowager had come home. And none too soon. None too soon at all.

"A goodly part of it is fourteenth century," said Serena, Lady Moretaine, to her young companion, whose nose was pressed to the coach window. "The cloisters around the courtyard were enclosed at a later date, though the Gothic style was imitated quite nicely, I think. Of course, the curtain wall, moat, and drawbridge were taken down long ago."

Katy knew her mouth was agape, her eyes reflecting astonishment. *Castle Moretaine.* Truly, she had thought it only a name given, perhaps, to some long-ago structure on the site. But it had towers, turrets, even a glimpse of crenelations. It was truly an enchanted castle, shining in light-colored stone, shaded pink by the last rays of the sunset. Surely such a place could not house a wicked witch who might be on visiting terms with Baron Oxley and his family.

They clattered through an opening in the front wall and entered a vast courtyard, the gravel drive illuminated by a veritable wall of torches. Obviously, they were expected. On the inner side of the castle, Katy noted, the windows were much larger, with Gothic arches and diamond panes of glass. She had fallen asleep and awakened in a fairy wonderland. This could not be real.

But she could smell the acrid scent of the torches, see the reality of an entire retinue of liveried footmen lined up to serve them, putting down steps, unstrapping luggage, directing the coachman to the stables. Katy thought she caught a shine in the very proper butler's eye as he solemnly welcomed the dowager countess to the home in which she had reigned for so many years. And, quite possibly, there was a suspicious moisture in Lady Moretaine's eyes as well. Then the colonel was beside them, offering his mother his arm. Katy trailed them, six feet behind, shrinking into her role, deliberately cloaking herself in invisibility. For at Castle Moretaine silence would not be enough.

Chapter Ten

Drucilla, Countess of Moretaine—they were informed by Rankin, who had been butler for nearly as long as Damon could remember—awaited her guests in the new drawing room, a designation used to distinguish the seventeenth century addition from the lord's withdrawing room, part of the original keep. The hall in the "new" wing was quite splendid, Katy thought, with a fine double staircase, painted white, leading to a first-floor gallery above. She was, however, disappointed by nary a sign of suits of armor, chain mail, or crossed swords and lances. But they must have been somewhere in this great sprawling pile for the colonel was saying, "I always liked the old part best. Ashby and I fought countless battles up and down the winding stone staircases with our wooden swords. Knocked over a good bit of armor as well, as I recall."

"And fenced," said his mother reprovingly. "Up and over the trestle tables—"

Damon chortled. "Ah, yes, we alternated knights with cavaliers and Roundheads. We drew straws to determine who must play the Roundhead, as neither of us wished to do so. Good memories," he said to his mother, who had halted beside him, with Katy Snow hovering in the background as a good companion should. "I am glad we came," Damon added softly. "I had thought to put childhood aside with the rest of my life, but it's good to see the old pile. And Ashby. He's a good man . . . he has done his duty here, as I did in the army."

His mama laid her gloved fingers over his arm. "I am proud of my sons. Of both of you."

Damon flashed a genuine smile that dazzled both females present. "Then onward!" he cried, as lighthearted as Katy had ever seen him. "Let us beard the castle's lord and lady in their den."

Rankin, stately in his livery, had been patiently waiting at the foot of the grand staircase. Ascertaining that the dowager and her son were once again ready to proceed, he led them up to the gallery, where he threw open a great studded oak door. He stepped inside, threw back his shoulders, and announced in stentorian tones, "The Dowager Countess of Moretaine, Colonel Damon Farr, and"—he lowered his voice to a near whisper—"Miss Katy Snow."

Katy, mindful of the many warnings she had received, tried not to wince at being singled out in this fashion. She should have stayed below, asked to be shown to her room. But when she had hung back with Briggs and Archer, who were directing the unloading of the luggage, the dowager had beckoned her forward with an imperious wave of her hand. So here she was, being announced in an earl's drawing room. As if she were a real person, not Katy Snow who was supposed to be unseen as well as unheard. A shadow figure unworthy of acknowledgment.

Polite but cool words were being exchanged. Katy, keeping her eyes fixed on the hem of the dowager's traveling costume, was surprised when her employer's voice suddenly rose. "And where," she demanded, "is my son?"

"Moretaine sends his regrets, my lady," said Drucilla, Countess of Moretaine, "but the doctor has confined him to his chamber until he is quite recovered from his chill. A ghastly place, Scotland," she added with a shudder. "Why he insists on going there each autumn I cannot imagine. We shall have tea, then I shall have a cold collation sent to your rooms. Moretaine will receive you in the morning."

The colonel had been studying their hostess with considerable interest. The younger countess referred to her husband of three years by his title. He supposed the formality was not uncommon, particularly in women who reveled in having snabbled a titled husband. Still and all, he could not like it. Perhaps his mama was not so far out in her opinion of the Dreadful Drucilla. And yet . . . a man would have to be blind not to be dazzled by the countess's sophisticated beauty. Her hair was the glossy black of a raven's wing, with the nearest of the room's two fireplaces burnishing blue highlights into the strands artfully arranged around her piquant face. Her eyes were a rich chocolate, he thought, though the flickering candlelight made it difficult to tell anything other than their icy indifference. Everything about her spoke of her position in the *ton*. He had no doubt her gown of burgundy satin was in the latest style, as was her coiffure, so much shorter than his mother's . . . or Katy Snow's. His brother's wife was lovely . . . and cold as a frozen pass in the Spanish mountains.

"Colonel Farr," said the vision of loveliness, proffering a sudden smile that would have had most men panting at her feet, "do sit by me and tell of your adventures in the war. Moretaine has so regaled us with your exploits that seeing you is quite like looking at a legend."

Damon—social façade firmly in place, if a bit grim—seated himself in a claret velvet armchair with ornately carved arms, then found himself as silent as Katy Snow—who, he noted, had slipped onto a upright chair set back against the wall in a corner as far away from the Farr family as she could get. Good. That was the proper place for the little minx.

"Colonel?" The younger Lady Moretaine, eyebrows raised, was holding out a cup of tea.

With an inward grimace at his wandering thoughts, Damon accepted the cup, noted that his mother and Drucilla already had cups in hand, so took a sip of his own. Ah . . . an aromatic brew of the finest quality. The next best thing to hot spiced punch after a daylong journey.

Guilt struck him. "Katy," he called, "come get your tea. You must be as parched as the rest of us."

As he watched her slink across the great expanse of carpet,

guilt struck from the opposite direction. Had the girl not been told to efface herself, to stay as far away from the younger countess as possible? And Katy had done just that. And he, the idiot colonel, was calling her forward, because innate good manners forbade him to drink tea while the child sat in the corner, undoubtedly tired and thirsty and— *Hell and the devil,* he'd set the cat among the pigeons. Or, more like, set the baby bird down in front of the cat.

With a careful precision that broadcast her disdain, Drucilla poured tea into a fourth cup. "Well, come and get it, girl," she snapped. "Don't just stand there as if you've never seen a teacup before. I am quite certain my dear mama-in-law has managed to teach you a few essential manners, at the very least."

Damon blinked. *How dare she?* He might criticize Katy Snow, but she was *his* waif. He could doubt her origins; Drucilla Farr could not. "Take the cup," he growled to Katy even as he glowered at the younger countess, who remained supremely oblivious to his displeasure.

Katy took the cup, scurrying back to her chair by the wall as fast as she could without spilling tea on the elegant thick carpet. She had not asked for cream or sugar. The thought of asking the Dreadful Drucilla for anything was quite appalling. If only . . .

The constraints of her long masquerade were beginning to pall. Not that she was some princess in disguise, she told herself bitterly. If she faced the matter squarely, the girl called Katy Snow was merely the overly indulged object of a doting grandfather's affections. In spite of one brilliant star on her family tree, the Drucillas of this world would always take precedence. She might have been raised to hold her head high, been given an education superior to that of most boys, yet, truthfully, she was the end result of a misalliance between the younger son of a younger son and the daughter of a wool merchant.

If only her papa and mama had lived . . .

But she had never known them. Both drowned when caught

by a sudden summer storm while they were sailing, leaving a six-month-old to be brought up by her grandparents. Katy had heard the story many times of how her grandfather the bishop, third son of the Duke of Carewe, had stormed into her parents' modest home and snatched her from the arms of her maternal grandmother, the wool merchant's wife. No grandchild of his would be raised by vulgar cits! And all connection between the families, tenuous at best, had been severed on the spot. For close on twelve years she had lived with her paternal grandparents, though she barely recalled her grandmother, who had passed on when she was four, leaving her to be raised in comfortable luxury by the scholarly but indulgent bishop.

And then he was gone, that light of her life, Cedric Challoner, Bishop of Hulme. And she had been delivered into the hands of her grandfather's second cousin, Cornelia Hardcastle, wife of Baron Oxley, in whom her beloved grandfather had mistakenly placed his faith.

"Katy. Katy, my child, come along. We are going to our rooms."

Katy? Katy Snow was a dream, a figment of the imagination of Farr Park's staff. She was not Katy, had never been Katy. Could not continue to be Katy. But what to do, what to do? Once, she had thought herself content . . . but no longer. She had only been content to bide her time, to grow up in peace—

"Katy!" the colonel echoed his mother, but more sharply. "Stop dawdling, girl, and come along."

Mortified, Katy bounced to her feet. With ingrained good manners, she crossed to the younger Lady Moretaine, who was still seated, and dropped into a curtsy whose depth indicated the proper respect and subservience expected from a lowly companion. *Which is all I am,* Katy reminded her rebellious inner self. Severely.

The colonel proffered a curt nod of approval. Once again, Katy trailed the Farrs, mother and son, as Rankin led them through a maze of passages to the guest wing, where the food and peaceful repose all three were anticipating encountered a sudden snag.

The dowager's pale complexion turned pink; her bosom swelled. Katy Snow was to be placed in the old governess's room? On the nursery floor? Indeed not! She needed the child close by at all times.

Fortunately, the elderly butler, who had served at the castle since—according to his frequent assertions to his staff—he was knee-high to a tadpole, seemed to have no difficulty ignoring his mistress's instructions. Katy was soon ensconced in a fine bedchamber next to the dowager countess, with Colonel Farr just across the hall.

Serena Moretaine savored her peace—laid down on a chaise longue with scrolled back and upholstered in brocade the shade of ripe peaches—for scarce five minutes before scratching was heard at her door. Archer, who had been hanging up the dowager's gowns, scurried to answer the summons. It was Katy Snow, looking anxious.

"No, no, child. Do not look so glum," said the countess, beckoning Katy to her. "Must I ring the bell and wait half an hour for someone to come up from the depths, then search for you, and finally see your presence an hour after I needed you? Absurd, quite absurd. Ah!" The countess frowned. "Yet still you look so solemn."

"As well she might!" declared the colonel, who had entered his mama's suite almost on Katy's heels. "Did we not agree that Katy must be invisible? That she would do nothing to raise the fair Drucilla's ire?"

"Fair!" exclaimed his mother. "Indeed she is not. That woman's heart is as dark as her hair."

The colonel groaned. "I will not mince nuances with you, Mama. You have likely brought Drucilla's wrath down on the child's head. She has no way to defend herself without your aid, and I cannot have the two countesses of Moretaine quarreling like fishwives during this visit. We are here to see Ashby—"

"*Fishwives!* Fishwives," the dowager repeated in a strangled tone softer than her initial shriek. Katy dropped to her knees beside the chaise longue and seized the countess's hand.

Colonel Farr shifted to Parade Rest, arms akimbo, and scowled at both women. "We are here to visit my brother, who, it seems, is too ill to greet us. Does that not strike you as ominous, Mama? Ashby has never been robust. I cannot like the sound of it. This is scarcely the time for female fits and fidgets—"

The countess burst into tears. Katy hugged her, fussed over her a moment, then bounded to her feet, fists clenched. Damon could almost see the words hovering on her lips, threatening to explode the myth that she could not talk. Indeed . . . a veritable torrent of words seemed poised on the tip of her tongue. The green eyes flared, the shapely lips quivered; her delicious bosom heaved. Almost, but not quite, enough distraction to deflect his worry about Ashby.

"Yes, I know," said Damon, holding up his hand, palm out. "I am a beast and a bully and not fit to claim the title of gentleman. Nonetheless, you will both obey me in this. Mama, you will not quarrel with Drucilla. Katy, you will be the drab mouse who inches back into her hole, as if she had never ventured out. No, you baggage, do not roll your eyes at me! I am determined it shall be so."

"We are not your troopers," the dowager forced out between sobs.

"Indeed not. My troopers would be far more obedient."

On a sudden surge of blue blood—or was it a vulgar display of tradesman's temper?—Katy charged across the room. The colonel, with a certain detached interest, allowed her to pound his chest with several quite ineffectual blows before he calmly seized both arms and put her from him. He shook his head. "A pity no one saw fit to tan your bottom when you were young enough that it might have done some good," he observed.

"Damon!" his mama cried, more shocked by his mention of such an intimate part of Katy's anatomy than by the implied threat.

"Goodnight, Mama." The colonel bowed, while Katy seethed, as horrified by her behavior as she was at being put aside as if she were of no more significance than a gnat. "Let us hope that the morning brings more sanguine news of Ashby."

And then he was gone, leaving the dowager and Katy Snow to console each other.

Chapter Eleven

"Sit, child," Archer declared, raising her eyes from her mending to follow Katy Snow as she paced the countess's sitting room. "You are exhausting me and wearing a path in the earl's Turkey carpet while you're at it."

Katy tossed her expressive hands in a gesture of frustration, then clasped them tight in front of her, head bent. Whether offering a prayer or willing her feet to be still, Archer could not tell. "'Tis nonsense to expect the worst, Snow. You are making yourself ill . . . and me along with you."

A fine London maid, Alice Archer had been with Serena, Lady Moretaine, since the year she was first presented to the queen. That a child of possibly base-born origins should capture her mistress's heart had not set well with Archer, but it had proved difficult not to like Katy Snow. The girl was appealing, ostensibly a lady, skilled in all the niceties of the upper classes. A take-in? Perhaps. But Archer was too wise to go against her mistress's wishes. Though not one of Katy Snow's avid supporters, as were the rest of the staff at Farr Park, she tolerated the girl well enough. Most of the time.

"Sit!" Archer repeated, more sharply. "You know quite well what curiosity did to the cat. Our lady will return shortly, and all will be revealed."

Katy stamped her foot, flounced to a comfortable-looking chair upholstered in blue satin brocade, and plopped herself into it. Archer shook her head. The colonel had it right when he said someone should have tanned her bottom long since.

The door crashed open. Serena Moretaine stumbled into the room. She leaned against the door, the back of her hand to her mouth, her entire body shaking as if she would sag to the floor at any moment.

"My lady!" Archer jumped to her feet, but Katy was already there, encircling the dowager with her arms, hugging her. Together, they steered the countess across the room, settling her onto the chaise longue. Archer rushed off to procure water from the pitcher on the nightstand in the bedchamber, while Katy fitted herself onto the edge of the chaise near the foot, wanting desperately to offer comfort, yet finding herself woefully inadequate in the face of such abject misery. Last night the countess had sobbed dramatically. Today, she was quite horribly silent, except for an occasional gasp for air. Last night had been a mere fit of temper. Today was anguish, pure and simple. Katy clasped both hands around the countess's own and hung on. Eighteen suddenly seemed very young, far from the wise adult she had imagined herself to be.

Lady Moretaine accepted the crystal goblet of water from Archer, took a small sip. A shudder passed through her. "He is dying," she said, looking straight ahead. "A chill from Scotland's cold rain, and my son is dying. He should never have made the journey home. Yet he insisted, he tells us. Foolish, foolish boy. Everyone knows Scottish doctors are superior to our own. If he had but stayed . . ." The dowager's voice trailed off. She took another sip from the goblet, her fingers shaking so hard the water sloshed from side to side.

"He says," the countess continued, "he knew he'd been given his notice to quit. That is how he put it—quite coldly, I thought. My poor Ashby," she added on a whisper. "He wished to come home to speak with Damon, for he says his brother will soon be Moretaine. He wanted time to instruct him." The countess's breath hitched in her throat. "For all his years at war, Damon took it as badly as I. Turned as white as my dear Ashby. He's still there. Ashby asked . . . asked if I would be so kind as to leave them alone. . . ."

As the three women huddled together, offering and seeking

comfort, Katy wondered about the younger countess, who had greeted them as if the earl were merely indisposed, suffering from nothing worse than a cold. Did she truly care so little? Or had the truth been kept from her? Or . . . was she one of those who saw only what she wished to see? Katy suspected the latter. Drucilla Moretaine was more selfish than venal. A woman who had married well and enjoyed flaunting her position at every opportunity—which was probably the source of her clash with the elder countess, the perfect Lady of the Castle, whom Drucilla would never be able to emulate.

But if Drucilla suspected the severity of her husband's illness, would she have been so calm, so cool, as she had been last night? If the earl were truly dying, she was about to lose her position. Surely a terrifying thought to someone who seemed to thrive on it.

As Archer answered a soft scratching at the door, Katy discovered her saddened heart could still leap at the thought of who was likely to be standing in the hall.

Damon.

The countess, who was lain back on the chaise, sat up with a jerk. "Have you seen the doctor?" she cried.

Glumly, the colonel nodded. "He confirms what Ashby told us. Each time he has had one of his bouts of illness, his lungs have grown weaker. He had been warned not to go to Scotland this year. He went anyway. Not something I would have expected our sensible Ashby to do," he added softly, "but there it is. The doctor holds little hope."

Lady Moretaine sucked in a deep breath, swallowing a sob. "I told Ashby I am an incompetent in governing my own lands, that I can understand Spanish better than I shall understand his steward—I was hoping to see him smile—but it seems to please him to attempt to stuff my head with all manner of things I never wished to know."

Abruptly, Damon sat in the chair Katy had vacated when she ran to the countess's aid. He plunged his head into his hands. "My apologies, Mama," he muttered. "I fear my unflappable military façade is crumbling in a most unseemly manner."

"Shall we leave you, my lady?" Archer asked.

"No, oh, no!" Vehemently, the countess shook her head. Katy squeezed her hand, holding on tight, willing her own youthful strength to the older woman's support.

Silence descended on bowed heads and inner anguish. Even Archer's customarily busy fingers were still. Wind rattled a shutter. In concert with their feelings, the already gray day grew darker, casting the sitting room further into melancholy.

"An odd thing," Damon said at last. "Ashby refuses to allow the doctor to speak frankly with Drucilla. Says he doesn't wish to see her plunged into gloom."

"Fustian! She must be prepared," declared the dowager, showing a spark of her customary spirit.

"And so I told him, but he was adamant. It is a masquerade I cannot like," Damon added. "I am a soldier. I am accustomed to fighting battles head-to-head, with no need to hide behind a false front."

Katy's fingers jerked against the dowager's hand. Warily, she looked from mother to son and back again.

"Indeed," the dowager agreed. "I cannot imagine involving myself in such a deception. I wonder that Ashby could expect it. Surely you can persuade him—"

"I have already tried. He claims he wishes only to protect her."

"Protect her! More like, she will suffer twice as much when he is gone."

Damon shook his head. "Deception is anathema. Only Ashby's illness could have caused him to sink to such an aberration."

Katy Snow sat staring blindly at the carpet. *Masquerade. Deception. Anathema.* She was trapped, with no way out. She must remain the mute Katy Snow—or lose her loving Farr Park family. Yet without the truth, she had no chance of ever being more than a servant—or, at best, a fleeting lover—to Colonel Damon Farr. A moot point, because at her revelation he would turn on her as viciously as all the others. *Katy Snow, deceiver. Liar. Lowest of the low.*

Outside, the gloomy day turned to a rain that pounded against the panes, augmenting the anguish within.

He was more than splendid—he quite took her breath away. Katy, following behind the dowager countess, came to an abrupt halt in the doorway to the Yellow Antechamber, where they were to gather before dinner. She stared, mouth agape. Uniforms of any kind were rare in the vicinity of Farr Park, even in time of war. But a cavalry officer in full dress? If she had not already adored Damon Farr, this would have been the moment of her fall.

Donning his uniform seemed to have added inches to the colonel's height. If he were wearing his shako, he would have towered over them like some ancient god. Katy snapped her mouth closed so hard her teeth cracked together. She feasted her eyes, watching the colonel greet his hostess and his mother before shaking hands with the earl's secretary, Philip Winslow.

Blue jacket with orange facings. Pointed cuffs. An intricate lacing of gold braid and gold buttons, pristine white breeches tucked into shining black boots. An orange sash . . . but no saber. Oddly disappointed not to see her hero in the full regalia of a wartime warrior, Katy peered more closely at his long, lean thigh, hoping her eyes had been playing tricks on her. Hoping no one was noticing the direction of her eyes. Hoping, quite despersately, she was not blushing. Alas, it was quite true. The colonel wore a diagonal sash across his chest, matching the one about his waist, but no scabbard dangled from the end of it. Colonel Damon Farr had not come armed to his sister-in-law's table.

But everything else was part and parcel of her heroic fantasies. Damon, dark and saturnine, leading his troopers as they charged across battlefield after battlefield, changing the boy she had worshipped ever since he had granted her a home into the man he was today. A man for whom the glory of war had worn away, leaving the hardened campaigner, somber . . . disillusioned . . .

And even more appealing in his hurt and vulnerability.

Katy closed her eyes, took a deep breath, then found her way to a seat in the corner, where it soon became evident that she was not the only female impressed by the colonel's finery. Katy had had little opportunity to observe a Diamond of the First Water fulfilling the role expected of her. Fascinated—if appalled—she watched as Drucilla, toast of the *ton* in her come-out year of 1812, demonstrated why she was still an outstanding gem in society three years later. Katy glowered. It seemed the Dreadful Drucilla could be shockingly charming when she wished, and with Colonel Damon Farr, she obviously so wished. The foolish man was lapping up the admiration quite as if he did not have the constant adulation of the females in his own household. *Ungrateful wretch!*

The dinner that followed was, as expected, strained, with the younger Lady Moretaine addressing the elder only to the length demanded by good manners, with nothing more than an occasional sniff of disdain hurled in Katy's direction. Between such dainty bites as indicated Drucilla could live on air alone, she regaled Colonel Farr with all the *on dits* he simply must know before rejoining society. To his mild protest that he had no interest in the *ton,* his sister-in-law responded with a tinkling laugh. Silly boy, of course he must take his place in society. Such a loss to the matchmaking mamas if he did not.

Drucilla fluttered her lashes. The colonel actually smiled. Philip Winslow kept his head down, his grip on his fork suspiciously like a man who was considering using it as a weapon.

Katy nearly bit through a chicken bone.

"We must have a dinner party," Drucilla announced, looking remarkably pleased with herself. "There are one or two families in the vicinity with girls the right age."

"My son is not well enough for company," the dowager declared, thoroughly shocked.

"I assure you, my lady, the neighbors are quite accustomed to Moretaine's illnesses. It will not be our first dinner party without his presence."

"But surely not this—"

"You are very kind, sister," Damon interjected firmly, "but I have no interest in marriage. I would not wish to raise any expectations."

"Nonsense! It must be apparent that Ashby and I are childless." For a moment the young countess actually appeared to be suffering from a genuine emotion. "Someone must ensure the title."

The colonel, looking pale, downed the remainder of his wine in one gulp.

"Perhaps afternoon tea," the dowager suggested, for as much as she was determined to dislike any suggestion made by her daughter-in-law, Damon must indeed marry and produce an heir. And before he could do that, it was necessary for him to be distracted from Katy Snow.

Drucilla considered the matter, nodded her acceptance. "Very well, afternoon tea. Three days hence. That is sufficient notice, I should think. The Richardsons and the Hardcastles have daughters. And I believe I heard something about another girl . . . some long-lost cousin or other, who has recently returned to the family. Splendid. You shall have three young ladies paraded before you, Colonel."

"That is . . . most thoughtful," said the dowager through clenched teeth. "Thank you." To be beholden to the Dreadful Drucilla was the outside of enough. Positively mortifying, but the opportunity was quite too good to be missed. The boy would have to marry, whether he liked it or not. The next heir in line was a London dilettante unworthy of the name Moretaine.

She must say something more, the dowager realized. Good manners demanded it. "Katy, is it not delightful?" she exclaimed. "You will have the opportunity to meet others your age."

The elder Lady Moretaine did not see Drucilla's lip curl or even hear her snort of disgust, for she was staring at Katy Snow, who seemed frozen in her place, fork poised halfway to her mouth, skin the color of parchment, eyes wide and unseeing. "Katy. Katy, my dear, what is wrong? Are you ill? Katy!"

Katy lowered her fork. Blinked. Cast a horrified glance at

the others, then struggled to get up, her legs seemingly too weak to stand. Damon thrust back his chair and was rounding the end of the table when Katy broke free, dashing out of the room and toward the stairs as fast as her shaky legs could carry her. The colonel followed, gaining rapidly.

Serena Moretaine slumped in her chair, her whole body quivering. It was all her fault. She had thrown the two of them together, hoping Katy's youth and high spirits would alleviate her son's somber melancholy. In her concern for Damon, she had not considered any other possible consequences. Certainly not Damon's lust or Katy's ruin.

Katy was on the first landing of the great mahogany staircase when Damon caught up with her. "By God, girl, you look as if you'd been sentenced to hang. What was said to upset you so?"

She tried to shove him away. A gnat against a blue stone wall. His gold buttons pressed into her palms even as his hands came down on her shoulders.

"It is not like you to fly into a pelter over nothing. So what is wrong?" He shifted his grip to one arm, turned her toward the remaining flight of steps. "Come, let us find some paper so you can tell me what has happened."

She struggled, he gripped her harder. She gasped.

Damon loosed his grip, stepped back, and crossed his arms. "Oh, ho," he breathed. "You just made a sound."

Even as the emerald eyes sparked, Katy's lower lip quivered. At long last, the colonel thought, she was at the breaking point. He should have felt triumph. Instead, he felt the worst kind of monster. This was Katy, the lost child he had given a home. Katy, who was closer to a daughter than a companion to his mother. Katy, his helper. His torment.

His bright, darling termagant.

His friend.

Damon sighed, the epaulettes on his shoulders subsiding along with his temper. "This has been a bad day, Katy—for all of us. You may keep your secrets. For now. We will finish this conversation another time. Go. I will tell my mother you were unwell."

For a moment, Katy bowed her head, almost as if offering a prayer of gratitude. He watched as she pulled herself up the stairs, grasping the banister for support, a far cry from the usual spirited Katy Snow. His avid gaze followed her along the gallery until she disappeared down the corridor.

Downstairs, they were waiting for him. Wondering. Speculating. What was Katy Snow to Damon Farr?

If only he knew. He feared this was the day his world had been turned upside down in more ways than one.

Chapter Twelve

Katy threw herself onto her bed, pummeled her pillow, then went as still as any small creature with hunters hard on its heels. Gooseflesh prickled her arms, every sense alert, ready for the ultimate disaster—which was surely approaching at breakneck speed, a runaway, out of control. She was doomed. And, outside of a full confession, she had no way to prevent it. Yet confession would be the biggest disaster of all. They would hate her, all of them. Even her dear, darling Lady Moretaine.

And Damon.

No . . . no, surely they would understand? She'd been so cold and hungry, so frightened that she would have done anything—*well, almost anything*—to find a safe haven. But deception was an insidious thing, swinging full circle to devour the deceiver. That she was no longer content with her simple, sheltered life had been hard enough to admit, but then, like the horrid rattle of a ghost walking the echoing halls of her past life, came the threat of a visit to Castle Moretaine, so dangerously close to the Hardcastles of Oxley Hall. Which was a mere bagatelle compared to the announcement that the Hardcastles were to be invited to tea for the express purpose of parading before Damon the dubious charms of the Honorable Eleanore Hardcastle.

And Eleanore's unknown long-lost cousin.

What unknown long-lost cousin? Could there be more than one?

Unlikely, most unlikely. Which meant . . . which meant problems Katy found too overwhelming to contemplate. *Long-lost cousin* could not possibly mean what she thought. Perhaps she had not heard correctly and was making much ado about nothing. Time enough to cross that bridge when she came to it. She had three days to discover a way to avoid that tea party, and avoid it she would. The Hardcastles would come and go and never know of Katy Snow's existence.

Katy's flurry of plans for escaping high tea went for naught, as not only did the dowager insist on her presence, the following morning Rankin roused Katy from the book she was reading and led her to the younger countess's morning room, a cozy chamber decorated in peach and gold, with tall windows revealing a formal walled garden with fountain. The sound of birds twittering could be heard even though the doors were closed. It was a lovely room, the most comfortable Katy had seen in this massive pile of stone.

"Ah, there you are, Snow," said Drucilla, glancing up from the parchment notepaper atop the D-shaped satinwood desk in front of her.

Bad enough for the colonel to call her Snow, Katy fumed, but for the earl's wife to address her mother-in-law's companion as no better than a servant was a deliberate insult.

"I am told you write a competent hand," the young countess said in a tone that indicated she did not quite believe what she had heard. "I have decided to add two more families to our tea. You may pen the invitations." Drucilla, elegant in a morning gown of jade green, with layers of ruffles at the hem and cuffs of her long sleeves, abandoned her seat at the desk to drape herself over a settee upholstered in ripe peach and scattered with tasseled pillows of amber satin.

A remarkable picture, Katy thought. *But why waste it on me?* Perhaps displaying herself as if posing for a painting was so ingrained in Drucilla's life that she simply conducted herself accordingly at all times, no matter if the vision she was presenting was only for the eyes of one so unworthy as Katy Snow.

"Sit. I shall tell you what to write."

Katy sat and did as she was told, beginning to have a better idea of why the dowager insisted on referring to her daughter-in-law as the Dreadful Drucilla. Yes, she was cold and more than a little toplofty . . . and had probably married the earl for his title and wealth, but until this moment Katy would not have called her Dreadful. Most young ladies of the *ton* could be said to have married for advancement rather than love. And being arrogant enough to be termed "high in the instep" flirted with being a compliment of the highest order. Drucilla was not a loving person—perhaps not even kind—but Dreadful?

Katy, finding herself almost sorry for the young countess, had not truly thought so. She had, in fact, been slightly ashamed, wondering at the ease with which she had taken the dowager's opinion for her own. It did not seem right that Drucilla remained ignorant of the severity of her husband's illness. She must visit the sickroom. She must see . . . must guess. Yet, despite what should be obvious to the most calloused observer, she was inviting neighbors to high tea.

"Snow," said the earl's wife quite conversationally, as if she were discussing menus with her housekeeper, "my mama-in-law seems quite determined that you shall attend our little gathering. She has some quaint notion of introducing you to the other young ladies . . . even to their brothers." Drucilla waved a languid hand, dismissing such an outrageous notion. Her lovely face was suddenly distorted by a sneer. "You are a servant, a child of the gutter, given shelter by my careless brother-in-law in a most indiscriminate manner, and raised far above your station by my mama-in-law, who must surely have been affected by the libertarian rantings of the Corsican Monster. An effrontery I will not tolerate. Introduce you to my guests indeed! When pigs fly, Snow. When pigs fly."

Drucilla adjusted a fold in her soft muslin skirt, flicked a disarranged ruffle back over her fingertips. Satisfied by the perfection of her appearance, she returned her attention to Katy. "At my tea you will efface yourself in a corner. You will not mingle with my guests. You will not cast your smile at anyone, do you hear? You will effect a blank countenance, as a proper servant should. You will serve the dowager and no one else. You will not encroach by passing tea cups or passing plates. You will not raise your eyes to your betters. Is that clear? Answer me, girl! Is that clear?"

What was clear was that in her cold-blooded anger Drucilla, Countess of Moretaine, had forgotten that Katy Snow was also known as Lady Silence. Inwardly, Katy smiled. Nothing could have played more neatly into her hand than being told to hide in a corner. Also, she had an answer to her doubts about the dreadfulness of Drucilla. The younger Lady Moretaine was beyond toplofty and high in the instep. The younger Lady Moretaine was, in fact, nasty.

Which, in this case, was good. The dowager would be furious, Katy knew, but could do nothing about her hostess's orders without causing a complete break at a time when she needed to be at her elder son's side. Drucilla was indeed queen of her castle—for now.

At the appointed hour for the Countess of Moretaine's high tea, the supposed guest of honor stood in a far corner of the seventeenth century drawing room, resting a hand on the back of a Queen Anne side chair where Katy Snow sat, hands clasped, making what appeared to be a valiant effort to be invisible. Even as the colonel was forced to agree that Drucilla could not introduce her guests to some unknown chit who wandered into his kitchen one night, Katy's resigned attitude touched his heart. She was eighteen, a lady in all but pedigree. Naturally, she wished to meet other young people. Ruthlessly, Damon curbed a rush of anger at his sudden vision of Katy flirting with the sons of the local gentry. If the chit wished to be like other young misses her age, it was perfectly understandable.

Devil take it! He actually felt sorry for her—which must be the reason he was standing here next to her instead of helping Drucilla and his mama greet the guests, as he should be doing. For the gentlemen, it seemed, had not scorned an invitation to

Castle Moretaine, even if the only beverage to be served was tea. The countess had summoned and the local gentry came.

From his sheltered position near the servants' entrance to the drawing room, Damon listened to Rankin's announcements attentively. For the sake of the House of Farr, he must put on what he thought of as his Wellington front, playing host in his brother's stead, addressing each of these strangers correctly, without faltering over their name or rank. Katy had provided him with an annotated list of guests. Baron and Lady Oxley, daughter Eleanore Hardcastle, and as-yet-nameless cousin; Squire and Mrs. Richardson, son Joel, daughter Joan. Mr. and Mrs. Swann and daughter Edwina, a schoolroom miss. Mr. Dearborn, the vicar, his wife Amanda, son Gabriel, and daughter Patience. A competent chit, Katy Snow—the meek façade she was presenting at the moment undoubtedly hid a veritable volcano of seething thoughts.

He leaned down, whispering, "The vicar's daughter looks as if she wouldn't say boo to a goose." Katy's lips twitched. "And Squire Richardson and his good wife appear to have reproduced themselves from the very same mold. One son, one daughter, as sturdily four-square and upright as any fine country family could wish." A flash of green fire warned him not to be unkind. "No, no, they are undoubtedly very worthy." Katy sat taller in her chair, turning her back, as it were, on his comments.

"Good God!" Damon hissed as a third family arrived, "does Drucilla think I wish to rob the cradle? That girl cannot be a day over fifteen. Though, on second look, it's fifteen going on twenty-five." He searched the list he had memorized and decided the newcomers must be the Swanns and their daughter Edwina. He looked to Katy for her reaction and saw that her hands were clasped so tightly together, the knuckles were white. Her face had turned the color of chalk. She looked, in fact, as if she were about to topple from her chair. She looked remarkably like the girl who had bolted from the dinner table just after Drucilla announced the tea party.

Damon laid a supporting hand on Katy's shoulder just as

Rankin announced, "Baron and Lady Oxley, Miss Eleanore Hardcastle, Miss Lucinda Challenor."

Katy whimpered. He'd swear on a stack of Bibles he heard her whimper. Later, later . . . he'd have to deal with it later. He'd already lingered too long; his presence was required. He tightened his grip on Katy's shoulder, hoping she recognized his attempt at comfort for what it was, then strode across the room, holding out his hand to Lord Oxley, a beefy man of close to fifty. Damon greeted the baron's wife with punctilious courtesy, turned to the two young ladies.

Now these two, he thought, were almost worth enduring Drucilla's party. The elder, Miss Eleanore Hardcastle, was tall and stately, with chestnut hair and amber eyes. Though her features were somewhat angular, she was a strikingly classic English noblewoman, precisely what a titled gentleman expected to have standing next to him at the top of his staircase. Miss Challenor, however, was of a different stripe altogether. Petite and blond, with a truly lovely face. And sparkling green eyes—bold and wise beyond her years. Odd, that. If put side by side with Katy Snow, the two girls might almost pass as sisters.

Colonel Farr, no one's fool, knew a mystery when he saw one. The strange resemblance, combined with Katy's reaction, refuted coincidence. Blast the chit! Surely she could have trusted him enough to tell him why this particular family caused her so much anguish.

"Do tell us about Moretaine, my lady," said Mrs. Dearborn, the vicar's wife, as she accepted a cup of tea from her hostess. "We have heard he is quite poorly." There was a general murmur of concern and sympathy from the other guests.

"As you may have heard," Drucilla said, "Moretaine took a chill while shooting in Scotland. Instead of staying until he was better, he insisted on coming home. It is his lungs again, and I fear it will be a long convalescence this time."

"Is he well enough to see me?" the vicar ventured. "When I called two days ago, the doctor turned me away."

"I think a visit today, while you are here, would be an excellent idea," Damon interjected before his sister-in-law could reply. "An excellent idea," the colonel repeated, exchanging a significant look with the vicar.

Mr. Dearborn put down his cup. "Perhaps now?" he murmured.

"Rankin," Damon said, "have someone escort the vicar to my brother."

And in that moment all but the most oblivious and self-centered knew that the earl was not expected to live. That power had already passed to his heir, the next Earl of Moretaine. Even the squire's son and daughter recognized the moment, as did the children of the vicar. Among those who missed the message entirely were the very young Edwina Swann, who was considering practicing her flirtation skills on Philip Winslow, the earl's secretary; Miss Hardcastle, who was still seething over the colonel's obvious interest in her cousin; and Miss Challenor, who was fully occupied planning her campaign to win Colonel Farr.

And Drucilla, Countess of Moretaine, who simply would not believe her reign could come to an end.

"Colonel," said Miss Hardcastle rather too brightly, "we are told you were in the cavalry. Do tell us about your experiences on the Peninsula."

"Believe me, Miss Hardcastle, you would not wish to hear them."

"Come now, Colonel," said Lady Oxley, an imposing woman whose voice boomed nearly as loudly as her husband's, "there must have been some lighter moments fit for a lady's ears."

"I fear our lighter moments were as ribald as our battles were bloody." Lord, what was the matter with him? Wellington would have pinned back his ears for such a gauche remark. "I beg pardon, my lady. My brother's illness has scattered my wits. There were indeed a number of moments that bear repeating." Damon launched into the tale of what had happened when the only available officers' billet was in a convent. Fortunately, it was one of the few times his troopers, mostly Irish, had behaved themselves—outside the convent walls, of course—

while the sons of British noblemen practiced almost forgotten restraint inside. With one or two of the younger, more winsome nuns, it had not been easy, but they had managed the thing, moving on after three days with nothing more than sighs of relief echoing behind them.

"Splendid," cried Miss Challenor. "A delightful tale. I can just see the column riding away, scarlet coats shining in the Spanish sun—"

"Blue."

"Blue?" Miss Challenor's green eyes went wide.

"My regiment—blue jackets with orange facings," Damon told her.

"Oh." Miss Challenor pouted. "'Tis not so striking a picture, I fear."

"Now, now, missy," said Squire Richardson, "soldiering is a hard thing. A pity young girls can't see beyond the uniform."

"Tell us about the Iberian ladies, Colonel," said Mrs. Richardson before her husband could launch into a tirade against the follies of the young. "Are they as dark and lovely as everyone says?"

"Indeed, ma'am," Damon replied easily, "but we were more likely to see the camp followers, who were—ah—seldom the best that Portugal and Spain had to offer. Most noble ladies were confined behind miradors, intricately carved wooden screens that shield the balconies overlooking the street. The ladies could see us, but we could not see them. It is, I believe, a conceit borrowed from the Mussulmen, who conquered the region at one time."

"Merciful heavens," murmured Mrs. Richardson, "I had no idea."

"Come, Colonel, don't tell us you never saw a single beauty?" said the squire's son, Joel, with a grin. Not much younger than Damon himself and confident of his position in the world, he did not hesitate to tease an earl's younger brother.

Taking no offense, Damon responded with a rueful grin of his own. "Wellington seemed to have an attraction for women. They flocked to him, like iron shavings to a magnet—why, when he was as cold as an icicle, I never could understand, but he enticed women from behind their miradors as easily as the Pied Piper led rats from Hamlin. No matter where we were—except for that time in the convent," he amended hastily—"there were always lovely ladies to brighten our days."

"Surely not on the battlefield," huffed Mr. Swann, father of the nubile Edwina.

"Ah, but there are always great gaps of time between battles," said the colonel, his spirits lightening somewhat as he recalled a number of moments of camaraderie, sparkling wit, dark eyes, lace mantillas, and sometimes, much more.

The squire harrumphed. The vicar's wife coughed. Joel Richardson laughed out loud. Gabriel, the vicar's son, turned his face away to hide a grin.

"Naughty boy," said Drucilla, but her eyes gleamed with mirth.

In her corner, Katy dug her nails into her palms. *Horrid man.* Why she liked him she could not imagine.

"My lady," cried an upstairs maid, bursting into the room, "vicar says you must come at once. Colonel, he asked for you as well. And for my lord's mama."

Katy, heedless of the presence of the Hardcastles, rushed to Lady Moretaine's side, helping her beloved dowager to her feet. The colonel took his mother's arm, and the three rushed out, leaving Drucilla, Countess of Moretaine, still sitting in her chair. Gradually, as shock settled into reality, Mrs. Dearborn, the vicar's wife, closely followed by Mrs. Richardson, rose and went to the countess's side. They might find the Countess of Moretaine a trifle sharper than they cared for, but it was their duty to be of help in times of crisis. With gentle words and great care, the two women brought the countess to her feet and escorted her from the room.

Chapter Thirteen

"You must stay by me every moment, child," Serena Moretaine said to Katy as they sat in the drawing room, two black crows perched in a vast field of green damask, cream satin brocade, silk wallcoverings hung with priceless paintings, and seemingly acres of gilt. "With Drucilla prostrate upon her bed, I must manage alone, for Damon will be obliged to move about, speaking to each of the guests."

Katy, who knew quite well that the Hardcastles would be among the mourners returning to the castle after the earl's funeral, shuddered. In the dramatic flurry that ended the tea party, she had escaped detection, but what if Oxley and his wife were using the funeral to take another look at the dowager's companion? Nearly seven years had gone by. She had grown up. Surely no hint of the spirited, overindulged child could be seen in Lady Moretaine's demure, drably garbed companion—

"I have never told a soul why I left the Dower House," the countess was saying. "It's a lovely house, not more than a mile from here, and I shall not begrudge Drucilla's use of it, if that is her wish. Poor girl . . . her grief seems more genuine than I expected."

More likely Drucilla's grief was for her loss of position, Katy thought grimly. For the ignominy of following in her mother-in-law's footsteps, becoming yet another Dowager Countess of Moretaine. If Drucilla had had a son, she could reign here in triumph until his majority. Without a son, she would be expected to vacate Castle Moretaine, leaving it to the use of the new owner. *Damon Farr, Earl of Moretaine.*

But Serena, her dear countess, was saying something more. Katy gathered her wandering wits and listened with increasingly avid attention.

"At first," said the dowager, "I thought Drucilla was only flirting, practicing her wiles as young women will. Ashby, dear Ashby, was . . . a quiet man. I fear he was not exciting," she added judiciously. "Drucilla craved more, always more, and men flocked round her like bees to a nectar-filled flower." The countess flexed nervous fingers that contrasted sharply with the stark black of her gown. "Ashby was indulgent, perhaps too much so," Serena sighed. "He had won a Diamond of the First Water and was delighted—dazzled—to see her shining at the apex of the *ton.*

"And then one day during the Season I paid a call at Moretaine House. A duty call, I must admit, as I had never taken to the girl. She did not value Ashby as she should. Oh, I saw it quite clearly. She was sometimes as sharp with him as she was with everyone else. That is why . . ." The countess's voice faded, obviously considering if she could have made an error about her daughter-in-law. She shook her head. "No, no, there can be no doubt. I saw what I saw. When I entered Moretaine House that day in London, Lord Redcliffe was coming down the stairs. . . . My dear, I know I should not sully your maiden ears with such things, but I need to say this out loud, for I have kept it from Damon, and I know he has never understood my desire to leave the Dower House, even though he was quite splendid about allowing me to move to Farr Park."

Katy, fascinated, never took her gaze from Lady Moretaine's face.

"A dashing rake, Redcliffe. Exactly the sort to catch Drucilla's notice. And"—the countess took a deep breath—"he looked as if he had just tumbled out of bed. Certainly his valet never turned him out in such a rumpled fashion! And Drucilla on the gallery above, en déshabillé. Oh, yes, my dear. Her dressing gown—no more than a thin layer of silk—was wrapped over what I swear to you was nothing at all. The windows are clerestory, and the sun was shining, revealing, I assure you, far more of that witch than I wished to see.

"Well might you be shocked," the dowager pronounced as Katy's eyes grew enormous. "That she should take a lover before giving Ashby an heir. Not done, my child. Simply not done. I turned and marched out of there, and wrote immediately to Damon for sanctuary, for I could not bear to see my dear Ashby a cuckold." Serena sniffed, fumbling for the handkerchief in her reticule.

"I suppose you think I should have told him," the dowager continued presently, "but I could not. It was better to hide myself in the country for ten months of the year than be tempted to break his heart. I hoped that when they had a child, she would be content."

Katy sat, hands in her lap, head down, ashamed to reveal so much as a hint of what she was thinking.

The dowager was not fooled. Or possibly she merely attributed her own suspicions to Katy. "I know what you're thinking, clever minx that you are," the dowager added on a resigned sigh, "though surely no one should be so skeptical at eighteen. But you are right—if there were a child, no one could be certain of its parentage."

Katy nodded. Access to servants' gossip had left her with few illusions, including exactly how babies were made. Though how anyone could wish to indulge in such an awkward and surely anatomically impossible feat she could not imagine. She supposed some people would do anything for a baby, but that did not explain the scandal and anguish when others found themselves with babies they did not want. Obviously, there was something she had not yet grasped about the mating of the sexes.

The rumble of carriage wheels sounded upon the drive. Footsteps. Rankin's voice, subdued but clear, announced the first of their guests. The funeral feast had begun.

* * *

"Fox!" Damon grasped the hand of a well-dressed gentleman near his own age, shaking it vigorously. He turned to the slightly shorter man beside him. "Thayne. Good of you to come."

"Barely made it to the church, I fear. Didn't see the announcement until yesterday," said Major Arthur Foxbourne, the taller of the two men of decided military bearing.

"Bit like one of Old Hooky's forced marches, don't you know," added Captain Chetwin Thayne. "But we're old hands at that, so here we are."

"What good are comrades in arms if they can't support a man in his time of need?" Major Foxbourne added.

"Though we may fail to 'my lord' you now and again," said Captain Thayne. "Hard to adjust, don't you know. Our colonel, a lord. Calling you Moretaine don't come trippingly off the tongue, I can tell you."

"Nor to mine," said Damon with a scowl ferocious enough to silence both junior officers. Ruthlessly repressing his surge of melancholy, the new Earl of Moretaine said to the men who had followed him through long years of war, men he knew far better than his own brother, "You will stay, will you not? Two more in this vast pile will scarcely cast a ripple, and old friends in time of need are not easy to find."

"Of course," said Major Foxbourne. "Thayne?"

"We're both on leave with only our mamas to miss us, alas," said the captain. "Can't say as I ever slept in a castle before, though parts of this place remind me of that convent—you recall the one, Farr? *Moretaine!* The one in Spain?"

"I remember." Damon's grim features lightened for a moment as thoughts of the almost surreal calm of the convent flashed through his mind. He and his officers had basked in it, savored it. It was there he had promised himself to capture that quality in his own life and hold it tight. For a while, an all-too-short while, he thought he had done it. "Rankin," the new earl called, "find rooms for these gentlemen. They will be staying."

After seeing that his friends were being properly attended, Damon moved through the crowd of mourners, accepting seemingly endless condolences, attempting to hide a wince every time he was addressed as "my lord," or "Moretaine." It wasn't right. It wasn't supposed to be this way. He didn't want it. Not the title, the responsibility, nor this monstrous sprawling castle. He wanted to go home to Farr Park and never see any of his ancestral properties again.

But he put on his best face, speaking with Squire and Mrs. Richardson, proffering cordial nods to their children. He moved on to other familiar faces, to Mr. and Mrs. Swann, who seemed to have left their precocious daughter at home, praise be. And then he plunged into a veritable sea of strangers, grateful to discover Philip Winslow at his side, making introductions, smoothing his way.

Ensuring his place in the new earl's household?

The vicar and his family popped up before his gaze, like an island in a storm. After proffering his sincere appreciation for Mr. Dearborn's tasteful service and inspiring eulogy, Damon slipped out the servants' door and into the plain ill-lit hallway behind. He leaned back against the wall and closed his eyes, breathing hard.

What if they had not come to Castle Moretaine? What if he had not had those last days with Ashby? The precious time to reestablish a bond never truly severed?

And now—among all the unwanted responsibilities of the estate—there was Drucilla. *Drucilla, the dowager*. Would she accept life in the Dower House? He doubted it. She was a creature of the city. He could only hope Ashby had provided enough for her to live in town. Would she rouse herself from her bed long enough to hear the reading of the will? Very likely. He was unconvinced that the excess of emotion she was experiencing had anything to do with grief.

As Damon slipped back into the immense drawing room, he glanced at the settee on which his mother was holding court, with Katy close beside her. She seemed to be holding up well. A true lady, his mama. He was proud of her.

Damon assessed the rest of the room, seeking those to whom he had not yet spoken. His gaze passed a large beefy man of vaguely familiar countenance. Why was the man staring at his mother and Katy with a mighty frown that twisted his features into the grotesque shape of a gargoyle? He'd met him somewhere. Titled . . . Oxley, that was it. Baron Oxley. The family had attended the ill-fated tea party. The wife was a friend of Drucilla's. Ah, yes . . . now it came back. The events of the last few days must have addled his wits. The man was father to Miss Hardcastle, the sharp-eyed female who had looked him over with the avidity of a hawk assessing prey. And some sort of connection to the petite blond who bore such a remarkable resemblance to Katy Snow. The one with the winsome face and knowing eyes. Eyes as green, but far more bold than his Katy's.

The baron was turning away, moving off toward the inevitable cluster of gentlemen forming in one end of the room, leaving the ladies at the other. Another oddity, that strange look. Damon filed it away for future analysis. There was something going on . . . flitting just outside his grasp. One more item in the host of problems he must confront.

But this one concerned Katy, of that he was nearly certain. Therefore, it was important. The clever little minx had wormed her way into his life like a barbed hook that refused to budge. Either he lived with her insidious itch or he cut her out. And, for some reason, the latter idea had no appeal at all.

"My dear boy." An elderly great-aunt tottered up, grasping his hand in both of hers. Damon managed a wan smile while frantically searching his memory for her name. He failed. If only Katy could have made a list. . . .

Much later, when all the guests had gone home and the house was quiet, the younger dowager countess of Moretaine descended the stairs, supported by two stalwart footmen. She allowed them to settle her black-clad figure into a wingchair in the library. Holding a black lace handkerchief to her nose, she sniffed—rather dramatically, Katy thought from her place beside the elder dowager. Drucilla then bowed her head, the very portrait of distraught widowhood.

There were no surprises. Ashby Farr's will was as well constructed and formally conservative as his life. His widow's jointure was generous, as befitted his wealth. Drucilla would be able to live more than comfortably in whatever dwelling she desired, short of the extravagance of the Carlton House set. The bequests to servants and the church also reflected the late earl's rank, wealth, and fine sense of *noblesse oblige.*

Joseph Benchley—the late earl's solicitor, down from London for the occasion—cleared his throat, allowing a moment of silence to emphasize the importance of the next portion of the will. In lieu of an heir of the earl's own body, he pronounced in clear and ringing tones, the bulk of the estate—the late earl's money in the funds, his speculative investments, his cash on hand—was left, along with the entailed properties and the family jewels, to his younger brother, Damon Wythorne Farr.

Drucilla shrieked. "The jewels are mine," she wailed as every eye in the room stared at her in amazement.

"Lady Moretaine," said Mr. Benchley a trifle sternly, "there may be certain pieces that the earl—the late earl—bought solely for you, but you must be aware that it is customary for family jewels to stay with the title."

"They are mine!" Drucilla cried. "I will not give them up. Ashby said I should have them. He promised!"

Damon signaled Rankin, who stood just within the doorway. The two footmen appeared almost on the instant. "Your grief does you credit, my lady," Damon said cooly. "When you are feeling more the thing, we will discuss this matter further." He nodded, and the two footmen scooped up the countess and led her from the room, her sobs rending the air until Rankin shut the heavy oak door firmly behind her.

Serena Moretaine did not bother to disguise her snort of disgust. Later, in the privacy of her sitting room, she announced to her son, with Katy listening as usual with her ears a-twitch, "If I could give up my magnificent jewels to that awful woman, then she can most certainly give them up to the next Lady Moretaine."

"And that may be when hell freezes over," Damon growled.

"Beg pardon, Mama, but this is a day I do not wish to relive. Marriage is the last thing on my mind at the moment."

"The jewels remain with the estate," Serena declared fiercely, "whether you are married or no."

All Damon wanted was to get away. Meet Fox and Thayne in the library, have Rankin mix punch with rum, brandy, and a myriad spices, talk about old times—anything but the present—and get roaringly foxed. *Foxed.* An old joke among the three of them. Foxy Foxbourne, foxed again.

Away. *Now!* Damon didn't even sneak a last lingering look at Katy Snow, as he so often did. After the briefest of farewells, he fled.

Chapter Fourteen

"A female who don't talk," declared Major Foxbourne, a man noted for his ability to catch ladies' eyes with his classic good looks, sharp hazel eyes, and sophisticated polish. At the moment he was sprawled in a brown leather wingchair, his booted feet supported by a matching footstool. "Now there's a phe-phe-*nom*-e-non worthy of another toast. Still able to lift an arm, Thayne? Pour me another, dear boy."

Obligingly, Captain Thayne picked up a bottle from the low table set before the three men in the earl's library, managing to pour brandy into his friend's glass with only a few drops spilled. With a long-drawn sigh he settled back into his chair. The captain was more addicted to humor than to brandy, his round face and mischievous blue eyes seemingly untouched by what he had seen and done in the war. "Astonishing," he murmured. "A woman who can't tell tales."

"Writes a fine hand," Colonel Farr drawled.

"A pity." Fox clasped his hands around his snifter and gazed hazily into the fire that was nearly burned down because none of the three had felt inspired to abandon either their reminiscences or the brandy bottle long enough to replenish it.

"A female secretary . . . ain't that a contradiction in terms?" Chetwin Thayne remarked. "No such thing. Daresay she serves well in other ways though, don't she?"

For a moment the atmosphere in Castle Moretaine's library crackled with the intensity of a thunderstorm. The colonel's strong hands gripped the arms of his chair, his snifter teetering dangerously. He started to get up, thought better of it. The brandy seemed to have turned his legs to blancmange. It had been a long day, a long nasty day. "She serves well as my mother's companion," he said coldly. "As she serves me well as my secretary."

"Don't be an ass," the major growled. "We are all friends here. You don't use a female who looks like that for nothing but writing your letters. Tell us what she's like. Don't credit that prim and proper exterior one whit. There's a great deal more, now ain't there? Come, man, don't be so obstinate."

Damon—who, like the others, had drunk far more than he should—tossed off the last of his brandy, plunked his glass onto the table. "Very well. She's a minx, a veritable minx. With a piquant sense of humor, even a mischief that bubbles up and over at the most unexpected moments. She drives me mad when she leans over my desk. Climbing the bookroom ladder is worse, with her ankles showing and her bum wiggling—"

The colonel broke off with a groan. "She's also my mama's pet and the darling of my household staff. Which means if I touch her, I'll likely find an emetic in my soup, if not arsenic or ground glass."

"Poor sod," Chet Thayne murmured, appalled.

"You can't mean she's willing but you ain't," Fox exclaimed, if a bit muzzily.

Damon swore. "Didn't say that. She's . . . enticing. Doesn't work at it."

"Said she waggles her—"

"Quiet!"

"So you ain't bedding her, but you'd like to," pronounced Captain Thayne judiciously after several seconds of silence broken only by the soft hissing of the fire.

Damon reached for the brandy bottle, found it empty. How fortunate he'd had the foresight to have Rankin place two extra bottles beside the decanter on the table before seeking his bed, for Damon doubted he could cross the room to find another bottle, let alone negotiate the precipitous stone steps down to the wine cellar. Alas, they were now down to the last bottle. In spite of being almost as foxed as the night the three of them had celebrated his leaving the regiment, he made short work of opening the brandy. He poured, sniffed . . . and discovered his nose was well past savoring even the finest French brandy. Odd that the English had such a taste for the enemy's brew.

He drank. "Demmed female," the colonel grumbled. "All I wanted was quiet. Time to be alone. And there she is, day after day, cutting up my peace. Even in Ashby's last days, when he was cramming my head with barley and sheep and drainage and God only knows what else, I could see her hovering, right there in his bedchamber, haunting me. At a time like that!" Mournfully, guiltily, the colonel refilled his snifter.

"Only one thing to do," Fox declared. "Must have her, dear boy. Only cure. So she tells your mama. Set the chit up in a cottage. Teach her all the right tricks. You'd be doing her a favor. Girl's far better off as a courtesan. All that beauty's going to waste here in the country. The best of everything awaits her in the city. She'll have all the fine gentl'men nosin' about. Fascinating concept, a female who don't talk."

Why wasn't he grabbing Fox up? Damon wondered. Planting him a facer? Why was he sitting here, actually listening to this . . . oaf, mouthing . . . offal.

An oaf mouthing offal. Amusing, Farr, most amusing. Perhaps he should set up a group of players for the next church fair.

Horrified. That's what he should be. Yet the picture Fox was painting was simply too tempting. It wasn't as if he hadn't had similar thoughts himself, but his last remnants of honor had prevailed.

Yet what was honor to a girl who was nobody? What right did she have to expect the treatment due a young lady of good family?

She'd earned it.

Hell!

He should be telling old Foxy what he could do with his advice. And with his salacious projections for Katy Snow's future. Yet he continued to sit, silent and glum. Knowing that in some twisted way his friend was right. Katy was the light trapped under a bushel. The country beauty confined by convention into a role that did not suit her. Oh, yes, Fox was right. Katy Snow had too much spirit to spend the rest of her days as a companion.

Not as companion to a *female,* Damon smirked.

The brandy fumes rose in his brain, circulating with insidious thoroughness until only the battle-hardened soldier, reacting to the urge to save himself, was left. "A test," Damon proposed. "Let us devise a test."

His fellow officers raised their heads, as befuddled by their colonel's words as they were by drink.

"You, dear sirs," said Damon, "may have the privilege of discovering how the chit reacts to a bit of flirtation. Let her choose her own fate. Track her down wherever she is to be found and do your worst. You may, I believe, even find her in the woods in the early morning, as my brother granted her a mount."

A slow, if lopsided, smile spread across Major Foxbourne's handsome face. "By jove, Farr, but that's good of you."

"Not *this* morning," said Captain Thayne, "for I believe it's morning already and I swear I'd have to be poured into the saddle."

"Wouldn't be the first time," said his colonel.

"No, but if I'm to accost a female, I'd like to be capable of enjoying it."

"Capable," Fox mumbled. "That's it . . . must be *capable.*"

In the end, not surprisingly, the three military gentlemen fell asleep in their chairs, where they remained until Rankin aroused them in time to set themselves to rights before nuncheon.

Katy, atop the lovely chestnut mare Lord Moretaine had said she might ride, scowled at a perfectly innocent rowan tree, whose red berries were as yet unfaded by the advent of fall. *Damon could not be earl! Surely, life could not be so cruel.*

But, of course, it was. Had she not learned that at an early age?

Katy urged her horse to a gallop, sweeping down a narrow track that meandered along a stream that marked the boundary of a field of knee-high hay. *Ah!* The wind buffeted her heated thoughts while threatening to dislodge the cavalry blue shako that matched her elegant new riding habit, resplendent with white braid. She leaned forward in the saddle, savoring these few moments of freedom after all the sorrow, almost as if she feared they might not come her way again. She reveled in pounding hooves, the freshness of the air, the rush of the small stream, the scent of rich earth, the closeness of life all around her—plants, animals, insects . . .

And a few moments of freedom from people and the vicissitudes of an outside world that would not leave her alone.

How very *small* of her to rail against Fate. She was a better person than that. But she was young and full of hope, however foolish. Mind and heart clasped her complaint close, refusing to let go. Damon, her Damon, should not be earl. During the month she had spent at his side in the Farr Park bookroom, her girlish fantasies of love had withered and died. And been reborn, full-blown, as hope. There were enough shining lights on her family tree—if a bit tarnished here and there—to allow the waif to build castles in the air. Damon of Farr Park, if truth were told, was not so far above her touch.

The Earl of Moretaine most certainly was.

A peer might look as high as he pleased for a wife. Every matchmaking mama and predatory daughter avid for a title was going to be after him—leaving the chances of a girl whose only claim to a title was the colonel's derogatory designation "Lady Silence" no hope at all.

Katy slowed her chestnut to a mincing walk, allowing the mare to approach the stream and dip her head for a cooling drink. Fortunate animal. She herself would have to wait until she returned to Castle Moretaine. Katy sniffed the breeze. Almost, it seemed, she could smell coffee, bacon, and hot muffins. But it was such an unusually fine day, rich with sunshine and crisp autumn air . . . and she had not been beyond the walls of Castle Moretaine for a full five days.

Not far ahead was a copse which, she had discovered, hid an intimate glen obviously designed for the pleasure of Castle Moretaine's residents and guests, for it featured a curved marble bench where one might sit and enjoy the view while basking in the beauty and solitude of the moment—the bubbling stream with water meadows beyond, birdsong of amazing variety, and glorious privacy—as if the world and its cares no longer existed.

There she could dismount and fill her aching soul with serenity, for the marble bench also served as a fine mounting block. Katy's lips curled in wry laughter at herself. Kate, the pragmatic. The girl who found a way over and around all obstacles.

Until now.

The glen was waiting. Perhaps, today, it held inspiration, a solution to her problems. Katy patted the horse's neck, drew up the reins, and headed her mount toward the distant copse.

After his abominably late start on the day after the funeral, Damon had vowed to do better today. But when he reached the stables, he discovered his friends were more spry than he. Gone out a half hour since, the groom told him.

Grief and alcohol were lethal enemies of the brain, but the colonel had not survived nearly seven years of war without developing keen instincts. Instincts that did not lay down, roll over, and fall asleep just because he was wallowing in a sea of conflicting emotions. An alarm shivered through him. There was something he should remember. . . .

The library. Brandy. He'd told Fox and Thayne about Katy. All about Katy, from her arrival at Farr Park to his doubts about her character . . . to his speculations that her demure exterior hid a questing spirit, deserving to be freed. *Hell!* He'd even told them about her morning rides. He'd suggested—*encouraged* them to test her, see how far she would go.

Drunken sot that he was, he'd set them on her!

To punish her for tempting him?

He should be drawn and quartered!

"Is Katy Snow riding this morning?" Damon snapped.

"Aye, col—m'lord. Hasn't been out since the poor earl—God rest his soul—passed on, but today she was here, same as usual."

"Which way?"

"She mostly goes east, m'lord. Path along the stream. Or so it seems from what I can see from 'ere," he added a trifle hastily. "Sometimes she rides into the village, but seems a tad early for that."

Damon leaped on Volcán, jerked the reins from the groom's hands, and galloped off. Even as he castigated himself for being in such a lather over what was likely nothing, he tried to recall his exact words. Flirtation. Surely he'd only mentioned flirtation. Test the chit, see if she made eyes at every man she met. Hadn't his own steward been caught in her snare? The doctor? That damned footman? Even the Castle Moretaine groom had kept track of her comings and goings.

Flirtation, he'd said . . . yet he had implied that Katy was a female of no discernible background, a servant without protection.

Do your worst.

He could not have said it.

Do your worst. Yes, he had.

Hell and the devil confound it! He'd all but handed her to them on a silver platter. A succulent treat complete with the piquant sauce of her mysterious background.

Gritting his teeth, Damon slowed to a trot as he entered the wooded ride at the edge of the park, then burst back into a gallop as a patch of sunlight signaled a clearing ahead. Hay fields to the left, the stream and water meadows to the right. *Here . . . she had to be here somewhere.* If he failed her, he was forever damned.

The land was nearly flat. He rounded a clump of willows drooping over a bend in the stream, fully expecting to see her—and his so-called friends as well.

Nothing. Just tall waving grass, the dirt path, and bubbling stream.

Damon pulled up his horse, swearing softly. If she wasn't here, he'd never find her. The grounds of Castle Moretaine comprised five thousand acres. *Blast the woman! Where was she?*

They'd found her, damn them. Fox and Thayne. They were hiding somewhere, doing God knew what. Damon's rage soared. She was *his. How dare they lay a hand on his woman?*

Or was she giving herself to them, embarking freely on a new life with a new set of protectors?

Blood pounded in his ears. Volcán, sensing his rider's unrest, snorted and stamped his hooves. Grimly, the new Earl of Moretaine brought him under control. Not far ahead was a small copse planted by his grandfather to add scenic beauty to this ride along the river. Very well, he'd go that far and not an inch farther. Why make an ass of himself, playing knight-errant? Foolish chit probably didn't want to be rescued anyway.

And then he heard the scream. A high-pitched penetrating ululation that sent even the battle-tested Volcán into a skittering caracole. *Katy! Katy was in trouble.*

And it was all his fault.

But somewhere in that hundred yards to the copse, a new thought clicked into place. The colonel who entered the woods was a very angry man indeed.

Chapter Fifteen

Katy was only partway into the stand of trees at the east end of the hay field, thoroughly enjoying the sun-dappled shade and delicious privacy provided by a fine mix of oak, mulberry, and elm, when she heard hoofbeats behind her. *Damon!* He'd followed her . . . was looking for her.

The hoof beats were rather loud. He wasn't alone. Her shoulders slumped in disappointment. Katy found she'd brought her mare to a halt. With the curve of the path obscuring her vision, she could only wait and wonder.

Major Foxbourne and Captain Thayne! In vain she looked for Damon. The light dimmed, the forest grew cold. Ridiculous to feel danger here, but Katy shivered. There was something about the way they were looking at her. Breath caught in her throat. *Dear God, she recognized that look!* But surely they wouldn't . . . not on the earl's own lands.

They closed in, one on either side, much too close for a conventional exchange of polite greetings. The three mounts were but inches apart. "Miss Snow," Major Foxbourne purred, "how delightful. We hoped we might meet you this morning."

Katy granted them a cool nod, even as she withdrew into herself, vowing to find a way to keep them from touching her. For that's what they wanted, she knew it. At twelve, she had run from that look. Later, the boys in the village had evidently decided that her position at Farr Park protected her from touching, but not from naked glimpses of what they would like to do. Oh, yes, she knew lust when she saw it. Cool, calculated lust, without a hint of hesitation. Which, in itself, seemed odd. Decidedly odd.

They had her pinned now, there in the narrow path, their large geldings intimidating her dainty mare as easily as the two officers were intimidating her. They were speaking, making incredible suggestions, not of using her for themselves, as she had expected, but of her becoming the earl's mistress, allowing him to set her on the path to life as a famous London courtesan. Such beauty was wasted in the country, they told her. She was destined for far better. The finest of everything laid at her feet. She would mingle with the men of the *ton,* the wealthy and powerful—noble men who had defeated Napoleon Bonaparte and were destined to rule the vast empire Britain was establishing around the world.

Now was the time to speak up . . . to tell them what she thought of their grand scheme. That they must be mad to wave whoredom before her as if it were a high treat.

But her lips refused to move. Her tongue sat like a lump of clay in her mouth. So long . . . too long. Whatever the mechanism that allowed people to talk, it had rusted over. Or was it her brain that was frozen, unable to transmit the command? Perhaps she simply could not believe two officers, supposedly gentlemen, could speak to her so.

"I believe she needs encouragement," Major Foxbourne said to Captain Thayne. "Hard to believe such a beauty's a skittish virgin, but there you have it. I suppose anything is possible."

"Virgins bring a higher price," Thayne agreed, pressing his mount directly into the mare's flank. "Colonel's panting so hard after you, you could have anything you want," he said to Katy. "A house in St. John's Woods, silk gowns, your own carriage and pair, diamonds draping every part of you." His salacious gaze examined her tight-fitting military-style habit from head to toe. Again, Katy shivered.

"A kiss," declared Foxbourne. "Warm her up with a kiss, that's the ticket. Try her out a bit, see if she's worthy of our colonel." He leaned forward, one arm snaking about her waist.

Katy thwacked her riding crop against the side of his head.

The major swore. Combat was short-lived. The riding crop disappeared into the underbrush, and Katy found herself twisted hard against Foxbourne's chest, his furious face descending toward hers. Her struggle to free herself was as effective as her attempt to hold on to her riding crop.

"I say . . ." Captain Thayne interjected, belatedly recognizing that their "flirtation" had gone out of control.

Harsh lips bruised Katy's. A kiss without even lust, it was punishment, solely punishment. When the major finally eased the fierce pressure, Katy snapped her teeth over his lower lip, biting down hard. Foolish, perhaps, but oh so satisfying.

He boxed her ears.

"Major!" Captain Thayne roared, but Foxbourne had gone beyond reason, back to the beserker days of the worst of the Peninsula. He leaped from the saddle, dragging Katy with him, his hands tearing at the buttons of her habit even as they fell.

For Katy, all the old horrors came back, bursting past the dam she had so carefully erected. She had promised herself she would not think of it, would not remember. And then the Hardcastles had come to Castle Moretaine. And now this. Yet she had saved herself once. She could do so again. She only had to open her mouth and scream. Surely someone would hear her. Someone would come.

If she screamed loud enough, perhaps the major would come to his senses. *Yes, surely it must be so.* Foxbourne could not truly intend to have her here, on the earl's own acres.

But to make a sound—particularly a loud sound—after so many years . . .

The front of her habit was open, exposing the fine lawn of the shirt inside. His hands were ripping at the thin fabric . . .

Katy summoned every ounce of courage, the spirit that had sustained her through the years.

But no sound escaped her mouth.

The major shifted his attention to her voluminous skirts, his hands frantically searching for a way beneath the layers of heavy twill and lacy petticoats.

Katy took a hard, heaving breath. Her scream rose and

echoed through the copse, silencing the birds, penetrating all the way to the meadow. Where Colonel Damon Farr had almost given up the search.

It was worse than he'd feared. When Damon charged up to the knot of horses on the path through the woods, Fox had Katy on the ground with her skirts up over her head, although, thanks to Thayne's determined hold on one arm, the major had not progressed any further. Damon thought he'd put the heated surge of battle behind him, but the satisfaction of clubbing Fox off Katy was as fine as any moment he could recall. A second blow sent the major crashing into the brush at the edge of the path, where he had the good sense to lie still.

Thayne was babbling, attempting to explain, making excuses. Damon paid him no heed. He picked Katy up, swung her into her saddle with not so much as a query about whether she was fit to ride. He took up her mare's reins, then turned to look down at the major, who was now sitting, a trifle lopsidedly, at the foot of an elderberry bush.

"I am aware of my guilt in this," Damon told him grimly. "Nevertheless, I will see you both in the library after breakfast." Colonel Farr addressing his junior officers.

The new Earl of Moretaine, leading Katy's mare, turned his horse away from the castle, leaving two ashen-faced officers who had never before doubted that they were gentlemen.

There was a clearing close by. A treasured remembrance of childhood. He'd even visited it more than a time or two while at Eton. A good place for a young man to contemplate the world—his fellow students, friends and those who were not; the harshness of his teachers . . . and later, the delights of wine and women. Oh, yes, he remembered the spot well. His great-grandfather had planned with care. There was even a curved marble bench, stuck incongruously in the middle of the wilderness. Was it still there? He hoped so.

Damon found the narrow sidepath, and there was the glen, perhaps even lovelier than he remembered. The last time he had been here, he had not yet learned how privileged he was, how so much of the world was ugly and harsh, bathed in sweat and blood. . . .

He swung Katy from her sidesaddle and plopped her onto the hard marble with the carelessness he might have used with a sack of grain. The breath whooshed out of her. Clasping her hands in front of her face, she stared blindly at the stream, rocking ever so faintly back and forth.

Damon tethered the horses, then stood over her, hands on his hips. "And now," he declared, "you will tell me about your long masquerade. Why you are a liar. Why you have deceived my mother, myself, and my staff for all this time. Why you have betrayed our trust. Well, speak up, girl! Your audacity overwhelms me. It is unfortunate you were too young to go as a spy. You would have been superb. I daresay you could give Mrs. Siddons lessons."

Katy's slight shoulders slumped, her head drooped forward.

"Answer me, dammit. I must know! I gave you shelter, food, allowed you to live a life of gentility. Open your mouth and speak to me, girl! I know you can, so stop your games. This instant."

Her whole body shuddered. She dropped her hands from in front of her mouth. "Sometimes," Katy breathed into the waiting silence, "late at night in my room or when I was out riding, I would say a word or two out loud. Just a whisper, to see if I still could."

Damon stared at the changeling on the bench. *A lady, by God!* Not a trace of the streets in a single word.

She was clever, adept. She could have learned proper speech from his mama.

No, every word was perfect. Katy Snow was a lady, born and bred.

"*Why?*" The word burst from him, raw and hoarse-voiced, for here was the ultimate betrayal. The residents of Farr Park had taken her in, offered protection, even love. And all along the miserable chit was playing a part. Hoodwinking them. Bamboozling the lot, numbskulls that they were. They'd *trusted* her, by God. Treated her like a princess. And this was the thanks they got.

He should have let Fox have her.

Katy coughed, cleared her throat. "Nearly every place I tried to find work . . . after no more than three words, I was suspected as a runaway from a noble house and they wanted no part of me." For a moment she seemed surprised by her spate of words, relapsing into silence. Her bosom heaved as she took another deep breath and tried again. "The few times I was taken on as a scullery maid, I was soon shunned for my fine speech and what they said were my lofty ways." Katy paused, eyes fixed on the tall water grasses swaying with the pull of the current. "Each time I was chased away or turned off. No one wanted me."

"I believe I've heard tales of your lack of domestic skills," Damon commented drily.

"That, too," Katy conceded softly. "I was hungry, exhausted . . . freezing. It had begun to snow. I had to find shelter or die. I'd lost the main road, you see, and ended up on the hill above Farr Park. When I looked down and saw the lights in the windows, the torches along the drive, I knew it was a miracle. This place was meant to be my new home . . . and I vowed I would do whatever was necessary to stay there."

"And if you didn't speak, no one would guess you were a lady."

Katy, falling back into old habits, nodded.

"Except my staff soon found you out . . . and then my mother, so that you were once again a lady by the time I returned."

Cream rises, Katy thought, beginning to recapture a bit of her spirit.

"But no one could be certain," Damon continued, "because, for some quite incredible reason, you maintained your masquerade long after becoming the family darling, making fools of us all. Betraying my mama's trust, the devotion of my staff—"

"Never!" Katy cried. "I love them. They are wonderful. But

I could not—I simply could not—risk being sent back where I came from."

"And where was that?" Damon inquired silkily.

"I was nearly . . . *ravished* just now," Katy declared after only the slightest pause for thought. "Though I appreciate your gallant rescue, my lord, surely you cannot expect the entire story of my life at this moment."

"Why, you arrogant, devious, self-serving little baggage, I ought to take you over my knee!"

"It is surprising what six and a half years of silence will do, my lord. Such ample opportunity for contemplation and self-reflection. I believe most people could benefit from being forced to keep their mouths shut and their minds open. You may do what you will with me, but I am not yet ready to tell you who I am or where I came from."

He had to give the chit credit for courage. And swiftness of mind and remarkable agility of tongue. "If I do not know where you came from, I am not obliged to return you, is that it?"

"Exactly."

"And if I should ask the Baron Hardcastle to identify you?"

Katy jumped up, took two steps toward him, her hands held out in supplication. She faltered, knees buckling. Damon caught her before she hit the ground. They rested there, on their knees, Katy quivering in his arms, her face buried against his shoulder.

"Do not think I am not still angry," Damon said at last, "but only a beast would press you now, and I am determined not to fall to Foxbourne's level. Come, we'll go home." He stood, drawing Katy up with him. "And once there, I must tell my two best friends to leave the castle." *Though the fault is mine.* "And you must tell my mother how shockingly you have betrayed her trust."

He felt a quiver pass through her. Grim-faced, he tossed her into the saddle. After loosening the mare's reins from a tree branch, Damon looked up at her, examining Farr Park's lovely, but deceitful, foundling as if he had never seen her before. "Tell me, Snow," he asked, "did you enjoy making mock of us all?"

Chapter Sixteen

Katy sat, hands resting in her lap, regarding the remains of her breakfast. If she had any sensibility at all, she would not have eaten every last bite. The meal, delivered to her bedchamber by Rankin himself, had been more than ample, and she'd downed it all. Seeking strength to face the earl and his mama? Courage to run away again?

Obviously, she had the constitution of her more vulgar ancestors, the good merchant stock on her mother's side of the family. Any proper young lady of the *ton* would be prostrated by the double disasters of unrequited love and discovered deceit, unable to eat or drink. Lost in an attack of the vapors . . . falling into a decline . . . fading away, doctors hovering, family gathered about, telling her they were so very sorry not to have given her a second chance . . .

Katy replaced the silver cover atop her empty plate with a decided thump, then stalked to the fireplace where she plunked herself down on a footstool and stared into the fire, chin propped in one hand. She was in trouble. Severe trouble. Damon had told her to stay in her room until he sent for her. A summons could come at any moment.

She had put on the least becoming of the four new gowns created solely for the journey to Castle Moretaine, a dark apology in gray kerseymere, relieved only by a quarter-inch strip of white piping on the high neck and edge of the cuffs. She had confined her blond curls into a tight bun at her nape and fashioned a makeshift headcovering from a lace-edged handkerchief. She could only hope she gave the appearance of a chastened, humble servant. Self-preservation—was that not her credo? Physically, she was prepared, but her mind whirled in chaos, like a child's round-about caught in an evil spell of circles without end. They would cast her out—or, worse yet, question the Hardcastles—and send her back to the hell she had escaped.

No! Before that terrible fate, she would run away.

To what? To the life the major and the captain had touted as they recounted what they considered the grand enticements of a career as a courtesan?

Or . . . was it possible the Hardcastles would deny her? Yes, of course! They had their Lucinda Challenor. What did they need with Katy Snow?

But *why* did they have a Lucinda Challenor? In the grief following the earl's death Katy had had little time to contemplate the puzzle. Her dear grandpapa, the bishop, had not been a wealthy man; at least, she did not think so. He must have left her something, however, for she seemed to be his sole heir. Was it enough to tempt the baron to—

Her skittering thoughts were brought to an end by a scratching at the door.

"The earl will see you now, miss," Rankin announced. "In Lady Serena Moretaine's chambers."

Next door! They were both there. Waiting. What had Damon told his mother? Enough to make her beloved countess hate her forever?

Whatever he had said, he was right. Katy Snow was a horrid, conniving liar—there was no way around it. She had deceived them. It could even be said she had played on their sympathies to make a home for herself . . .

She had given good service.

Head high, stomach churning, Katy followed Rankin the few feet down the hall to Lady Moretaine's suite.

They stood there like a portrait, mother and son, the Dowager Countess of Moretaine seated on the chaise, the new earl standing behind her. From force of habit, Katy bobbed a curtsy, feeling as if she'd left her stomach at her toes while her heart was stuffed into her throat.

"I believe you have something to say to my mother," Damon intoned. "Please do so."

Did the countess know? An anguished glance revealed little. Her dear countess did not look shocked or angry. Perhaps he had not told her.

"*Now*, Snow," said the earl. *"Tell her!"*

"My dear," said Lady Moretaine, "Damon has told me of your accident while out riding this morning. Though why he should be so cryptic about it I cannot imagine. Nor why he has insisted on bringing you to me when you should be laid upon your bed. Dear child, do sit down before you fall. You look quite dreadful. Damon, help her to a chair!"

The earl remained fixed behind his mother, even as Katy swayed.

It was cruel not to have told his mama. Cruel to her as well. The countess deserved to have the news broken gently. And as for herself . . . poor Katy Snow needed to be spared this barefaced revelation to the only mother she had ever known.

But it seemed military men were rigid, even more inflexible about rules and ways of conduct than the starched-up, unforgiving *ton*. . . .

Katy clasped her hands under her chin, planted her feet more widely apart, willing her legs to support her. She longed to throw herself at the countess's feet, as she had done with Mrs. Tyner so long ago . . . but she was grown now, and full of pride. The colonel would call it arrogance.

"I am so very, very sorry," Katy whispered. "I was alone and terrified. If I had not found a way to stay here, I fear I would have died."

"Oh, my dear child!" the countess gasped. Tears rushed to her eyes. Katy was close enough to see them quite clearly. And the deep, abiding anger that followed. *"How could you?"* Serena Moretaine breathed. "All those years . . . the love we gave you . . . the advantages . . ."

"You may wait for me in the library, Snow," the earl said.

"But I must explain—"

"Out! Have the grace to allow my mother to recover from the shock you have given her."

If you had prepared her, the poor dear lady would not be suffering so!

"The library, Snow."

Without a last look at the countess, whose anguish she could not bear to see, Katy left.

The library was not empty. *The beast!* He had sent her here quite deliberately, casting her into the den of iniquity. For Major Foxbourne and Captain Thayne had bounded to their feet the moment she entered, standing parade-ground stiff, faces frozen in masks of red, as if they were being strangled by their cravats.

"Miss Snow," Foxbourne croaked, "I offer my most sincere and humble apologies. Even too many years of war are no excuse for my behavior."

"I offer my apologies as well," said Captain Thayne. "It was a moment of insanity. I pray you will be able to put it from your mind."

There they were, the swine—two officers and gentlemen who had not hesitated to attempt to drag her into the life of a high-paid whore. But *why*? Although she had just met them, Katy suspected their behavior was out of character, for bounders would never be numbered among close friends of Colonel Damon Farr.

I am aware of my guilt in this. Damon had said that. Indeed, he had.

The officers still stood, red-faced, stiff as pokers. "Tell, me *gentlemen*"—could she help it if the word came out a bit askew?—"did the earl use you to test me? To see if I were susceptible to such a heinous offer?"

"Oh, no!" the two men protested, nearly in unison. The colonel's officers were nothing, if not loyal.

"The sad result of a drunken evening, miss," said Captain

Thayne. "Thought you was such a beauty, don't you know—shame to see you hidden here in the country."

"Just a bit of flirtation, a hint in your ear," said Major Foxbourne. "That's all we intended. No sense why a female with your–ah–qualities shouldn't try to better herself."

"Better myself? A strange way of putting it, is it not, Major?"

"Strange indeed," said the earl, who had entered the library in time to hear Katy's remark. "Let us declare an end to this," he continued briskly. "Our guests will leave us now, and when we meet again, the matter will be forgotten."

With brief, frozen-faced nods to their colonel and to Katy, the two military gentlemen marched out of the room.

"The matter was rape," Katy pronounced through gritted teeth.

"Not quite."

"Close enough."

"Attempting to distract me from your own guilt?" the earl inquired, soft and insinuating.

"Stating a fact."

"They are my friends," declared the earl, his stance as uncompromising as Katy's own. "Comrades through horrors you cannot even imagine. What happened was the result of the drunken ravings of three old soldiers who have not yet shut the war out of their lives. As angry as Foxbourne was when you hit him, he tells me he would not have gone through with it."

"Ha! The captain kept him from it . . . until you rescued me." Which he most certainly had. She had to give him credit for that.

"Then Fox must live with his guilt. As must you, for now you know what an anomalous situation you have created by avoiding your proper place in the world. Whatever that place may be. By being Miss Nobody from Nowhere you invited amorous attention, importunate suggestions—"

"It is not my fault! Never say it is my fault!" She had promised herself she would be accommodating, swallow her hurt, her outrage. As always—anything to secure her position. And now, look at her, fighting tooth and nail against her own best interests, when she should keep her tongue between her teeth, as she had for so long.

"You are a deceiver, Katy Snow. You betrayed our trust. I will not sacrifice years of friendship with my officers for an arrogant adventuress."

"I was twelve years old!"

"And could have revealed your secret any time these past many years."

Katy collapsed into the nearest chair, her legs less steady than her courage. "I dared not chance it. As long as everyone assumed I was a poor wounded creature ejected from the nest, I was safe. No one would force me to reveal myself. But if it were discovered I was . . . normal, I might have been sent back."

"Back where?"

Katy shook her head. "I can't go back, truly I cannot."

"The Hardcastles?"

"You must believe me! *I cannot go back.*" Katy drew a shuddering breath. "If your mama could be prevailed upon to write a character . . . If you would but let me stay until I find another position . . ."

"Recommend a liar? I think not."

"Damon?" Katy stretched out a hand, returning it abruptly to her lap as she realized what she had let slip. Dear God, he would know she thought of him by his Christian name.

Silence stretched, the yawning chasm between them widening with every second. Or so she assumed.

"I am sending you back to Farr Park," the earl said at last. "My mother and I will be situated here for some time. When we have time between settling my brother's affairs and fixing Drucilla in her new home, we will discuss what is to be done with you. Meanwhile, you may return home in disgrace, to make your deception known to your doting admirers among my staff. I fear, however, they may be as displeased by your duplicity as are my mother and myself."

Hands behind his back, brows lowered over his piercing

dark eyes, the earl scowled at her. And, inwardly, at himself. Whatever her duplicity deserved, it had not been the treatment foisted on her by his own lapse into idiocy. He led, his officers followed.

Betrayal was a double-edged blade, slicing at them both. With results far worse than intended and repercussions that shamed them all.

With his luck, the little minx would turn out to be a royal by-blow or, worse yet, the long-lost legitimate daughter of a duke. Certainly, she was arrogant enough.

Devil a bit! Excuses weren't necessary. He could not very well cast her out into the street, no matter how appalling her long masquerade. She was, after all, Katy Snow.

His Katy.

Though, damn and blast, that could not, of course, be her real name. *Miserable chit!*

"That is all, Snow. You may go. Begin packing immediately. I shall order the carriage for an hour hence. You will be back in Farr Park tonight."

Chapter Seventeen

It was gone nine o'clock and long since dark when Katy's coach pulled up at the service entrance to Farr Park, the now infamous kitchen door by which she had first arrived. Katy thanked the coachman—an old acquaintance who would spend the night in his own bed above the stables before returning to Castle Moretaine. He had not been as shocked as she'd expected when she spoke to him. In fact, she thought she caught a sly twinkle in his eyes, as if he rather found the trick she had played on the family more amusing than outrageous. Katy could almost hear him thinking, *Put one over on 'em, she did. Clever girl.*

It gave her hope. If only the others at Farr Park might feel the same. Katy stared at the solid oak door, flanked by windows glowing softly with light, just as they had so long ago. She had asked the coachman to bring her to the kitchen entrance. Why, she wasn't certain. Easier on the servants—fewer footsteps than the long trek to the front door?

Less pretentious? A suitably humble homecoming suited to a wandering waif?

Tonight, it was snowing only in her heart.

The Moretaine footman who had accompanied them brought up her portmanteau, rapped sharply on the door. The snick of a bolt . . . memory threatened to overwhelm her. Once again, she had returned a beggar. But this time, she feared, she would not find acceptance. Farr Park, no longer a refuge, was likely to become a house of torture.

The door swung open, revealing the rotund outline of Betty Huggins, the cook.

"Katy! Child, it *is* you, is it not? And pray tell, what have you done with the master and the countess? Never say they sent you round to the kitchen while they're waiting at the front! Well, don't just stand there, child, come in, come in. Mrs. Tyner! Mr. Mapes!" Cook bawled at the top of her lungs. "Come see what's at the kitchen door again."

The years flooded back, drowning Katy in memories. Words stuck in her throat. *Not tonight.* She could not reveal her secret tonight. She needed a few final moments of having them fuss over her, care for her.

Love her.

Katy stepped into the flagstone-tiled kitchen, where warmth enveloped her. The scent of ginger and vanilla, fresh bread, mutton, drying herbs, and exotic spices. *Home.* Her place of safety.

The footman plunked down her portmanteau. Katy touched his arm, managed a smile of thanks. She did not speak.

"Dear child!" cried Millicent Tyner, dashing in from her room just down the hall. "Have you come alone then? What is wrong?" The housekeeper glanced at Cook, then turned to Humphrey Mapes, who had entered the kitchen a few steps behind her. "Something has happened, I know it. Else they would not have sent her back all alone. You, boy," she called to the potboy who slept in an alcove off the kitchen, "fetch paper and pen from my office. We must discover what has happened."

"It's the colonel," Cook declared stoutly. "Must be. Was he after you, Katy girl?"

"Earl," Mapes corrected, but his heart wasn't in it, for he very much feared Cook might be right.

"Merciful heavens!" said Mrs. Tyner, "can that be it? Has her ladyship sent you home to keep you out of his clutches? The vile wretch. And such a fine little boy he was. Fair breaks my heart."

Vehemently, Katy shook her head. *No, no, no,* she could not allow them to think—

"Deny it all you want," said Cook, "anybody could see you had an eye for him, but protect him you'll not. The truth will out," she added with a dramatic flourish.

The potboy plunked paper, quill, and inkpot onto the long kitchen table. Katy found herself hustled across the room and into a chair. *A few more hours, a few more minutes*—that's all she asked.

But it was not to be. The long masquerade was truly over.

Katy folded her hands on top of the paper, bowed her head.

"You'll not remain mum about this, child," Mapes declared with a hint of sternness. "We must know why you have been sent home."

"Katy, dear," added Mrs. Tyner, "you know we wish only to protect you. We must know the truth."

Worse and worse.

Slowly, Katy removed her bonnet, inched off her gloves. Farr Park's primary staff, sensing a drama, if not understanding its cause, remained silent. Waiting. Katy shoved paper, ink-stand, and quill to the center of the table. The whoosh of three shocked breaths—Mrs. Tyner, Mapes, and Cook—echoed through the kitchen. She was *refusing* to answer?

"I don't need them, you see," Katy said quietly and evenly, "for I can talk quite well. That is why I was sent home. I am in disgrace."

Chairs scraped on stone as Katy's three mentors, legs turned to jelly, groped for places to sit.

"'Tis a miracle, then," breathed a wide-eyed Betty Huggins.

"I am afraid not," Katy told her sadly. "I could always talk, you see, but everywhere I went, I was sent away because I spoke too well. I was desperate . . . and I liked it here. You were all so kind. I never, ever wanted to leave . . . so I lived the lie, knowing so much as a single word would put me back out on the street. I am sorry—truly sorry—for deceiving you . . . but I am not sorry for all the wonderful years I had here. You may think me a liar and a cheat, but knowing you all, being part of this household, was worth whatever I must suffer now. Without Farr Park, I am convinced I should be dead."

"Oh, my poor dear child," Mrs. Tyner sighed.

Betty Huggins sobbed out loud, her mounded bosom heaving.

"This is serious, Snow," Mapes intoned. "Did the earl say what we are to do with you?"

"No. Merely that I am to stay here until his return."

"Are you confined to the house? To your room?"

"He did not say. I presumed—which I should not have done, of course—that I would be allowed access to the bookroom, the stables, the village. Truly, nothing was said about my being a prisoner. Only that I was to stay here."

"Very well. If the earl has any other instructions, I am sure he will write." Mapes selected a bell rope, gave it a pull. "You may retire, Snow. I will have Wiggs bring up your baggage." He paused, unaccustomed uncertainty crossing his angular face. "Are we to be given your true name and background, miss, so we may know how to address you?"

"I hoped you might still call me Katy."

"Inappropriate," Mapes returned gravely. "But if anyone wishes to address you as 'Miss Katy' rather than 'Miss Snow,' I shall allow it."

"Thank you," Katy murmured.

"Surely you do not intend to continue your deception . . . Miss Snow," said Mrs. Tyner. "We are—have been—your friends. How can you still refuse to tell us who you are?"

"Please understand that I have very good reasons why I cannot go back to . . . to the place where I was living before I came here. It was *not* my home."

"Poor lamb," Cook choked out. "You've had a bad time of it, have you not?"

"Enough!" Mapes snapped. "You may leave us, Miss Snow. The kitchen, as you have always known, is not the place for a lady. No matter how devious and conniving she might be."

When Katy reached the haven of her bedchamber, she knew she could not bear the sight of one more disapproving face. So she nodded her thanks to Jesse Wiggs and flashed him the smile he had always seemed to like so much. His answering grin and words of welcome were a spark of warmth in Farr Park's sudden chill. Let him find out from others. She'd suffered enough from convicting herself with every word out of her own mouth.

And what now?

Perhaps the vicar would write her a character? He had known her for years. A good man, surely he would not hold her deception against her?

Yes . . . she very much feared he would.

The doctor or Mr. Palmer? A character from an unmarried man was out of the question, as good as a recommendation to the life proposed by Major Foxbourne and Captain Thayne.

Did she really *wish* to be gone when Damon came home? Was pride that important? Was fear of being sent back where she came from enough to send her running from all she loved?

But Farr Park was only a minor property now. Castle Moretaine was the primary seat of the earls of Moretaine. Perhaps the Park was to be her prison, after all. She had been exiled, to grow old here, abandoned to her misery.

She was eighteen! With a whole long life to live. And live it she would. Though the how of it reminded her forcibly of that biblical verse about seeing through a glass darkly.

What about her mother's family? She was not destitute now. Other than an occasional ribbon or sweet, she had had no use for the wages earned at Farr Park. So she had the wherewithal to go adventuring. Her mother was an Alburton, and there had once been grandparents who had taken her in, ready to bring her up as their own. No matter the Bishop of Hulme's opinion of their fitness to do so.

Yes, perhaps that was what she should do. In all honesty, it was, quite possibly, what she should have done long ago. Except . . . she had not wished to leave Farr Park. Or her glorious imaginings of the master of Farr Park, who, someday, would come home.

And now, with those dreams scattered by the winds of reality, she must face up to the invidiousness of her position. Yet how did one find a wool merchant, named Alburton, who was likely long dead?

Katy, resting on her favorite chintz-covered window seat, broke off her musings, her speculations suddenly bowled over by the realities of this long, horrid day. Was it possible she had begun it in eagerness, feeling the wind in her hair as she rode beside the stream at Castle Moretaine? She had been so thrilled to be out of the house at last, leaving behind the oppressiveness of grief, compounded by Drucilla's dramatic posturings. For a few fleeting moments, she had been free, the whole world laid out before her. Free to dream of ways to conquer an earl, now risen so far above her touch.

And then . . . her whip struck the major's face . . . the retaliating sting against her cheek . . . clawing hands at her breasts . . . skirts up over her head.

The discipline of years broken at last, she had screamed. And ruined her life.

And now they all hated her. By tomorrow, when word spread, she would not have a friend left. Worse yet was the one thing she had not allowed herself to think about. It was too much, much too much. A problem far too complex to be analyzed in the strained conditions of a house of mourning. A problem that, perhaps, defied analysis at any time or place.

Who was Lucinda Challenor? And why had the Hardcastles claimed her?

Talk about deceit! For if there was one thing that bold hussy was not, it was Lucinda Challenor.

Katy Snow was Lucinda Challenor.

Chapter Eighteen

"Clover!" Katy, catching a glimpse of her friend disappearing down a side corridor, threw ladylike behavior to the winds, hiking up her skirts to chase after the Farr Park maid. But when she turned the corner, the hallway was empty, every door shut. "Clover," she called more softly. "Clover?"

Not Clover, too.

Already this morning, Katy had encountered no more than a stiff back and poker face from Jesse Wiggs. Dear Jesse, who had offered blind adoration for years, not to mention staunch support whenever her high spirits had forced Lady Moretaine, Mapes, or Mrs. Tyner to scold her. And now . . . Clover. *Et tu, Brute?*

Katy opened each door in turn. Clover Stiles was not going to elude her. The fourth door revealed a young woman in a gray gown with crisp white apron and cap. She was busy, suspiciously busy, running a feather duster over the high wooden tester above the bed. She did not look up from her task.

"Clover . . . please . . . I would like to explain. . . ."

The feather duster paused, descending slowly as the maid stepped away from the bed and dropped an exaggerated curtsy. "Was there something you needed, miss?" she inquired, her eyes focused somewhere past Katy's shoulder.

Katy bit her lip, tears threatening. So far she had managed to endure rejection rather well, she thought, but Clover . . . the girl so determined to better herself. Surely she could understand. She *must*!

"Yes, I need something," Katy told her. "I need someone to listen to why I—"

"Excuse me, miss, but Mrs. Tyner'll have my liver and lights if I don't get this whole corridor done this morning."

"Clover . . . you're my friend . . . for years."

"Well, that was before, now wasn't it, miss? Can't be friends with a real lady like yourself. Talkin' so hoity-toity, words just rollin' off your tongue. Fooled us all, didn't you? Made game of us. Thought we weren't good enough for the truth. Friends for years, indeed, miss," Clover spat. "And not a drop of trust."

Katy retreated into the silence that had been her refuge for so long. She had no rebuttal to Clover's words. Guilty as charged. She wanted to try again, to *make* her friend listen, but her tongue seemed to swell, choking off any possibility of speech. Katy managed a slight nod. A gesture of apology . . . acceptance of Clover's rejection. Good-bye.

Blindly, she stumbled back to her bedchamber and closed the door on the outside world. She had planned to take her hoard of coins and go into the village today, to consult Mr. Trembley, the local solicitor. The one possession remaining from her childhood was her mother's Bible. And above the names of her parents, Harold and Belinda, were the names of her maternal grandparents, Matthias and Emily Alburton. Throwing herself on the mercy of the lofty and distant connections on her father's side of the family, headed by the mighty Duke of Carewe, seemed quite impossible. But a wool merchant—or son or daughter—might be more willing to take pity on a long-lost relative.

At this moment, however, her courage failed her. She must give the villagers time to absorb the news, reel with the shock . . . and possibly find a modicum of pity, deep down in their souls, for a poor lost child.

For now, she would ride out on Mehitabel, dear Mehitabel—very likely her last true friend in all the world. Katy tore at the buttons of her gown as she rushed to change into her habit. But when she threw open the wardrobe door and saw the cavalry blue jacket and white braid she had once adored, the habit she had worn so proudly into the woods only the morning before, she cringed. Her old one must be here somewhere. . . .

Garbed in the forest green habit that threatened to burst its seams at any moment, Katy guided Mehitabel to all her old haunts, making a valiant effort to recapture the joy she had known here for so long. Inevitably, she and the bay mare found their way to the fateful hill overlooking Farr Park, where Katy suddenly slumped in the saddle and burst into tears.

It was lost to her now, her glorious, wonderful Farr Park, its beauty and comfort dust without the love of those within its borders. The only honorable course was to leave. Never darken the doors of Farr Park ever again.

Never see Damon.

Serena, her dear countess.

Mrs. Tyner, Mapes, Cook, Clover, Jesse . . . all those who had been so dear.

She must let her dreams of Damon go. Katy Snow was not for the likes of the Earl of Moretaine. Nor was Lucinda Challenor, overly indulged granddaughter of the Bishop of Hulme. Nor the great-granddaughter of the Duke of Carewe. Katy's claim to gentle birth—tainted by trade and a shockingly unconventional upbringing, not to mention deceit—was far too tenuous.

Two days. She would give the village of High Henton two days before she drove the gig into town and consulted Mr. Trembley. If they mocked her, reviled her, so be it.

She could not say she had not earned it.

Katy's meeting with Mr. Martin Trembley went well, almost as if he were asked to find long-lost relatives on a weekly basis. She could only suppose that solicitors encountered a great many strange things in the course of their profession. Her lingering hopes of sympathy from the villagers did not fare as well. Even the vicar's wife gave her the cut direct.

She was anathema—cast out.

The eyes of the village boys, now grown to young men, grew bolder. Narrowed with speculation, their avid gazes bored into her back as she drove by. She had no protection. The staff at Farr Park might address her, coldly, as Miss Snow, but to these ruffians she was the lying chit who'd managed to pull the wool over the eyes of the gentry, a spirited miss who was likely up to all the rigs and rows and ready for anything, including a roll in the hay. Katy shivered, and urged the cart horse into a trot.

She escaped the village, only to be brought up short a half mile from the gate to Farr Park when another gig suddenly swerved across her path.

"How fortunate we should meet like this," declared William Rowley, the doctor, who, as usual, was dressed in the height of fashion, his burgundy jacket pristine, his beaver at the perfect tilt in spite of driving on rough roads in an open carriage. "My dear girl, is it true you have found your voice at last?"

"As you may have heard, Mr. Rowley," said Katy, very much on her dignity and recalling every grope of the handsome doctor's hands, "I have always been able to speak. I simply did not choose to do so."

Mr. Rowley did not bother to hide his spark of anger. "So you include me among your victims, Miss Snow. Did you think to attach me? I assure you I would never stoop so low as to pick up vermin off the street."

"Back your gig, doctor. I wish to be on my way."

"Home to Farr Park, is it?" he taunted. "Do they still treat you as a queen then?" Rowley snorted his disbelief. "By all means, return to your cage, sly weasel. I trust the earl will see you are properly chastised when he returns." After a mocking salute with his whip, the doctor deftly backed his horse, allowing her to pass.

Katy's hands were shaking so hard she was grateful the old cob knew how close she was to a nice sack of oats, setting off briskly for the turn into Farr Park.

She must leave, she must leave.

A runaway, once again.

No! This time she would be running *to*.

Surely, oh surely, the Alburtons would want her. . . .

*   *   *

"I beg your pardon," Damon said, knowing his mouth was agape. Indeed, knowing full well he sounded as much of a fool as he felt.

"I spoke quite clearly," declared Drucilla, Dowager Countess of Moretaine, who was enthroned in a gilded chair, whose seat and back were upholstered in a heavy satin brocade only a shade or so brighter than the countess's suspiciously red lips. Her gown was a half dress of black lace opening over a shimmer of black silk. Diamonds glittered at her throat and dangled from her ears. She looked magnificent and knew it. With a thin smile and a flutter of her long lashes, she purred, "You cannot possibly have mistaken my meaning."

The colonel's eyes narrowed to slits, his voice taking on a grim quality his officers would have recognized as boding no good for the person on the receiving end of his wrath. "I did not mistake your words, my lady," he replied coldly. "I merely question their veracity."

"How dare you?" Drucilla shrieked, hitting her fan so hard against the arm of her chair that the fragile carved ivory sticks cracked.

"I dare because you have been childless for three years. Because the timing of your grand announcement is far too convenient to be believable."

"You are no gentleman!"

"I am a colonel. It would appear that will have to be sufficient," Damon returned, knowing from painful experience when to concede a battle he could not win. If Drucilla, wife of Ashby, late Earl of Moretaine, declared she was enceinte, then the title would go into abeyance. Damon Farr would still control the estate as executor, but his tenure as earl would be short-lived. For if Drucilla was delivered of a son, the infant would be the new Earl of Moretaine.

"Drucilla," he added quietly, "if this child is indeed my brother's, I should be the happiest of men, for I do not want the title. I never have. If this is a figment of your hysterical imagination, then I can only offer my pity. Time will surely solve our dilemma. But if you are planning to put some cuckoo in my brother's place, beware. You will find me an implacable foe."

"Such a fierce scowl, brother—when you know quite well that half the nests in the *ton* have cuckoos in their midst."

"Not for heirs!"

Drucilla sighed, running her fingers lightly over the folds of the silk and lace overlying her abdomen. "Perhaps not. But poor Ashby . . . I had almost given up hope. Such a delightful surprise!"

"Drucilla, I swear to you—"

She laughed, a light tinkling sound, as if she hadn't a care in the world. "As you well know, there is nothing you can do, *Colonel.* My son will be the next Earl of Moretaine."

Damon very much feared that was true.

Except it was highly doubtful the child would carry a drop of Farr blood. *Ashby, I have failed you. Forgive me.*

"You have a caller, miss. Mapes says for you to come at once. He's shown him into the morning room." The maid bobbed a curtsy, as if Katy were a mere guest at Farr Park, and took herself off. A caller? Someone was actually willing to speak to her? Perhaps it was Mr. Trembley. But four days seemed much too soon for the solicitor to have acquired any news of her grandparents. Defiantly, Katy wrapped a colorful fringed shawl over one of the dark Castle Moretaine gowns that served as semi-mourning, and hurried downstairs. The morning room. Evidently, she was no longer thought fit to receive guests in the drawing room.

Or perhaps the caller did not meet the butler's standards for the drawing room. Katy's steps faltered as Elijah Palmer rose at her entrance. So far since her return, she had managed to avoid Farr Park's steward. She liked the blond, broad-shouldered and good-natured Mr. Palmer and knew quite well he liked her. She could not bear to see the look of betrayal in yet another dear friend's eyes.

"Katy. Miss Snow, " he amended hastily. "I hope you do not

object to my call. I have not had the pleasure of encountering you since you returned."

"Not at all. I am pleased to see you." Was he not angry? All she saw in his fine blue eyes was a touch of sadness. Katy settled into a barrel-shaped klismos chair, indicating with a wave of her hand that Mr. Palmer should return to the chair he had occupied when she came in.

"I . . . I . . ." Elijah Palmer hesitated, tried again. "It has come to my attention that you are in an awkward situation, Miss Snow. That everyone seems to have forgotten you were but a child when you came here, that you could not be expected to understand what you were doing."

"But I grew up, Mr. Palmer. I should have rectified the situation."

"Eighteen is still very young. Far too young to venture out into the world alone."

So much emotion swept through her, Katy swayed, clutching the arm of her chair for support. What a good, kind, perfectly *wonderful* man. Had he heard about her visit to Mr. Trembley? Or did he merely guess her intention to once again run away?

"I would not have the courage to speak else," Mr. Palmer was saying, "though when I mentioned the matter to the earl—the new earl—I felt I had his blessing." The Farr Park steward leaned forward in his chair, his good countryman's face alight with hope. "Katy . . . I offer you my name and my protection. I have wanted you for my wife for years now. Marry me, Katy. I will never let them hurt you, and in time the gossip will die." He reached out, seized her hand. "Please, my dearest girl, say you will be mine."

Chapter Nineteen

It was the best offer she would ever have. And she had sat there like a ninny, gaping at the poor man as if he had suddenly grown two heads.

Once again, Katy scrunched down on a footstool before the cozy fire in her bedchamber, chin cupped in her hands, and railed at her sad lack of common sense. Elijah Palmer was a fine man . . . and a friend. How many women would consider themselves fortunate to marry a friend instead of a stranger chosen for title, wealth, or ancient family name?

He was the only person who understood.

Love and desire were ephemeral, though where she had acquired such a cynical notion Katy was unsure. But friendship was forever. . . .

Not in her case. Her friends had fled like rats from a sinking ship.

No one likes a liar.

Yet Elijah Palmer understood.

And so, knowing quite well she should tell him he deserved a woman who would love him as he should be loved, she had compounded her deceptions by asking him to give her time. The dear man had looked so pleased that she had not rejected him outright—he had even raised her hand to his lips in a marvelously old-fashioned gesture that had nearly broken her heart. Why, *why* could she not love such a fine specimen as Mr. Palmer? As Lucinda Challenor she might have looked higher, but Katy Snow had no such expectations.

Lucinda Challenor, the wretched imposter, was firmly ensconced at Oxley Hall, and even if Katy could prove her claim, she would not do so. For her overly trusting grandfather, the bishop, had named Baron Oxley her guardian. A disaster of catastrophic proportions.

She would never go back!

Yet it was not right to keep Mr. Palmer waiting, like a second string to her bow. Particularly when the first string was snapped in two, as irretrievably shattered as her heart.

Sounds of scurrying in the hall, the faint lilt of voices broke Katy's reverie. More visitors? Impossible. No one but Elijah Palmer was speaking to her.

Footsteps on the stairs, Mapes's ringing tones giving orders to the footmen. A sharp command in a female voice. *Archer?* A thud in the corridor. A trunk. *The countess's trunk?*

The dowager was back! But why? Katy rushed toward the door of her bedchamber, stopped abruptly with her hand on the knob. Her forehead sank against the wood. She was no longer the countess's pampered pet. She was the disgraced deceiver, the all but prisoner awaiting her fate. She no longer had a right to pop in and out of the countess's rooms at will.

And yet . . .

Katy inched open the door, peered into the hall. At the moment all was quiet. Damon had not returned, of course. His responsibilities were too great. Unless . . . he had made the journey solely for the purpose of dealing with Katy Snow.

She tiptoed down the hall, turned down a side corridor, and cracked open the door to the narrow gallery above the bookroom. Not a sound. Well, of course it was empty. Even if Damon had come home, he would scarce make the bookroom his first stop.

Nonetheless . . . moving silently as a mouse, very like the Katy of old, she slid past the rows of dark leather bindings engraved in gold until she could see behind Damon's desk, which had been partially hidden beneath the overhang of the gallery. *Ah! He was there.* Katy fell to her knees, clutching the balusters, peering down at her infuriating love.

Slumped in his comfortable chair, his face dark with misery, he was glaring at the brandy decanter perched before him, his fingers beating a tattoo on the leather blotter. He looked . . . defeated. At the end of his tether. Almost as bad as the soldier who had returned to Farr Park last summer.

Damon. Her love. Who had once also been her friend.

There was only one thing to do.

Katy rose and tiptoed to the narrow spiral staircase at one corner of the gallery. Ever so softly, she descended.

But he was a soldier. She was only halfway down the dizzying staircase when he barked, "For God's sake stop pussyfooting! Come over here and sit." Like a gimlet-eyed predator stalking prey, he watched her every step of the way.

Katy's chair was exactly where it had been before they left for Castle Moretaine—at his right hand, not two feet from his own. She sat. Questioning green eyes met turbulent gray. "What has happened?" she asked.

The colonel steepled his fingers, his lower lip jutting into self-mockery. "It seems," he told her, "that I am to be an uncle."

It took her a moment. *Uncle?* "Drucilla?" she breathed.

Damon snorted. "Of course Drucilla. Could anyone else manage to stir up such a bumblebroth?" After being pierced by Katy's steady, accusing gaze, he qualified his remark. "Believe me, child, your crimes pale in comparison to this. The day after the funeral, with Drucilla still demanding the entire collection of family jewels, my mother decided to tell me about her escapades. Redcliffe, it seems, was far from her only lover. It is likely the House of Farr is about to hatch a cuckoo. Moretaine will be lost to us forever."

Katy bit her lip, offered the only comfort that came to mind. "But you said you did not want it, the title or the lands."

"I do not! But I'll not see that rapacious whore sitting in my brother's home, laughing over her triumph."

Inwardly, Katy sighed. They both knew he had absolutely no choice. "We have nine months to pray for a girl," she ventured.

"Seven. It seems Drucilla very graciously waited until she was certain. Or so she says."

"Is she shamming it?"

"Doubtful. She is a schemer, inclined to hysterics only when they serve her purpose." Damon tapped the tips of his fingernails against the glass decanter. "And to think I wondered why my mother called her the Dreadful Drucilla."

"You are home to stay then?" Katy asked, her voice little above a whisper.

"My brother's many affairs require a veritable bevy of solicitors to settle the estate, but I am executor, so I fear I must return to Moretaine on a regular basis. I cannot like it, but I have no choice. The least I can do for Ashby is make certain his affairs are not mismanaged . . . until the outcome is clear."

"But surely you will be Trustee, and still in charge, even if the child is a boy?"

"Indeed. How absolutely delightful. Twenty-one years of hell fighting Drucilla's whims every step of the way."

"It *must* be a girl!" Katy cried. Then she scowled, her chin firming into that determined line Damon had come to know so well. "Though it is not at all fair," she qualified, "that girls should be so scorned. Our laws are archaic. Even the monarchy may pass to a female, but not some peer's entailed acres."

"Enough, child. A discussion of the rights of women has no appeal at the moment." How very strange, he thought. In this dark moment it was Katy Snow who stood his friend. A Katy Snow who no longer had to settle for nods or shakes of her head, to cryptic notes scribbled on scraps of paper. Katy, who understood his moods, tolerated his temper. Katy, who refused to give in to his lust.

Katy, the deceiver.

Whom he had wronged.

He must send her away. There could be no place for her here. Yet what would they do without her? She had infected the very air of his house. When she was happy, Farr Park sang. The rooms were bright, faces wreathed in smiles. When Katy was sad, as she was now, the atmosphere was cold and dark. People crept about with long disapproving faces, as lugubrious as gravediggers.

Would Farr Park come back to life if he sent Katy the deceiver away?

Hell's hounds! It wasn't supposed to be this way. Damon shoved the brandy decanter to the far side of the desk. "Miss Snow," he pronounced, "it is my considered opinion that my mother has suffered enough. If she is willing to tolerate your presence—not forgive, you understand, merely tolerate—then I believe we should go on as we did before. At least until I can think what must be done with you. I accepted you into this household, however foolish that may have been, and I feel responsible for you. I cannot simply thrust you out the door and forget about you." Now there was an admission he should not have made! He'd never control the arrogant little minx now.

"I am, as you must know," Damon hedged, "immensely sorry for the incident at Castle Moretaine. In effect, I precipitated the actions that revealed your perfidy. There are, of course, many so-called gentlemen who would be willing to cast the entire burden of guilt on your shoulders, but I am pleased to discover I am not numbered among them. Therefore . . . for a while at least, you will remain my mother's companion, if she agrees . . . and my secretary."

Confound it! She was doing it again. On her knees in front of him. Seizing his hand. Kissing it. Her lashes brushed his skin. A teardrop splashed the back of his hand.

Hell and damnation! He was putty, to be molded at her will. Encroaching little demon. But he, too, had known desperation. In battle and again now, when he was powerless to save the title from passing to a bastard. Desperation was a harsh taskmaster, frequently resulting in words and actions one could only wish unspoken and undone.

The fingers of his free hand dug into the arm of his chair, lest he twine them in the shining blond curls bent over his lap. God forbid his imagination should soar any farther toward the edge of sanity! "I will speak with my mother," Damon rasped. "Do not go to her until the morning. Hopefully, by then I will have smoothed your path."

And once again turned his refuge into a den of temptation. *Bloody hell!*

Katy dashed back to her room, heart soaring, head awhirl. A miracle had occurred. Everything was going to be all right. She did not have to leave. All thoughts of her grandparents fled from her head. And Elijah Palmer? She would tell him the dowager needed her. As surely the poor dear lady must.

But was it right to leave him hanging, just because her inner self knew it was all too good to be true? That in seven months' time Damon Farr could once again be Earl of Moretaine. Mr. Palmer deserved far better than a heartless chit who kept a beau in reserve until she had need of him.

So tomorrow she would reject his suit, as gently as she could. And pray he would find a woman who truly loved him.

As for herself . . . she would take her chances. Damon Farr, for all his faults, was worth the risk.

Chapter Twenty

Life was never going to be the same—although it was more than a month before Katy was willing to admit this unpleasant reality. The shock of grief, the threat of a possible bastard earl, compounded by betrayal from the viper in their midst, had thrown a pall over Farr Park as dark as the black hatchment over the front door. The dowager—in the past a lady of vivacity and decided opinions—spent much of her time in her suite of rooms, her Bible, embroidery, or a novel lying untouched in her lap. Katy could only hover, grateful for a nod, a faint thank you, a tiny twisted smile.

Belowstairs Katy found even less tolerance, Farr Park's staff remaining almost universally unbending. No more tea in Mrs. Tyner's cozy room. No more sage advice from Clover Stiles or flirtatious grins from Jesse Wiggs. Mapes was so formal she might as well have been a visiting duchess. Yet at times he seemed not to see her at all, as if she had simply vanished from his sight. Miss Nobody from Nowhere, unworthy of a proper butler's attention.

It was very lowering. A good many salty tears were washed from Katy's pillowcase each week.

And Damon—her glowering demon—was the worst. Each morning in the bookroom, he kept his head down, so studiously avoiding looking at her that Katy longed to whack him over the head with one of the library's larger volumes. And yet, sneak that he was, there were times when she could feel his gaze boring into her back. But when she peeked, he was always head down, quill poised, quill scribbling, or feathers idly tapping against his mouth.

It was Miss Snow this and Miss Snow that, with only a rare absentminded slip into Katy. In short, Damon, like Mapes, was so formal his manners practically squeaked. She'd swear that after the incident with his officers, he had buried lust so deep it might well be in China. And yet she could feel scorching heat in the dark eyes fixed on her back. More likely, she told herself sternly, a manifestation of heat from within herself, a product of the overactive imagination she was trying so hard to repress.

The truth was, she had destroyed Damon's desire, as well as his trust, in one fell swoop. Or should she say scream? He wanted nothing more to do with her except her convenience as a secretary. His periodic journeys to Castle Moretaine were almost a relief. Even though he returned each time surly as a bear, the absence of tension for a few days was more than welcome.

She was indeed a liar! So addicted to deception she even lied to herself. For each time Damon was gone, she missed him most dreadfully. Even when a glower emphasized the lines at the corners of his eyes, the slashes from nose to chin, she wanted to be near him. She wanted to gaze her fill at his dark head bent over his desk, researching, writing, puzzling out what to say next. A man of action struggling to fit himself into the confines of the world of words.

He might be a stiff-rumped, buffleheaded idiot where she was concerned, but she loved him anyway. She had betrayed his trust. He had betrayed hers. Surely that made them even.

If the granddaughter of a wool merchant and the potential heir to an earldom could ever be said to be even.

In mid-November Katy turned nineteen. The day was gray, cold, and blustery, presaging a long difficult winter. The dowager did not forget, although her gift of soft bone-colored kid gloves was a mere token compared to her customary effusion of presents. Katy's eyes filled with tears, however, when Cook made all her favorite foods for dinner that night. Damon, gruff and forbidding, evidently disturbed by the sight of a tearful

Katy, handed her a guinea—a munificent gift if she had not felt like a servant being handed a vail at the end of a gentleman's weekend in the country.

Conscience money, that's what it was.

She nearly thrust it back at him, but remembered in the nick of time that money gave independence. So she curtsied, even as she hoped he could not mistake the fire in her eye. Love him she might, but accept his behavior meekly she could not.

Late that night, just as she was climbing into bed, there was a faint scratching at her door, and Clover slipped into her room. Standing proud and straight, she announced, "I've come to offer best wishes for your birthday." Her lips quivered. "Katy," she added softly.

A pause . . . and the two girls fell on each other, Clover's stiffness dissolving in a flood of tears to match Katy's own.

"It's cruel we've been," Clover sobbed. "Right cruel. You were a child, a babe on your own without kith or kin. Who was there to tell you how to go on?"

With shuddering breaths and tearful faces, the two old friends built up Katy's fire and curled up before it for a coze that lasted until pre-dawn tinged the sky with silver.

The only other riffle in the quiet melancholy days at Farr Park was heralded by a message from Mr. Trembley. Katy drove the gig into the village on rutted, almost frozen roads that jarred her teeth and threatened to throw her from her seat until she slowed the old cob to a walk. Why should she be eager to learn what Trembley had to say? She no longer needed the grandparents who had given her up after only a few short weeks. Her situation at Farr Park might still be a bit awkward, but Damon was there, and her dear countess needed her. Nothing else mattered. What could some ephemeral connection to a wool merchant's family mean to her now?

But somehow the old cob kept picking up the pace, seemingly sensing a barely controlled excitement Katy was unwilling to admit.

Martin Trembley stared at her from across a desk piled with

leather folders tied with string and stacks of papers, some high enough to be in imminent danger of tumbling to the floor. The solicitor appeared to be measuring her in a far more penetrating manner than he had when she had made her initial request. "Miss Snow," he said at last, "in conducting the search you requested, I have encountered far more than I expected . . . even a bit of a mystery."

Ah! A quiver shook Katy's stomach. A village solicitor—she had not expected him to be quite so astute.

"I regret to inform you that the person you wished to find is no longer among the living. Matthias Alburton passed on almost a year ago."

A man she had never met, and yet she felt grief. Now she would never know her maternal grandfather.

"However . . . his wife, Emily Alburton, still lives. There is also a son and grandchildren, all living most comfortably in an area not far from Derby."

A grandmother? She had a living grandmother?

"There was once a daughter," Mr. Trembley added. "Belinda Alburton, who married up, as the saying goes. Harold Challenor, son of the Bishop of Hulme, and grandson of the old Duke of Carewe. But Challenor and his wife perished in a sailing accident, leaving a child, a girl barely six months of age. Lucinda. The Alburtons promptly took over care of the child and were just as promptly relieved of the baby by the Bishop and his wife, who declared the child should be raised to a life befitting her father's station. The Alburtons were heartbroken, but believed they were doing the right thing when they let the babe go."

"Mr. Trembley . . . I am astonished you have learned so much," Katy murmured. The dratted man had obviously come to conclusions she had never dreamed of his discovering.

"The tale of the Alburtons' grandchild is the talk of the entire midlands, and as far south as Peterborough and the Cotswolds," said the solicitor, leaning forward as if to better gauge her reaction. "For it seems the child went missing shortly after the Bishop died and she was consigned to the guardianship of a Baron Oxley. Whose wife, I am told, is connected in some way to the Challenor family."

"Surely old news, Mr. Trembley. Of little interest outside the family." *Blast the man!* This was the worst, the very worst that could have happened. Why had she been so foolish as to open the path to ancient wounds?

Mr. Trembley could not know she was Lucinda Challenor, Katy reminded herself. She had not asked him to find her grandparents. She had asked only that he find a Matthias Alburton, wool merchant.

"The talk is current," Mr. Trembley continued, his gaze never leaving Katy's face, "because Lucinda Challenor has made a miraculous reappearance and been reunited with her family. Lord and Lady Oxley are ecstatic, as are the Alburtons." The solicitor paused, dropped his gaze to the topmost paper on his desk. He pursed his lips, leaned back in his huge brown leather chair. "The Bishop of Hulme was not a poor man. He provided quite well for his only grandchild, though what has become of the money is a bit of a mystery. I have experts looking into it—"

"I cannot afford it," Katy interjected. "Truly, I shall be hard pressed to pay your fee. You have more than done as I asked. You are, in fact, most amazing in your thoroughness. I am infinitely grateful, but—"

Mr. Trembley cut her off with a wave of his hand. "Hear me out, Miss Snow. There is more . . . and I assure you I find this matter intriguing enough that I am pursuing it for my own edification. A village solicitor is not often given a puzzle of this complexity."

Inwardly, Katy echoed one of Damon's more colorful oaths. Outwardly, calling on the discipline of her years of silence, she appeared perfectly calm. Clasping her hands in her lap, she prepared to listen. What else had she been doing since the age of twelve? She had a talent for listening.

"Matthias Alburton and his wife never gave up hope their grandchild was alive," said Mr. Trembley. "Alburton was so convinced of it, he left the missing child a sum of sixty thousand pounds."

Katy gasped.

"Well might you be surprised if you thought Alburton an ordinary tradesman. The bulk of his estate, of course, went to his son, who is a very wealthy man indeed. And powerful. The family expanded from wool to weaving to owning mills throughout the midlands. Sixty thousand pounds was an easily affordable token thrown out to lure a missing child."

"Which it did," Katy breathed.

"Which it did," Trembley agreed.

Dear God! She was an heiress.

Lucinda Challenor was an heiress. And the alleged Lucinda Challenor was currently residing at Oxley Hall—when not ogling Colonel Damon Farr. For he had told his mother that the Hardcastle family were regular visitors to Castle Moretaine, supporting the bereaved and increasing widow in her hour of need.

"My investigator reports that Miss Challenor bears a remarkable resemblance to you, Miss Snow."

He knew! Or suspected. Dear Lord, who could have expected to find a shark swimming in the shallow stream of the village of High Henton. But he was *her* solicitor, was he not? Pledged to silence. Unless Mr. Trembley had considered how much blunt a few well-chosen words might acquire from the baron . . . or from the Alburtons.

How much would they offer for news of the long-lost heiress? How much to lose her forever?

Katy fumbled to open her reticule. She summoned a smile, even though her jaws ached with the effort. "You have exceeded my expectations, Mr. Trembley." Most horribly. "Pray tell me what is needed to settle your fee."

He named a sum she suspected would not cover his investigator's time for more than a few days, with nothing left over for himself. Solemnly, Katy counted out the coins. Through a narrowed mouth and a throat that threatened to swell shut, she thanked Mr. Martin Trembley and left, head high. But not before accepting the paper he held out to her, on which was written in flowing script the names and direction of the Alburton family. Her grandmother, her uncle, and her cousins.

Caught on the horns of a dilemma, that was the right phrase for her situation. Or *teetering on the brink. Damned if she did, damned if she didn't.* Any one of the old expressions would do.

She feared the Hardcastles. Yet she could not allow an imposter to fool the Alburtons. Or seize the fortune her grandfather Alburton had left her. Although it would appear the Hardcastles had already helped themselves to the funds left her by her grandfather Challenor.

She could not even be certain of Mr. Trembley's support. This was not a situation a girl of nineteen, with no legal rights, could handle alone. She had no choice—she would have to confess all to Damon and pray that he would protect her. But how? He, too, had no legal rights where she was concerned. He was not her guardian. Any efforts on her behalf would embroil him in an arcane plot created by *her* relatives, just when he was suffering from grief for his brother, attempting to deal with his mother's melancholy, and handling the far-flung affairs of the Moretaine estate.

Katy allowed the cob to meander at its own pace along the road back to Farr Park. If she had any sense, she would keep going. Straight out of the lives of everyone who knew her.

Which, of course, she would not. She would not leave those who had given her shelter, given her love, just when they truly needed her. *Never!*

So she could not tell a soul. And she could only pray Mr. Trembley was an honest man.

But when Katy arrived home, she found a fresh wind sweeping through the Park. The dowager raised a wan face to hers and declared, "Damon wishes us to remove to Bath after the holidays. He thinks I should take the waters."

Bath! A marvelous notion. Exactly what the countess needed to coax her back to life.

And yet . . . Katy shivered. Bath was only a short distance

west of Farr Park and not far south of Castle Moretaine. And Oxley Hall. With Damon as the lure, the Hardcastles would not be far behind, increasing the many languid visitors to the Pump Room by four.

And spelling disaster for Katy Snow.

Chapter Twenty-One

Would Wellington applaud his compromise? Damon wondered. Or damn him for a buffleheaded idiot?

Bath. Instead of sending Katy Snow packing, he was sending her to Bath.

And his mother, so fixed in her melancholy that he had not thought to be able to budge her, had welcomed the scheme with surprising alacrity. *Suspicious* alacrity. Now why . . . ? Had she gone back to her determined, if self-sacrificial, plan of finding Katy a husband? Surely, without being able to vouch for the chit's character, the dowager had long since abandoned that notion . . .

Unless . . . *Hell's hounds!* Unless she was seizing the opportunity to part him from his secretary. Unless his mama actually thought he would be fool enough to . . .

If she had heard the truth of what happened in the woods at Castle Moretaine, she could easily suspect the worst. Or if she had intercepted one of his glances at Katy—perhaps an unguarded moment when the shutters had lifted, revealing the naked truth . . . Ah, yes, his mama could easily suspect her once-cherished foundling was in danger. Even with Katy no longer the darling of her heart, the dowager would feel responsible, obligated to whisk her companion out from under his constant presence.

Or had his mother's speculations gone beyond fear of Katy's ruin? Did she actually think he would stoop to a nameless waif for a bride? Marry a conniving little sneak? *Was she mad?*

Or did the countess fear he would never marry as long as Katy Snow flitted before him, pulsing with youthful beauty, vivacity, and intelligence? Even the sound of her playing the pianoforte could send his wits to grass, whether he was in the room with her or hearing the notes drifting in from the music room.

Truth was . . . his mother very likely had the right of it. Katy Snow was close to becoming an obsession. When he visited Castle Moretaine, Miss Hardcastle, Miss Challenor, and Lady Oxley inevitably arrived hard after. He forgave the young ladies their flirtatious manner, their simpering, fan-tossing, and forced giggles in a house of mourning, for they were young and not well acquainted with the late earl. But find them enticing, he could not. In an heroic effort to be gracious, he had even returned their flirtation in a halfhearted manner, yet experienced not an iota of stirring in head, heart, or loins.

The same could not be said for the time spent with Katy Snow. If he did not send her away, he was going to drag her down to the bookroom carpet and . . .

A swish of skirts, a deep indrawn breath. Damon looked up into twin pools of green fire. "Is it true?" Katy demanded. "You are not accompanying your mama to Bath?"

Damon leaned back in his chair, crossed his arms. Swallowed. If it were possible for Katy Snow to look any more delectable, he could not imagine it. The chit fairly quivered with outrage, cheeks flushed, even her tumbled blond curls seemingly aquiver. He knew her to be a scheming little baggage, yet he could scarce keep his hands off her. Even now, his fingers tingled as they longed to free themselves from where he had tucked them. "I will, of course, escort the countess and her party to Bath," he responded coolly.

"But you will not stay?"

"I will then go on to Moretaine."

"Pray cease the roundaboutation, Colonel. Will you, or will you not, be joining us in Bath?"

"By what right do you ask, Miss Snow?" Damon inquired silkily.

She huffed a long breath, then quite deliberately crossed her arms in imitation of his own. "By right of caring about your mama," she retorted, enunciating each syllable with awful clarity.

He raised a dark brow, looked down his strong, aquiline nose. "And you think I do not?"

"I am shocked you could abandon her in her hour of need."

"May I point out we are past mid-January, with more snow on the ground than the night that gave you your name. My brother has been gone for nearly four months. With the exception of my visits to Moretaine, I have been close by for all that time, and it has made very little difference that I can—"

"It has made every difference! Your mama adores you."

"*Hound's teeth!*" He abandoned his crossed-arms pose to wave a commanding hand at Katy's customary chair. "Sit down, and let us discuss this in a civilized manner. Now let us face the facts of the matter," Damon continued after his all-too-bewitching secretary was seated. "We are both aware my mother has fallen into a melancholy and is in sad need of distraction. In Bath she may take the waters and talk to old friends. She may go shopping, take a drive in the country. When the weather improves, there are some splendid parks to be explored. All without any hint of disrespect for her period of mourning."

"Yes, but she needs your support—"

"My library is here, Snow. This is where my work is. No one can be more aware of that than yourself." Katy opened her mouth, closed it again, shoulders hunching in defeat. "I believe we have already retrieved from the shelves all the books I will need." Damon swept his right arm in an arc, pointing her attention to the chaos surrounding them. There were piles of books on every table and chair, books stacked on the floor around his desk and in towers on each side of the broad mahogany surface. "And did you not send off to London for the others I need not a sennight ago?" Dumbly, Katy nodded.

"So there you have it. I will go on here in perfectly splendid peace and quiet, bringing you my latest for a fair copy when I visit in Bath—" The colonel broke off, uttering—fortunately only to himself—a very bad word. Katy had pokered up so badly, he might as well have kicked her.

"You preferred me when I didn't talk," she accused. "Is that not so?"

"I preferred you when I didn't know you were a liar and a cheat." He should not have said it, of course, but the opening was too tempting—a man must defend himself, must he not? This beautiful young creature, the epitome of virginal innocence, blessed with intelligence and internal fire . . . infinitely tempting. She had been everything that was wonderful . . . a light shining in the darkness of his days, dimming the pain of war, the pain of grief . . .

Then, lo and behold, he discovered his goddess had feet of clay. Yes, he hurt. And would be well rid of her.

And, deep down, he knew his mother agreed. Serena Moretaine was going to Bath—and taking Katy with her—as much for his sake as for her own. And, perhaps, in spite of his mama's dim view of her companion's betrayal, she was doing it for Katy as well. The child deserved something better than the fate of becoming the plaything of a roughened, disillusioned old soldier. Even a colonel.

Especially a colonel.

Lucifer! She was sitting there, head bent, once again Lady Silence, crushed by his harsh words. Good. No more arguments. That was as it should be. "Before you go, Snow, please organize my sources, each stack with a similar topic, then draw a key so I may find things easily." His bookroom would be cold and dreary . . . and an incoherent shambles within days of her departure.

"Of course, Colonel." A subdued Katy rose, bobbed a token curtsy, and went to work, attacking the stacks on the burl elm side table first, meticulously reading each title and rearranging as necessary.

Damon knew she longed to run off, out of reach of his sharp tongue, but she wouldn't. Not his Katy. She would stick like a burr, doing her duty, as she had for all the years she had been at Farr Park. . . .

Where else did the chit have to go?

Damon picked up his quill, dipped it in ink. The words he had written not half an hour ago blurred before his face. Who really cared about Hannibal and his elephants anyway?

His vision cleared enough to reveal his last sentence. It would seem, that according to Colonel Damon Farr, someone named Katy had led an army across the Alps. He stared at the page, blinked, looked again. Furiously, Damon scratched out the offending name—so well, in fact, that he put a hole through the page. Good! There mustn't be so much as a trace of his mistake for Katy to pounce upon when she wrote out the fair copy.

The colonel gritted his teeth, ostentatiously consulted one of the volumes on his desk, then settled down to write. The first day of February was scheduled for his mother's move to Bath. It could not come soon enough.

Bath was much like a lopsided bowl, Katy decided as their coach wound its way down the precipitous slope into the city. Ancient tribes had settled inside the bend of the Avon at the base of the bowl, as drawn by the warm bubbling springs as all those who came after. The Romans had followed, building bathing structures and villas, of which a glimpse or two could still be seen. How much, Katy wondered, was still underground, waiting to be discovered?

The city now spilled out of its ancient walls, with beautiful buildings in the Palladian style creeping up the steep hillside above the river, above the baths, the Pump Room, and the impressive Gothic spires of Bath Abbey. It was not Katy's first journey to Bath. The countess usually paid a short visit to an old friend there at least once a year, but this would be their first extended stay. The first time they would have a house of their very own, and time to explore the marvels of a city that was infinitely fascinating, if no longer fashionable.

If only the colonel were staying with them . . .

If only she could be certain the Hardcastles would not decide to take the waters . . .

Without Damon's presence, there was no reason for the Hardcastles to make a winter journey to Bath. How could she not have realized that before?

Katy brightened. Damon would be a regular visitor to their residence on Brock Street, but since the Hardcastles had access to him at Castle Moretaine, they were unlikely to pursue him further. Once again, Fate had been more kind than she deserved. Katy sat back against the squabs and closed her eyes, vowing to do her very best to show her dear countess that she was not an ungrateful wretch. She cared, she truly cared, about Serena Moretaine. Katy had no recollection of her mother and grandmother Alburton, only hazy memories of her Grandmother Challenor. The Dowager Countess of Moretaine had been her mentor since she was twelve years old, the closest to a mother she had ever known. Katy loved her dearly. With narrowed eyes and lower lip extended into a pugnacious pout, she vowed that, no matter what the risk, she would do her best to make the countess's stay in Bath as pleasant as possible.

And there it was! The magnificent vista of the Royal Crescent, overlooking a vast sweep of parkland, the lower portion dotted with grazing cows and sheep. Then they were turning into Brock Street, each narrow townhouse distinguished by a colorful door or distinctive architectural touch. How delightful that Damon had been able to lease a house here, tucked on the narrow street between the Royal Crescent and the Circus and only a few steps from the Upper Assembly Rooms. Not that they would be attending the assemblies, but perhaps the countess would care to take tea there and talk to friends. They could listen to the music drifting in from the ballroom. Perhaps, by the end of six months of mourning, the dowager might even visit the card room.

Only a short ways down the hill were a choice of baths—though Katy doubted the countess would be willing to indulge in total immersion in the midst of winter, despite the hot temperature of the water. But the new Pump Room, built some twenty years before, was just beyond, facing the Abbey churchyard, and only a few niggling steps from a shop selling the famous Bath buns. Katy's mouth watered at the thought. Beyond that were streets of small shops selling nearly everything under the sun to the many hopeful people who came to Bath to take the waters and plunge their aching bodies into the hot springs. A far cry from the meager offerings of the village of High Henton. Oh, yes, Bath was truly a delightful place.

If the colonel did not care to join them, that was his loss. Foolish man!

"I fear you will find it a trifle cramped," Colonel Farr told his mother as he ushered her from the carriage, "but a house to let in this part of town is so rare, it was an opportunity I could not ignore."

"Do not be absurd," Lady Moretaine pronounced as they stepped up to the front door, which was painted a rich burgundy red, accented by a shiny brass knocker, and topped by an elegant fanlight. "It is charming and could not be more conveniently located, for we are above the miasma of the baths, and with only a few steps to the Royal Crescent, the entire vista of the city and surrounding hills is spread out before us." She patted his arm. "And it is not as if we will be entertaining."

Fine words, Katy thought a short while later, but compared to Farr Park, their new residence was a doll's house. The townhouse was a mere two rooms wide, with a long narrow hall down the center. Drawing room, dining room, and two parlors on the ground floor, with four bedrooms above and servants rooms in the attics. The basement, with no more than high thin windows letting in the light on the lower side of the slope, contained the kitchen, a modest wine cellar, laundry, and a box room.

She would recover from this feeling of being shut in, Katy assured herself, but somehow her explorations continued straight out the rear door, where, to her delight, she discovered a walled garden. Though the plants were brown and dusted with snow and the flagstone path glimmered with patches of ice, the garden extended the full width of the house, with perhaps as much as a hundred feet to the far wall, where a wooden door led to a street behind. There did not appear to be a mews, as in London. Horses and carriages must be kept elsewhere, Katy supposed, and sent for when needed. Not surprising in a city where streets were so steep sedan chairs and shank's mare were more common transport.

In spite of the shelter of the garden's six-foot brick walls, Katy could only take pleasure in picturing its awakening over the next few months. At the moment, she had no desire to linger in air cold enough to frost her breath. The garden was, in fact, as cold and drab as her heart when she thought of Damon leaving them on the morrow.

Miserable man. He had parked them here, where he could conveniently forget about them while he chased about the countryside, hotly pursued by Eleanore Hardcastle and the alleged Lucinda Challenor.

And fended off Drucilla's latest dramatic fits and starts.

Poor man. Perhaps she should feel sorry for him.

Pooh! If he was taken in by the Hardcastles' maneuverings, he deserved his fate.

No. No one deserved the dire destiny of being attached by a Hardcastle. And Katy Snow née Lucinda Challenor would protect him, even if it meant a full confession.

Chapter Twenty-Two

"There you are!" Drucilla, Countess of Moretaine, swept into the estate room as a footman stood at attention, holding open the door.

Chairs scraped over a well-worn rug as the three gentlemen occupying the room leaped to their feet. Colonel Farr noted with some interest that Ashby's secretary, Philip Winslow, appeared to be strangling on his cravat, his face an interesting shade of strawberry puce, as Lady Moretaine's well-rounded belly preceeded her into the room. Castle Moretaine's steward, a gentleman well along in years and accustomed to the vagaries of the aristocracy, turned a face of bland inquiry toward the young countess.

With an impatient gesture—remarkably like a farmwife shooing chickens, Damon thought—Lady Moretaine said to her steward and her late husband's secretary, "You may leave us. I wish to speak with Colonel Farr in private."

"My lady," Damon protested, "we are nearly finished here. I will come to you in the drawing room as soon—"

Drucilla skewered him with a glare of outrage. "*Now,* Colonel. I wish to speak with you now."

Even as Damon ground his teeth, he proffered a polite bow. While seating his sister-in-law in the most comfortable chair the estate room could offer, a scratched and faded leather of venerable age, the other two men scurried out, Philip Winslow still suspiciously red above the high white collar of his shirt.

"Well, Drucilla?" Damon inquired, finding he was having

some difficulty reining in his temper. He should not let her rile him, but she did. Every time. Making his visits to Castle Moretaine on behalf of estate business a duty he longed to eschew. How he could endure another twenty-one years of this agony until the babe reached its majority, he could not imagine.

There his nemesis sat, in yet another new gown of mourning with falls of black lace at neck and cuffs, each banded at the top in jet beads that seemed to have the same shine as her raven hair. As usual, Drucilla's cheeks and lips were rouged, standing in sharp contrast to her almost ghostly pale face. And again—as usual—she was unhappy with him. An attitude she adopted whenever she was not openly gloating about her triumph over him.

She looked up, amber eyes seething with a fine combination of fury and disdain. "My father tells me that you and he are named co-guardians for my son. That I have been completely ignored. I cannot believe Ashby could have been such a fool. Surely he was not in his right mind. I was so certain of being named that I did not even question the matter until Father mentioned it during a visit last week. It is vile, Damon, perfectly vile. I will not have it!"

The colonel, who was still standing, thrust his hands behind his back and stared down at the countess, making a valiant effort to mask his loathing. "The will was quite clear on the subject, my lady. Your father and I are guardians for any child, boy or girl, born posthumously to the late Earl of Moretaine. Ashby's clarity of mind was never in question. He knew exactly what he was doing. You are not named. Ashby's friend, Lord Hervey, and Mr. Benchley, the solicitor, are also named as Trustees, to help oversee the estate's finances until the child should come of age."

"At twenty-five!" Drucilla huffed.

Damon shrugged. "Hopefully, an age of reason. I shall be most happy to relinquish my guardianship at age twenty-one, I assure you."

Drucilla pressed three fingers to her forehead, then flicked them dramatically into the air. "Am I to have nothing to say about the rearing of my son," she cried, "my dear boy who will be earl the moment he is born?"

Damon almost applauded. For some seconds silence hung between them while he rejected the succession of pithy comments that chased through his mind. "Drucilla . . . no one wishes to take away your rights as a mother," he said at last. "And I am sure your father and I will listen to your opinions about governesses, schools, and such. But it was Ashby's decision to make us guardians, and we will exercise that right with care. We want only the best for Ashby's child."

"Liar!" Drucilla spat at him, her fingers clenching the arms of her chair. "You wish my babe to the devil. My Moretaine, my little earl. How can I possibly trust you to take proper care of him when you would be earl if he is gone."

Damon's hands tightened into fists. He closed his eyes, took a deep breath. "Drucilla, I fear grief has addled your wits. I will do my best to forget you ever made such an unwarranted remark. My duty to my brother is first and foremost in my life. Whether you are delivered of a boy or a girl, I will endeavor to see the child is raised in the rank, luxury, and education befitting a Farr. Even . . ." Damon added softly, enunciating every word with cutting clarity, "even if I have grave doubts about the child's paternity."

The countess opened her mouth, but got no further than a sibilant hiss of outrage before Damon overrode her indignation. "I will be watching, Drucilla. If the heir to the House of Farr grows up to resemble Redcliffe or Philip Winslow or any other on a considerable list my agent has compiled, I will make life as difficult as possible for you. I loved my brother and would love and protect any child of his body. I will even respect the rights of any child of doubtful paternity. But *you* I will not forgive." Did he look as implacable as he felt? He could only hope so. Drucilla, he noted with some satisfaction, had turned as uniformly crimson as her painted cheeks.

"Come!" Damon responded to a scratching at the estate room door, exceedingly grateful for the interruption. Berating a woman so obviously enceinte was not the act of a gentleman, no matter how venal her actions might have been.

Rankin entered, his customary butler's façade spoiled by a slight flush about the ears. How long had he been listening at the door? Damon wondered. Not that it mattered. No household's secrets were safe from its staff.

"Lady Oxley, Miss Hardcastle, and Miss Challenor are here, my lady. Shall I ask them to wait?"

Drucilla's hands fluttered. "No, no. Tell them I will be with them directly." She turned to Damon, a mean little smile curling her lips. "You need not look so pained, dear brother. Either girl would do quite well for you. Daughter of a baron or sixty thousand pounds. A fine consolation prize." She levered herself to her feet with some grace and started for the door.

"It has never occurred to you the babe may be a girl?" Damon inquired softly.

Drucilla paused, turned halfway toward him, chin high. "Do not be absurd," she declared. She exited with all the dignity of Anne Boleyn confronting the headsman.

Damon shook his head. Drucilla Moretaine was a trollop, but no one could say she did not carry it off with style. What mortification would be his if the babe were a boy born in Ashby's image. He would rejoice. But the thought of humbling himself before Drucilla was too terrible to contemplate. He swore, with feeling, and steeled himself to face the phalanx of female visitors in the drawing room.

Katy was reading aloud to the dowager countess when the thumps and thuds began. The poetry of *The Lord of the Isles* was swiftly cast aside, as neither lady cared for it as much as the author's previous works, and the strange noises were loud enough to warrant investigation. A cold breeze wafted down the central corridor, insinuating itself into their cozy parlor overlooking the winter-ravaged garden.

The front door was open.

The ladies' heads swiveled toward the parlor entrance, faces alive with speculation. Not only was the outside door open, but it was remaining open for an unwarranted amount of time for February. At Serena Moretaine's nod of approval, Katy sprang to her feet and rushed into the hallway that bisected the house on Brock Street. Then, unable to believe her eyes, she dashed toward the front of the house, where four stalwart carters were attempting to wrestle something very large through the front door.

It wasn't possible. Surely not. Yes, it was! A pianoforte. Not as large as the one in the music room at Farr Park, but an instrument that would fit perfectly into the modest confines of their present drawing room.

"Ah, Miss!" Jesse Wiggs spoke from just inside the drawing room door. "I was coming to find you. Clover and me are ready to move furniture about, but we need to know where you wants it."

Jesse, Clover, and Archer, the countess's maid, were all the servants they had brought from Farr Park, as the owner of the house on Brock Street had taken only his butler and valet on an extended visit to London, leaving the remainder of his staff in Bath. Jesse had been momentarily struck dumb when informed he had been chosen as temporary butler for the dowager's household in Bath.

Katy sidled past the pianoforte that was now taking up most of the corridor and examined the drawing room. She looked back at the instrument, frowned. What an odd shape—the keyboard set at an angle to the long case holding the strings . . . and, yes, one side of the beautiful rosewood case was completely flat. . . .

Of course! That side of the string case was meant to sit flush against the wall. How exceedingly clever. "Let us clear the wall next to the corridor," Katy said. "If we set it against the outer wall, I fear it might disturb the residents next door."

In a trice three pairs of willing hands had cleared a space, while the four carters stood morosely by, giving no sign that sight of a lady moving furniture shoulder to shoulder with her servants was aught but a daily occurrence. Then Katy, eyes shining, directed the carters to the precise spot where the pianoforte should be placed. *Oh, it was so beautiful!*

"Quickly, Clover, run to the Upper Rooms and ask who tunes their pianofortes. I want to sit down and play this very minute, but I know moving loosens the strings. Clover!" Katy called as her old friend rushed from the room. "I did not truly mean for you to run. With the streets as icy as they are, you will surely break your neck. Walk carefully, if you please. Somehow I shall manage to contain myself." Clover, with the flash of a grin and a wave of her hand, resumed her errand.

Gingerly Katy touched one key. The tone was mellow and surprisingly strong for an instrument half the size of the one at Farr Park. She struck a chord. And made a face. Behind her, Jesse Wiggs chuckled. "Sounds like you was right, miss. Off with you now. I'll rearrange this jumble until all looks right and tight again."

He was smiling. Another forgiveness? Katy wondered. Did she deserve it? Her deception had been very long and very thorough. And she had experienced little guilt until it was far too late. "Thank you, Jesse," she murmured, and hurried back down the hall to tell the countess her grand news. But of course it could not be news—the dowager must have ordered it as a surprise. A startling, wonderful surprise . . .

Katy burst into the back parlor, profuse thanks spilling so eagerly from her tongue that she was close to stammering. Alas, Lady Serena Moretaine did not appear best pleased, an anxious frown soon replacing her initial smile of pleasure. "My lady?" Katy said. "Is there something wrong? Did you not order the piano? Is it a mistake?"

"No, not a mistake, child, but I did not order it."

"Oh." Katy thought for a moment. "Do you suppose the owner ordered it some time ago and it is just being delivered?"

"I think not."

"My lady?"

"Sit down, Katy."

Katy, now thoroughly alarmed by the severity of the countess's expression, sat. Her fingers sought each other, clasping tightly together in her lap. Whatever the dowager was about to say, she was not going to like it.

"Katy, you *are* aware that there is still a strong possibility my son may become the next Earl of Moretaine?" Katy, falling back on old habits, nodded. "Even as Mr. Damon Farr, it is important that he marry well. I cannot have him so infatuated with you that he does not look at suitable young ladies."

"O-oh!" Katy drew a long shuddering breath. Her fingernails bit into her palms. "You think Da—Colonel Farr—ordered the piano . . . and that he . . . no, no, that cannot be true. He may like to hear me play, but he is still angry with me, I assure you. He *glares.* He ignores me. No more than a grunt do I get for all my fetching, carrying, and writing out fair copy. Truly, you are mistaken."

No, she wasn't. Katy's heart was singing at the thought that Damon had presented her with this magnificent gift. For surely he had. And she recalled all those times when she was certain his eyes were following her about the bookroom, even if she never caught more than a glower from beneath his dark brows.

"No, Katy, I do not believe I am mistaken," the dowager returned gently. "It is the primary reason I agreed to remove to Bath. No matter what I think of your conduct, I have known and cared for you too long to thrust you out into the streets, but I have determined you must give serious consideration to finding a husband here in Bath. At worst, another position . . . I fear my son will never marry as long as you are under our roof." Lady Moretaine paused, pursed her lips, then plunged on. "And, truth be told, as much as I love Damon and know him to be a gentleman, I fear for your safety as well, child. I see—there is no disguising it—I see passion fly between you. When you are in a room together, even at the dinner table, I feel a tension like some great storm disturbing the air. You must leave us, Katy. By marriage or a new position . . . but you will not return to Farr Park."

Katy, unwilling to reveal the stark horror that must be reflected in her eyes, bowed her head over her clasped hands. She could not move, could not think.

"And you will not marry Elijah Palmer," the dowager continued inexorably, "even though the match is suitable. If Damon does not become earl, I cannot have you forever beneath his nose."

Was it possible, Katy wondered, that only moments earlier she had been as happy as she had ever been in her life? This was her comeuppance, of course. The end result of her own actions. For all that the Hardcastles were the root of her own personal evil, it was the twelve-year-old Lucinda Challenor who had disguised herself as a mute and wormed her way into the affections of the residents of Farr Park. It was she who had never uttered a word, no matter how severe the provocation. It was she who had made a fantasy hero of Damon Farr. It was she who had not hesitated to lean toward him or over him while they worked, displaying her nicely rounded bosom. She who hiked her skirts a mite too high when climbing the bookroom ladder.

"I am not speaking of your immediate departure," said the countess, softening her tone. "We are fixed in Bath for some time, certainly through Drucilla's confinement in May. What happens after that, of course, will depend on who is the next Earl of Moretaine."

Katy scarcely heard her. *Marriage, a new position* . . . but she had a third choice. She had a grandmother, an uncle . . . *if* she could convince them she was Lucinda Challenor and not that—that *imposter* who was undoubtedly making sheep's eyes at Damon this very moment.

Mr. Trembley. Yes, she must write to Mr. Trembley. Katy shot to her feet. "If you will excuse me, my lady?"

The dowager's ravaged face held Katy poised in mid-flight, as it clearly revealed the anguish the countess's words had caused her. "I am sorry, so sorry, child," she cried. "I fear the ways of the world are not at all fair." A tear spilled over and fell onto Sir Walter Scott's poetry, which she had continued to read after Katy dashed off to investigate the noise in the hallway.

Katy's chin went up. Her green eyes sparkled, as suspiciously moist as the countess's own. "I will survive, my lady. I always have." With rigid dignity she left the parlor. Her feet made no noise as she climbed the well-carpeted stairs to her room.

Chapter Twenty-Three

"Colonel, how delightful!" cooed Lady Oxley, as if surprised at finding him in the countess's drawing room, even though the regularity of her appearances hard on Damon's every arrival at Castle Moretaine seemed to indicate she employed a lookout on the road from the south. At the very least, Damon grumbled to himself, the baroness must have a spy in the Moretaine household.

And if he had ever been tempted to admire Miss Hardcastle's slim and stately beauty, he had only to look at her mother to see what Eleanore would one day become. Lady Oxley, molded by long years of complaints, of looking down her nose at lesser mortals, and shamelessly toad-eating her betters, had become the pattern card for a hatchet-faced shrew. As tall as her daughter, the baroness was two or three stone heavier. Her suspiciously bright chestnut hair showed not a hint of gray, and her gown of burgundy puce seemed singularly inappropriate for a call at a house of mourning. To top this distasteful image, Lady Oxley's voice seemed even more loud and shrill each time they met.

The colonel executed a bow as stiff as his smile before turning to the two young ladies. "Miss Hardcastle, Miss Challenor." Each girl, seated side-by-side on a scroll-armed gold- and cream-striped settee, extended her gloved hand, Eleanore with cool aplomb, Lucinda with that slightly wicked smile in the back of her eyes that always intrigued him. The mysterious Miss Challenor, miraculously recovered into the bosom of her family. Damon had niggling suspicions about where the young lady had been and what she had been doing all the years she supposedly was missing. Her façade, perfectly turned out in a carriage dress of a green only slightly darker than her eyes, said one thing; the tilt of her shoulders, the liveliness of her eyes, something else entirely.

Yet her resemblance to Katy Snow was truly remarkable. Not in bone structure—never that. Now that he knew Lucinda better, he recognized they could not pass for sisters. But in build, hair color, eye color—a near perfect match. Of the two, however, Katy's features were the finer. The height of her forehead, the small but clearly aristocratic nose, the edge to her cheekbones, the well-drawn lips. And when mischief shone from Katy's eyes, innocence surrounded it like a halo. Miss Challenor's eyes, when not lowered to disguise her true nature, brimmed with worldly knowledge tinged with cynicism. Colonel Damon Farr had seen too many barques of frailty not to recognize one when put before him. And if Miss Challenor had just turned nineteen, he should be able to disregard his years as a soldier and claim to be not more than two and twenty again.

There was a puzzle here. For all that he told himself it was none of his business, Damon could not stop worrying the problem. Like a terrier with a rat, he could not let go. Somehow Katy was concerned in this. Ignore it, he could not.

"Your dear mama is removed to Bath, I hear," Lady Oxley boomed. After the colonel had agreed and expressed his hope that the change would help the dowager recover from her melancholy, the baroness plunged on to her true goal. "And will you be joining her there, colonel?"

"I am much occupied at Farr Park, my lady, but I shall, of course, make frequent visits to Brock Street to see how the ladies go on."

"The ladies?"

"My mother and her companion, Miss Snow."

Lucinda Challenor's trilling laugh rang over the tea cups.

"Ah, yes, the little mute peahen hiding in a dark corner. Surely she cannot be of much use to your mama—"

"Indeed," Miss Hardcastle echoed, "the poor child seemed dreadfully out of place, as if frightened into immobility by exposure to her betters."

"Companions are such a sorry lot," Lady Oxley declared. "Scarce worth the cost of feeding."

"Miss Snow has been with my mother for years," Damon responded stiffly, startled by the strength of his urge to defend his erstwhile secretary. "I believe the countess is quite pleased with her."

"Miss Snow," Drucilla stated, replacing her delicate Worcester tea cup in its saucer with a decided clink of fine porcelain, "is a little minx who changes her appearance to suit her circumstances. She is a nothing, a nobody my mama-in-law has been foolish enough to take to her bosom. There was an incident the last time she was at Moretaine—and you needn't look so surprised I should hear of it, brother. Mute she may be, but the girl is no better than she should be. Why dear Serena should persist in giving her house-room, I cannot imagine."

Lady Oxley suddenly looked thoughtful. "I believe Oxley may have mentioned her. You call her a girl. Is she a *young* woman then? I confess I did not notice her at all."

Damon, assuming his most inexpressive face, allowed the conversation to surge, unheeded, around him. *Katy's fear of the Hardcastles. Lord Oxley staring at Katy at the reception after Ashby's funeral. The striking resemblance to Lucinda Challenor.*

Or Lucinda's striking resemblance to Katy . . .

It was quite possible the answer to the mystery of Katy Snow lay right here in this room. Yet he was too much the soldier not to sense danger. That day at the tea party—and again after Ashby's funeral—Katy had not simply feared recognition. She had been terrified of the Hardcastles themselves. Of Baron and Baroness Oxley, whose noble rank should have placed them above suspicion.

Was this, then, the home Katy had fled?

Nonsense! If Wellington had been so fanciful, they'd all still be camped outside Lisbon. Or driven into the sea, as they'd been at Corunna. With Napoleon preening at the head of troops marching past Piccadilly Circus to Carlton House.

Yet, despite everything, he could not betray Katy by mentioning her mysterious origins. Not his Katy. He had already considered stopping again in Bath on his way back to Farr Park, just to make certain the ladies were comfortable. Had the pianoforte arrived? Mehitabel and the groom?

Fool that he was, he was being shamefully indulgent. His mother was like to comb his hair with a joint stool. The chit was definitely a menace. He should breathe a sigh of relief that she was out of the house and out from under his nose. So why was he so pleased over an excuse to return to Bath, to question Katy more closely about the Hardcastles?

He knew damned well why. He was besotted. His mother's needs had come in a close second to his desperation to be rid of Katy Snow so he could get some work done. It was nothing but lust, instigated solely by propinquity. That was all. He would recover. Undoubtedly, the blasted minx was already eyeing every gentleman in the Pump Room, looking for a mate.

And what about Palmer and the doctor? There were candidates for her hand close to home as well. All he had to do was offer a modest dowry. . . .

Damned if he would!

"I beg your pardon!" Disconcerted, Damon realized Miss Challenor had asked him a question and was now looking up at him from limpid blue eyes that still managed to remind him of his last visit to a brothel.

Lucinda Challenor waggled a finger at him and repeated her question. Damon gathered his wandering wits, though reserving a deep well of doubt, and replied with the smoothness of a gentleman to the manner born. Beneath the surface, however, he determined to cut short his stay at Castle Moretaine. He would return to Bath as soon as possible. Unfortunately, everything from a way to avoid spring floods to fixing leaky roofs and making plans for spring planting must be dealt with before he was free to leave. Silently, the colonel indulged in a succinct oath that had no place in a countess's drawing room.

The third week of February was not, perhaps, the best time to go for a long walk on the precipitous streets of Bath, but it had not taken Katy long to discover she was, at heart, a country girl. Each morning she accompanied the countess to the Pump Room, dutifully fetching a glass of the sulphurous water from the hand of the liveried footman attending the fountain. Each morning she sat and attempted to look interested as the dowager chatted with friends or joined the parade of elderly men and women circling the elegant Palladian room with its tall arched windows and gracefully curved alcove with musicians' dais and gallery above. For the first few days, Katy had found it colorful and exciting, a far cry from their quiet life at Farr Park. The seamed faces, gouty feet, quavering voices, and shaking hands had excited her sympathies, even as she had been fascinated by the colorful, if unfashionable, display of clothing that did not acknowledge the advent of the nineteenth century. But now, after nearly three weeks, there was only one word for the Pump Room and its parade of elderly and infirm. *Stultifying.*

Indeed, as far as she could tell, this dire situation was true of the entire city. Except for a smattering of servants, a few clerks in the shops, and a rare glimpse of a smart dandy driving by in a curricle, she had not seen a single soul less than a quarter century her senior. Even the companions who attended the array of invalids were at least twice her age. Katy escaped one afternoon, charging down the hill past Queen Square, past the old city wall all the way to the Avon, just downstream from Pulteney Bridge, where she leaned over the rail above the river, enjoying the river's gentle ripple over the three cascades of the weir and the elegant Palladian lines of the bridge itself. But when she finally strolled onto the bridge, she was amazed to discover it was impossible to tell she was not simply walking down a street, for Pulteney Bridge was lined with shops on both sides, with not so much as a shimmer of the river to be seen.

Intent on exploration, Katy passed the shops by. Perhaps on the way back . . .

And then she was traversing fashionable Laura Place and, soon, Sydney Gardens lay before her. A pause to find a coin in her reticule, and then her feet were nearly flying down the broad gravel path. Past empty tennis courts and a bowling field, past the labyrinth, whose tall, shadow-filled hedges had no appeal on such a brisk day—and, besides, who wished to be lost, all alone, in a maze? But sight of the narrowboat traffic on the canal was too much of a temptation. In spite of the cold, Katy stood for a while, watching the needle-thin boats pulled by plodding horses, delivering essential goods to the heart of the city. Ah, yes, this alone was worth the walk. This was real life, not the sheltered paradise of Farr Park, the arrogant pleasures of the London *ton,* or the doddering ancients of the Pump Room.

Astonishing! Was this her grandfather, the wool merchant, talking? Was her tradesmen's blood so hale and hearty that it manifested itself despite all her efforts to be a lady? Katy grinned, and waved to a passing boatman. She was forever destined to *see* people, she feared. She could not look *through* the less-than-noble, as was the habit of the beau monde. When she looked at Farr Park's parlor maid, she saw Clover Stiles. When she looked at the footman, she saw Jesse Wiggs. She saw Alice Archer, Millicent Tyner, Humphrey Mapes, and Betty Huggins. She saw people, not servants.

It was a curse. She would never make a proper mistress for Farr Park. And, of course, a lifetime as the next Countess of Moretaine was quite out of the question—even though her Grandfather Challenor had been a bishop and son of a duke. It was all very lowering. She was Katy Snow, who held her head high so she could not see her feet of clay.

Katy lifted her gaze from the traffic on the canal and took a good look around her. Gray clouds were roiling to the west. Not only was the winter afternoon turning to early dusk, but it seemed a storm might be threatening. She was a long way from

Brock Street! And the return journey, all but Pulteney Street, was an uphill climb.

Katy settled her bonnet more firmly on her head, stuffed her hands as far into her red fox muff as they would go. If only her feet were encased in fur as well. The chill from the gravel path had seeped through her sturdy half boots until her ankles seemed frozen in place, reluctant to move.

She had, of course, brought it on herself. No one had made her walk so far on such a cold day. Wielding a figurative whip over her reluctant body, Katy set a brisk pace back toward the gate. Pulteney Street stretched out before her, surely twice as long as it had been earlier in the day. As she approached the bridge at last, the sky grew darker, the temperature plunged. She could almost smell snow in the air. The enticing items in the shops along the bridge would have to wait.

Ahead of her were several relatively unchallenging blocks to Gay Street and then the long icy climb to the Circus and Brock Street. The first snowflake fell, displaying its crystalline pattern on her forest green pelisse before melting into the heavy wool.

Snow. She had indeed brought this imbroglio on herself.

Snow. So like the huge flakes that had fallen the night she arrived at Farr Park.

Katy Snow. The girl the cat dragged in.

Katy took a deep breath, firmed her lips, straightened her shoulders, and set out for Gay Street. But as she walked resolutely past what was left of the old Bath wall, she caught a glimpse of shoppers still thronging Milsom Street. Surely Milsom was as short as the other . . . and not quite so lonely. Nor, perhaps, so steep. And with less ice underfoot, as the throng of shoppers tromped it into shards that soon melted. Head down against the increasing snowflakes, now great dollops of stinging wet, Katy started up the slope of Milsom Street.

Chairmen, too, were hunching their shoulders against the storm, hurrying home with their patrons snug inside before the snow began to stick to the cobblestones. Wheels rattled and hoofs clomped, as the few who kept carriages on Bath's steep streets scurried home as well. Katy narrowly avoided slipping on the slick walkway as she backed away from a lamplighter who suddenly stopped in front of her, his long pole swinging high to light a lantern. Muttering one of the colonel's more meaty epithets, she hurried on. It was still a long way to Brock Street.

"Katy, Katy Snow! Is that you, girl?"

Katy grabbed for her bonnet as a gust of wind threatened to send it tumbling back down toward the river. Peering through the lacy curtain of fat wet crystals, she saw the outlines of a curricle and four great horses stamping and snorting their disgust over being brought to a sudden halt when visions of a nice warm stable must have been dancing through their heads. *Damon!* It had to be Damon. Only a through traveler would be driving four horses in the heart of Bath. And Damon, she knew, preferred to drive himself on his frequent trips between Farr Park and Castle Moretaine.

Crossing the broad expanse of Milsom Street with her vision obscured by snow and the broad sides of her bonnet was perhaps not the wisest thing she had ever done, but Katy dashed forward with enthusiasm, dodging sedan chairs, carriages, and pedestrians with all the alacrity of a steeplechase. She pulled up, gasping, at the side of Damon's sporting vehicle, grinning up at him with pure joy. A moment to catch her breath before she could leap up beside him.

"Of all the lame-brained, totty-headed, idiotish nonsense," the colonel roared. "What in the name of God and country are you doing out in this weather? And all alone. Are you mad, woman?"

Her toes were numb, lips blue, her nose bright red. Katy didn't need a mirror to tell her it was so. Her clothing was white with a dusting of snow, her nose was going to start to drip at any moment, and he wanted to read her a scold! She gripped the side of the curricle, willed her frozen foot to rise to the narrow little strip of metal that served as a boost. Damon was alone and could not leave his horses, of course . . . but, blast it all, that small foothold was so much higher than it had ever seemed before. The angle of the hill? Or was it just that she was cold and tired, and filled with fury?

Her foot found the metal bar. Gritting her teeth, Katy dragged herself up . . . and up. A strong hand reached out, hauling her firmly and safely onto the seat. Was that an echoing sigh of relief she heard from her employer?

"What are you doing here?" Katy demanded as soon as she'd caught her breath. Her conscience niggled. This was not at all the gracious thank-you she should have been extending.

"I arrived from Moretaine to discover you gone out for a walk some hours ago. The entire household was up in the boughs. Mama had already sent the servants to every nearby park, the Pump Room, even as far as the Marine Parade. She was quite beside herself. And Clover was certain you'd been snatched up by an Abbess."

"Oh, dear. I never thought—"

"You never do," Damon snapped. "You are the most outrageous child."

"I am nineteen."

"Really?" Sarcasm dripped, even as Colonel Farr neatly turned his horses in the middle of Milsom Street, bringing all other traffic to an abrupt halt. With a nod of satisfaction, he urged the perfectly matched animals back up the hill.

The horses labored. Lady Silence, seething, lived up to her name as they reached the end of Milsom, turned left onto George, then right onto Gay Street, leading them straight up to the graceful curve of the Circus and finally into the narrow confines of Brock Street.

"Change your clothes, then meet me in the bookroom," Damon ordered curtly as he pulled up in front of the burgundy red door. "I wish to speak with you."

"I do not need your scold," Katy told him as she pried her nearly frozen self off the seat and began to edge over the side.

"No scold. I daresay you have suffered enough for your folly. I wish to discuss another matter entirely."

Now there he had her. Only slipping on the ice that lurked beneath the snow and breaking her neck could keep her from the appointed meeting in the room with a meager selection of books that passed for a library. Katy tossed a brief nod of assent and slid down, ostensibly ignoring the colonel's admonition to be careful, even as she made certain her boots had a good grip on the cobbles. Light suddenly pierced the gloom. Jesse Wiggs rushed out, offering a sturdy arm. *Home.* Whatever Damon had to say, surely it could not take away this sense of belonging. No matter what the countess said, this was her family. These were her people.

Katy turned to say thank-you to Damon, but he was already trotting off, preparing for the turn into the narrow side street that led to the stables. She shook off as much snow as she could onto the tiled foyer floor, then hurried up the stairs to change.

Chapter Twenty-Four

"'Tis the sharp edge of his tongue you'll be getting, my girl," Clover Stiles declared as she fastened the buttons on one of Katy's most demure gowns. A silver gray of softly woven wool, it featured long sleeves and a high neck and gave off the aura of the cloister. A silent order of nuns, of course. Katy's lips twitched into a half smile. *Ah well.* Succumbing to vanity, she wrapped a bright paisley shawl about her shoulders, then examined herself in the pier glass. Damp curls escaped the ruthless confines of the conservative coiffeur Clover had fashioned. An adequate compromise, Katy conceded. One that fit her peculiar status in the household and echoed the confusion in her heart.

Katy turned to Clover, who was regarding her with considerable anxiety. "He has already called me lame-brained, totty-headed, and idiotish. He says he wishes to speak with me about something else entirely."

"Oh." Unaccountably, Clover appeared stricken.

"Clover . . . Clover, what is it? Do you know something I do not?"

Katy's old friend stared at the carpet, shifted her feet, shook her head. "Ah, no, miss. It was just an idea I had . . ."

"Well, out with it."

Clover, who never blushed, turned bright pink. "I—I was wondering if Mr. Palmer had made an offer."

Oh, dear. "And it matters to you?" Katy inquired gently, while struggling to reverse her perspective.

Clover toed the carpet, offered a reluctant nod. After several moments of awkward silence, she drew a gasping breath and plunged into speech. "I know he's had an eye on you forever, miss, and it'd be a good match for a girl who had no family and couldn't talk, but now . . . now we know about you . . . well, truth to tell, I thought you was above his touch, and I've . . . we've . . ." Clover hung her head and faltered to a halt.

"You have an eye in that direction yourself," Katy finished.

"Yes, miss," her old friend whispered.

Katy wondered if it were possible to start this day over, to wave a wizard's wand and have dawn repeat itself. What to say? And how to say it? It was, after all, no more foolish for Clover to long for Elijah Palmer than for Katy to dream of Damon Farr.

Useless, perhaps—in both cases. But perfectly understandable.

"As much as I have always admired Mr. Palmer," Katy said, taking great care not to betray Elijah Palmer's offer, "he would not do for me. He is too good a man to have a wife whose heart is given elsewhere."

"Ah, Katy, I'm that sorry," Clover breathed, instantly recognizing her friend's dilemma. "The world is surely a cruel place."

Ignoring the pain in her heart, Katy asked, with an attempt at a smile, "And what of your plans to be a fine dresser in London?"

"The heart is a wondrous organ, they say—with a will of its own." Clover pursed her lips in self-mockery, then enveloped Katy in a hug. "Go now and see what his nibs be wanting. Probably naught compared with what we've been conjuring. Put on your brave face now and be off. We'll do, you and me. Like the colonel himself, we're survivors."

Damon was waiting for her, warming himself before a roaring fire which occasionally hissed as snowflakes found their way down the chimney, only to be vaporized into oblivion. Like her own, his dark hair was wet, glistening in the leaping firelight.

Harsh-faced he might be, but Damon Farr took her breath away. To Katy he was still the hero, the most handsome and desirable man on earth. And she was confined with him in a room about the size of his mahogany desk at Farr Park. The warmth that surged through her was not from the fireplace.

He waved her to a chair comfortably upholstered in floral tapestry and seated himself opposite her. As much as she wanted to look him straight in the eye, Katy feared of what he might see in her own. At the moment her emotions were far too raw for scrutiny.

Katy accepted an etched glass mug of hot spiced wine. She sipped, feeling the hot brew all the way down. Damon could not be going to ring a peel over her head—she would not believe it. The moment hovered—intimate, perfect, and infinitely precious. Dazzled by his presence, Katy fought her sluggish mind. There was something essential she had forgotten . . .

"I must thank you for the pianoforte and for Mehitabel. Especially when I know you cannot think me deserving of such generosity."

"You are mistaken," the colonel responded cooly. "Your misguided actions do not preclude my being aware of your service to my mother . . . and to me. A musical instrument and access to a horse are small recompense for your many years of service."

So that was it! She was being paid off. Like a mistress receiving a gift of jewels when her usefulness had come to an end. "I see," Katy murmured. "Your mama has already warned me that I am not expected to return to Farr Park."

"Indeed." It was the colonel's turn to look away. From what she could see, the frown he turned on the fire was inexplicably fierce.

"I am to find another position . . . or to marry."

The colonel drained his wine, poured another glass. He seemed to have forgotten her presence.

"Cat got your tongue?" Katy teased, taking shocking advantage of the intimacy established by the many hours they had spent alone in the bookroom at Farr Park.

The colonel's head came up. His wine mug clinked as it hit the brass inlay of one of the room's quartetto tables. "What are the Hardcastles to you?" he hurled at her like a shot. "No more pretenses, I beg you. I fear you may need my help, and I cannot give it if I remain in ignorance. Now is the time to tell all." Damon leaned forward, capturing her gaze with his. "You will note I do not call you by name," he enunciated not more than eighteen inches from her face, "as we all know it is not your own. *Now,* girl. No more roundaboutation. I will have the whole story."

Katy's mug tilted, ruby red drops splashing onto the silver of her skirt. Damon took the glass from her and set it beside his own. Wordlessly, he offered his handkerchief. When she had mopped up the spill as best she could, Katy kept the handkerchief, clutching it in both hands in her lap. "I cannot," she whispered. "You would have to send me back."

"And if I swear to you I would never send you back . . . ?"

"Legally, you would have no choice."

"I would have the choice of whether or not I ever revealed what you say to me now."

Of course he had that choice. She had always known it, but she had never been able to trust anyone, not even Damon, with such an all-encompassing decision for her life.

The smell of roasting meat drifted in to mix with the smell of woodsmoke and the damp chill of a snowy night. "Come, child," Damon urged softly. "If you do not speak up now, I shall have to order dinner put back."

The implied threat was clear. He *would* know before they left his room.

"There was once a child," Katy said at last, "born of good family, but her parents dr—died when she was a baby. She was raised by her grandfather, younger son of a noble house. He was unusually well educated, a true scholar, and the girl was given the education of a boy. She was even encouraged to think for herself, to express her opinions. In many ways it was an idyllic life—and, like most idylls—over far too soon. Shortly before her twelfth birthday, the grandfather died, and she was sent to live with her father's cousin, a woman who was considered to have married well and who had a daughter of nearly the same age. The grandfather's family was pleased. The solicitors were pleased, the trustees were pleased. All agreed the solution was ideal." Katy's voice trailed off. She looked pointedly at her wine, sitting at the colonel's elbow.

Grimly, he handed it to her. "But the situation was not ideal," he said.

Katy shook her head, took a gulp of her wine, still warm, thank goodness, for she had turned to ice. "No . . . it was not."

"Tell me."

"I—the girl was everything the lady of the house did not want in a child. She was shockingly well educated, a full-blown bluestocking. She expressed her opinions freely. She even dared object when told not to speak unless spoken to. She was told in no uncertain terms not to correct her governess, even if she said Timbuktu was in China. She was not to spend her days reading nor was she to ride her horse above a ladylike trot. She was not to hobnob with the servants. She was, in short, a *trial.* She betrayed the vulgar traits of her grandfather, the wo—the tradesman, as well as the bookish and misguided traits of her other grandfather . . ."

"And?" Damon inquired softly.

"The girl's relatives, a lord and his lady, were . . . tall. They towered over her. They *boomed* at her. They punished her."

"How did they punish her?"

Katy held her glass mug in both hands, searching for warmth. "At first . . . they simply shouted. To a child who had never heard a harsh word, they were very . . . intimidating. Then they began to shake me. They were both so large. After that, it was a willow branch or a riding crop. My hands, my arms, my . . . derrière"—Katy was too lost in her story to blush or notice she was no longer speaking theoretically. "And, finally, my bare back. There was no one to care. Eleanore, in fact, seemed to gloat each time. Perhaps because my beatings spared her what she herself may have endured. I never knew. The servants, of course, had no choice but to look the other way." Katy trailed to a halt, her gaze fixed on the draperies shutting out the snowy night.

"There is more, is there not?"

Katy proffered an infinitesimal nod. "I did not recognize the look then, but I know it now. I only knew that when he looked at me, I was frightened." Grim-faced, Damon nodded. "I went to the vicar, and he called me a spoiled ungrateful wretch to make up such lies about family connections who had been kind enough to provide me with a home. So I made my plans carefully—fortunately, my grandfather had been a man of the world as well as a man of the cloth, and he'd taught me well. I'd been wise enough to hide my hoard of coins, and one day I simply walked to the village, boarded a stagecoach, and kept on going."

"Until you came to Farr Park."

Katy nodded. "That was several weeks later, after I had learned that opening my mouth only brought great trouble and sent me flying back onto the road."

"And you actually thought I would send you back to that?"

So softly spoken, yet clearly he was angry. Very angry. "You were far away," she reminded him. "And I feared your mother could not stand against the baron and his wife. Legally, I am theirs to do with as they will."

Slowly, he nodded, his mind already leaping ahead. "And by the time I returned, you had dug a hole so deep, there was no way out."

"Yes," she admitted on the whisper of a sigh.

"I think," Damon said, his mind moving forward with military determination, "it might be awkward for Oxley and his wife to discover you at the moment. Is that not so?"

"The situation is, indeed, very strange," Katy admitted, recognizing at last the futility of continuing any portion of her long deception. "A twelve-year-old child has no access to proof of her birth. There is no way I can say, 'I am Lucinda Challenor, and she is not. My Challenor grandparents are gone, and my mother's family has not set eyes on me since I was a baby. So, truly, I am nothing but Katy Snow. The waif the cat dragged in."

"On a night much like this," Damon mused.

"Yes." Katy's lips curled at the edges. "Though I doubt you were as sober, for you still appeared foxed the next day when I first saw you."

Oh, yes. What a stupid young cub he had been. But not so uncaring he had had a homeless waif thrown back out into the cold.

"Dinner is served, Colonel, Miss Katy." Jesse Wiggs stood stiffly in the doorway. Katy, head whirling between gratitude for the interruption and a wish that these intimate moments with Damon would never end, allowed the colonel to draw her to her feet and lead her toward the dining room.

What had she done? Her life was in his hands.

And it felt good. So wonderfully right.

Katy sat, toying with her food until Lady Moretaine declared she must be sickening for something. And no wonder, after her ill-conceived walk to the far side of town. Katy allowed herself to be sent from the table, fed a hot posset sent up from the kitchen, and be tucked up under heavy quilts after liberal use of the warming pan. She wound her arms around her pillow and thought of her hero. She smiled . . . and forgot to be afraid. She dreamed the secret fantasies of her innermost being.

And woke to find Damon gone. Off at first light to Farr Park, saying—according to Jesse—that a mere dusting of snow would not keep him from home.

Home. Home was where the heart was, was it not? But Damon was at Farr Park, and she was in Bath. Katy sighed.

At least he had not gone straight to Oxley Hall.

But what would Damon do tomorrow? Next week? Next month?

Katy looked out on a world sparkling with fresh white snow and felt only dread in her heart.

Chapter Twenty-Five

Marriage was the only possible solution.

After a sleepless night of examining Katy's problem from every possible angle, Damon had had his horses put to, driving out of Bath as if the four horsemen of the Apocalypse nipped at his heels. The brave soldier, fleeing the field. He had tried to pen a note of reassurance to Katy before he left, but each combination of words that chased through his mind seemed as inadequate as the blob of ink that dripped from his quill, leaving a mark on the pristine page as ugly as Katy's situation.

All will be well . . . I will not reveal your secret . . . I am master of Farr Park, not my mother . . . you will always have shelter there . . . You are my Lady Silence. We will never be parted.

Foolish fantasy. They could, and they would.

So Damon had pulled on his gloves, clapped his beaver to his head, grabbed his whip from the waiting groom, and bowled out of town as swiftly as if it were a glorious spring day. And now, two weeks later, he sat in the chaos of the bookroom that had been his personal haven from a world of war and admitted that nothing was ever going to be the same again. His life was as higgledy-piggledy as his stacks and stacks of research books. It took him hours to find a needed reference. And he could not find himself at all.

Where was the daring soldier? The shining knight to defend

a fair maiden? Was Katy Snow not entitled to a dragon-killer when she needed one?

But she was not threatened. Even if Oxley suspected Katy's identity, a second Lucinda Challenor was the last thing the baron wanted. Surely.

Yet Katy—if her story were true, and every instinct shouted that it was—could be a decided inconvenience to whatever rig Oxley was running.

Money—it had to be about money. Damon itched to investigate, but feared that questions could stir the dragon into action, precipitating Katy into exactly the danger she must avoid. So here he sat, staring at four walls, when he longed to engage the enemy, piercing the dragon's heart with one great swing of his cavalry saber.

Marriage would do that rather effectively. No muss, no fuss, no blood or nasty magistrates. But without the consent of her guardian it would have to be Gretna Green. And he could not have that stigma hanging over his Katy, not with all the doubts about her parentage. She would be an outcast from the *ton* for life. His gallant rescue all for naught.

But . . . could anything that placed Katy by his side for the rest of his life be so bad?

Devil take it! He not only lusted after her, he *loved* her. He was rattling around Farr Park like a lost sheep in a deep pit. Utterly miserable in the privacy of his own carefully crafted hell. He not only had to have her in his bed, he had to have her in his life. Each and every day. He wanted to watch her bloom into motherhood. He wanted to watch their children grow. Whoever Katy was—however suitable, or unsuitable, a bride she might be—she was his.

And at the moment she needed protection. He must go to Bath at once—

"Colonel," Mapes announced, "there is a Mr. Trembley to see you. The solicitor," he added in response to his employer's blank expression.

Damon's skin prickled, his military instincts springing to the fore, wiping away the bittersweet vagaries of a lover's confusion. "Show him in, Mapes." The colonel stood to greet his unexpected guest. Somehow he knew this would be no ordinary conversation.

Katy stared at the letter Serena Moretaine was holding out to her, nearly snatching her hand back, for she recognized that atrocious scrawl. How could she not? Now, after three whole weeks of agony, of living on tenterhooks each and every day, the abominable beast had at last written to her. She could kill him, absolutely kill him!

> Miss Snow,
>
> I wish to inform you that steps are being taken to resolve the matter we discussed when last I saw you. Do not be anxious. I will elaborate on my next visit to Brock Street.
>
> Respectfully,
> Farr

Respectfully, Farr! The man was mad. Not that he knew she loved him to distraction, but to send such a letter to someone he knew so well. Odious! He could go straight to the devil for all she cared. That was the problem, of course. She cared most dreadfully. So instead of ripping the missive to shreds, Katy carefully folded it and tucked it next to her heart.

March was rapidly approaching April, and even the not-so-young residents of Bath were moving about with greater enthusiasm. The walled garden behind their house was coming back to life. White primula, golden narcissus, anemones, violets, even the exquisite bloom of a pink camellia, while a forsythia lit one whole corner with a waterfall of yellow sprays. Nearly every morning Katy rode Mehitabel on the downs above the city, always properly attended by the groom sent from Farr Park, whose presence she did not protest. She still took long walks—sometimes as far as the Marine Parade along the river; more frequently, slipping out the garden's rear door to explore the vast green below the Royal Crescent and Brock Street. But she had not returned to Sydney Gardens, which would forever be associated in her mind with Damon. Even shopping on Milsom Street with the countess by her side took on an air of sad nostalgia for dark clouds and drifting snowflakes.

In mid-March, at the end of six months of mourning, Lady Serena Moretaine had allowed herself the pleasures of tea and an occasional round of whist or loo at the Upper Assembly Rooms. While the dowager countess was occupied with friends her own age, Katy frequently climbed the stairs to the musicians' gallery, where, hidden at the back behind the cello, she listened to the lively music and watched the dancers swing down the lines or swirl about the room to the *one*-two-three of the waltz, the ladies' skirts flying as if in a brisk wind. It was glorious.

Oh, to be able to do just that. To dance . . . dance with Damon.

Dance with the devil, more like!

She could not have him. Even as Lucinda Challenor, she could not have him, particularly if Drucilla should be delivered of a girl. Katy was ever conscious she should be brave and do as the countess wished—make a serious search for a husband . . . or a new employer . . .

The thought of either made her ill.

Katy sank down on an extra musician's chair, with its classic simplicity of red velvet upholstery and softly curved gilded wood. She could no longer ignore the niggling bit of hope that kept her from doing as her beloved countess wished. If Drucilla's child were a boy . . . if Damon were not the next Earl of Moretaine . . .

Nonsense! No amount of fantasizing would put Damon Farr within her reach.

Nonetheless, she would wait. The countess would be forced to ask Jesse Wiggs to thrust Katy Snow out the door, bag and baggage. And *that,* Katy thought grimly, she would believe when she saw it.

* * *

Then one morning in early April, when it seemed as if the sun had never shone so brightly nor the birds sung so sweetly, when pedestrians seemed to float over the cobbles, and even the chairmen seemed to have a new lease on life, Colonel Damon Farr returned to Brock Street. Katy, who was reading to the countess, heard his voice in the hall. She faltered, swallowed, bit her lip, and began again.

"No, no, child, it is quite all right," Serena Moretaine said. "It has been far too long since he paid us a visit. You may tell my son I wish to see him immediately, even in all his dirt."

In the flurry of the colonel greeting his mother, Katy simply stood back and stared. Damon looked . . . good. Much better. As if the cares of the world had lifted from his shoulders since she had last seen him. She should be pleased, but indications that he thrived without her were not . . . were not . . . *Oh, devil take it!* She was everything she should not be. Selfish, self-centered, arrogant. Hopelessly in love.

"I am here for a longer visit than usual," Damon was saying as he bent over his mother's hand in old-fashioned courtesy. "I am in need of an infusion of city life to stir me out of my country ways."

In stodgy old *Bath*? But Katy's heart soared.

Then plunged to her toes. The Hardcastles would come. Of course they would.

And she would be afraid, every moment of every day.

To no one's surprise, it took only three days for Baron and Lady Oxley, Miss Eleanore Hardcastle, and Miss Lucinda Challenor to descend on Bath. Katy, happy as a grig, was circling the Pump Room, her arm tucked through the colonel's, when the Hardcastle family came sailing in, four pairs of eyes on the *qui vive* for the object of their interest. The baroness's gaze alighted on Lady Moretaine, and she charged across the room toward her, even though Eleanore, who had spotted the colonel and Katy not fifteen paces away, tugged at her sleeve, attempting to hold her mother back.

"Serena, my dear!" Lady Oxley gushed. "So delightful to

see you here. The waters have surely been a blessing, for you are looking splendid, quite splendid."

"Ah . . . thank you, Cornelia," Serena Moretaine murmured, looking up from the Bath ladies with whom she had been enjoying a comfortable coze. After introducing the newcomers to her friends, she added, "Are you passing through on your way to London?"

"Indeed, we are fixed here for some time," Lady Oxley replied. "Always wise to give young ladies a taste of society before taking them to London, do you not agree?"

Since Miss Hardcastle had already had one Season and Miss Challenor gave the appearance of being able to teach the *ton* a thing or two, Season or no, the countess clamped her teeth over the obvious reply. "A wise idea," she murmured, while frantically wondering what had happened to her son and her ever-resilient right arm, Katy Snow.

At that moment Damon was rushing Katy down a corridor, his goal a possible side or rear door out of the building housing the Pump Room. "Ah-hah!" Baron Oxley's boom of triumph echoed hollowly around them. "Escaping, Colonel? Can't say as I blame you. Frightening thing, women. Particularly when all three have set their caps at the same man."

Damon tried for humor. Raising an eyebrow and proffering a thin smile, he said, "Surely not Lady Oxley?"

"Hah! Worse than the gals, that woman. A better pointer than my best bitch. She'll snabble you for one of 'em before you can say Jack Robinson. You there," the baron barked at Katy, "what's your name, girl?"

Keeping her eyes on the polished wood floor, Katy bobbed a curtsey. "Katy Snow, my lord."

"Ain't you the one couldn't talk?"

"'Twas a miracle, my lord."

Damon squeezed her arm. Hard.

The baron harrumphed. "Look at me when you speak, girl!"

"Miss Snow is my mother's companion, Oxley," Damon intervened. "She expressed an interest in the Abbey's fan-vaulted ceiling, and I agreed to escort her there. A mission we must complete, so we can escort the countess home in time for nuncheon. If you are fixed in Bath for more than the day, I am sure we will have opportunity to converse at another time." The colonel bowed and started to turn away.

Lord Oxley's hand shot out, pulling up Katy's chin. His fingers bit into her flesh. "Enough!" Damon's tone was as quietly deadly as a bolt from a crossbow. Defiantly, Katy's green eyes stared up into the baron's ruddy scowling face. It was far too late for dissimulation. And then, oddly, his burly body seemed to deflate, like a balloon on a sudden descent from the sky. With a small sigh and a slight shake of his head, he turned back toward the Pump Room.

Dear God! Katy shivered.

"He knows," Damon acknowledged. "No doubt about it, he recognized you." He gripped Katy by both arms, scrutinizing her as intently as the baron had done. "He has lost, Katy. He knows it. We have only to put all our pieces in play, and we have him."

"He is a bully and a cheat," Katy replied tonelessly. "That does not mean he is stupid."

"His only way out is murder. Can you actually think he would stoop that far?"

Katy gave an infinitesimal shrug. People were murdered for sixty shillings . . . sixty *pence.* Why not for sixty thousand pounds?

Right there in a rear corridor of the Pump Room, with maids and footmen scurrying to and fro to the kitchens, Colonel Damon Farr took his secretary into his arms, holding her tight. "I told you this matter was being investigated," he murmured into her hair. "I promise on every oath an officer and a gentleman can give, that Oxley shall not have you back. Until I can get all the pieces of this match lined up, however, you will not leave the house without my escort. Is that clearly understood? And no equivocations, mind? Well . . . answer me! Do you understand your life may depend on doing as I say?"

Understand? She was positively basking in his protection. Removing her from her legal guardian was quite impossible, of course, but somehow she had never felt so protected since the moment her Grandfather Challenor died. It was quite, quite wonderful.

Even if Damon had not a legal leg to stand on.

If only he would continue to hold her like this . . . and never, ever let her go.

Chapter Twenty-Six

While Katy waited for the ax to fall, life in Brock Street ran at an agonizingly sedate pace. Mornings in the Pump Room, walks in the park, shopping, visits to the lending library, an evening in the Lower Rooms with a string quartet so somnolent that Katy was unable to keep her beasts at bay. While the music droned on, her head whirled with every misguided decision she had ever made, every disaster she had surely brought down upon herself, and visions of the appalling events that might occur if she were to reveal herself as the true Lucinda Challenor.

The warmth of Damon's embrace was not renewed, though Katy clung to the memory, hoping against every reality that it was an augury of things to come. The colonel did, however, accompany her on her morning rides. Though he said little beyond punctilious inquiries about her health, her plans for the day, or the vast improvement in the weather, somehow they recaptured much of the camaraderie that had frequently marked their days at Farr Park. Yet beneath this smooth façade Katy felt the tension. It was as if they were suspended in time, waiting . . . waiting for something momentous to happen. The birth at Castle Moretaine, expected within the month? Or was the colonel waiting on Baron Oxley? Waiting and watching . . . daring him to attempt to take Katy back.

Yet how could he? Lord Oxley already had a Lucinda Challenor. Which explained why Damon seldom let her out of his sight. And never outside the walls of Brock Street alone.

If only he would say something . . . tell her what was going on.

The colonel bowed and nodded to his mama's friends . . . he tolerated the predatory thrusts of the Hardcastle ladies with commendable graciousness—or so twittered Lady Moretaine's friends. The colonel did not, however, sample the waters. The countess's friends took a good long look at his erect carriage, broad shoulders, and decisive manner, and decreed that it was quite obvious Colonel Farr did not need the waters.

And then one perfect spring day everything changed. With the brilliance and unexpectedness of a lightning strike out of a clear blue sky, Katy Snow's world was turned upside down. Her first inkling that this day would be different was when she woke to unusual bustle in the house on Brock Street. "We are expecting guests for tea," Serena Moretaine informed her. "Wear your rose muslin with the lace inserts, child. And have Clover do your hair. I wish you to look your very best."

Katy blinked. "Yes, my lady." But when she questioned Damon, he would say nothing beyond the mild observation that he believed a rather large number of guests was expected. *Maddening man!* He and the countess were keeping something from her, she knew it. She was nineteen years old, no longer a child. They had no right to be so mysterious.

They had every right, of course. They were her employers.

Katy shook her head, withdrawing into herself. The arrogance of her childhood seemed to cling forever. Would she never learn that, to these people—for all their charity and condescension—she was nobody?

"Mama, you will please sit in your usual place at the tea table," Damon directed later that afternoon as the countess and Katy arrived in the drawing room. "And, Katy, since there is to be rather a large crowd for such a modest-sized drawing room, would you kindly sit on the tabouret by the pianoforte? There you will look quite at home and make more room for our guests."

She was not to have a chair, when the room was spilling

over with them, with at least six chairs from the dining room brought in to augment the fine upholstered furniture that customarily graced the Brock Street drawing room? *Goodness!* It appeared attendance at this tea party would rival the one at Castle Moretaine, but in one-tenth the space. Katy sat tall and straight on her backless bench, carefully adjusting her rose muslin skirts around her. She might be shunted off against the wall, but she would follow the countess's admonition to look her best. There had to be a reasonable explanation for all this.

"Lord and Lady Oxley," Jesse announced. "Miss Hardcastle, Miss Challenor."

Oh, no! The Hardcastles *here*? What had Damon done? For a moment, Katy swayed on her bench, then, gritting her teeth, she lifted her chin and stared into space as the four guests were seated. Out of the corner of her eye she saw the dowager pouring tea. When Damon brought her a cup, Katy's hands betrayed her, shaking so hard the colonel was forced to place the cup on a side table. With his back to the room to hide his gesture, he put his hand over hers. "Courage," he whispered. "All will be well."

She was in a room in close quarters with the Hardcastles and a female pretending to be herself. She might love the blasted man, but Katy was not reassured.

Oddly enough, as the guests drank tea, sampled delicate pastries, and chatted, the other chairs in the room remained empty. Where were the other guests?

Oh, yes, something was happening here that did not meet the eye. Katy sat with her hands in her lap, unable to swallow so much as a mouthful of the fragrant tea. Her throat was dry, but if she attempted to drink, she would undoubtedly commit the heinous crime of spilling tea into her saucer. So she sat and suffered. And waited.

Colonel Farr rose to his feet, waved his hand about the room at the empty chairs. "Undoubtedly, you are wondering about our other guests," he said in the mildest of tones. "And you are quite right. This is a very strange sort of gathering. Our other guests are currently enjoying tea in one of our rear parlors."

Baron Oxley set down his glass of Madeira with a decided thump.

"We are about to attend my own version of an assize," the colonel continued. "For this special private session I have brought together a fine collection of dei ex machina, for whose testimony I find myself organizer, moderator . . . and judge. Though I expect by the time we are finished here, no one will be in doubt about the truth."

He was going to expose her! Katy clutched the sides of the tabouret and hung on tight. She had never fainted in her life. She would not now.

The colonel moved the imposing petit-pointed armchair brought in from the head of the dining room table to a prominent position just to the left of the door from the corridor. "Wiggs," he declared, "you may bring in the first witness."

The only sound to be heard as a well-dressed man of middle years entered the room was a gasp from Katy Snow. The Hardcastles were expressionless. Evidently, the so-called witness was a stranger.

The colonel waved the gentleman to the prepared seat. "Will you please be good enough to state your name, your occupation, and why you are here," Damon said.

"I am Charles Farleigh, Rector of Pembridge-on-Steyne," said the gentleman in the rounded tones of a man accustomed to delivering sermons. "But at one time I was privileged to assist the Bishop of Hulme. And there I was acquainted with the bishop's granddaughter, Lucinda Challenor. A remarkable child, fully worthy of the information the bishop stuffed into her head. Though the purpose of Latin for a female, I admit I never could understand."

"Precocious, was she? Miss Challenor," the colonel purred, "perhaps you would care to translate *'Veni, vidi, vici,'* for us."

"Do not be absurd! I do not do tricks like some circus monkey." But the alleged Miss Challenor had turned decidedly pale.

"Katy . . . perhaps you would care to tell us."

The fiend! But had she not once been the obnoxious little

bluestocking who loved to demonstrate her knowledge. "I came, I saw, I conquered," Katy stated clearly.

"Indeed." The colonel nodded his approval. "Mr. Farleigh, I realize it has been some years since you saw Miss Challenor, but do you happen to see her here in this room?"

The rector turned a slow, indulgent smile toward Katy Snow. "I had thought it might be difficult after so long, but the young lady has changed only in becoming more of a beauty than she was as a child. There, sitting on the bench, that is Lucinda Challenor."

Not bothering to hide his smile of triumph, Damon thanked the rector and directed him to another chair.

Katy's eyes shone as a second acquaintance was shown in.

"Please state your name and why you are here."

"Martin Trembley, solicitor," said the man now seated in the witness chair. "During the course of an investigation requested by a client, I became aware of certain—ah—irregularities in regard to Miss Lucinda Challenor. Her long absence from the shelter of her family, her miraculous rediscovery, the seeming disappearance of the dowry left to Miss Challenor by her grandfather, the Bishop of Hulme."

"Was this a large sum of money, Mr. Trembley?"

"Large enough. The bishop willed some of his fortune to charity and to the church, but a dowry of twenty-five thousand pounds was reserved for Miss Challenor."

"And it is gone?"

There was a strangling sound from the upholstered chair occupied by Lord Oxley. He tore at his cravat, his face turning purple.

"I went to London and consulted with the bishop's primary solicitors," Mr. Trembley continued. "Not a sign that the money was ever held in a separate trust account for Miss Challenor. It simply . . . disappeared."

"Thank you." Damon waved the solicitor into one of the empty side chairs.

"Mrs. Matthias Alburton, Mr. John Alburton," Jesse Wiggs announced from the doorway.

Katy stared . . . but could not see them for the tears that rushed to her eyes. Her grandmother? Her uncle? *Oh, no, not possible. It could not be.*

The colonel stepped forward to draw up another chair, but Mr. Alburton waved him aside. Although a middle-aged man not much over medium height, he had the dignity and bearing of one accustomed to authority. Here in this bastion of the *ton,* he stood four-square beside his mother's chair, regarding the colonel with proud attention.

"Ma'am," said Damon, addressing the white-haired woman seated in the witness chair, "would you please tell us your relationship to Miss Lucinda Challenor?"

"She is my dear granddaughter, who was taken from me after only a few weeks in our care. I was heartbroken. First my daughter, then the baby." Emily Alburton faltered. Her son gripped her shoulder, and after a moment she continued. "We tried so hard to keep watch over her, to know all was well with her. When the bishop died, we thought to get her back at last . . . but she went to a Challenor, of course. To Lady Oxley. In spite of our disappointment, it seemed a just decision, for there was a girl her own age, but . . ."

This time, when Mrs. Alburton faltered, Jonathan Alburton took up the tale. "Lucinda had been gone from the Hardcastles for nearly a year before word got back to us. A child of her years, alone. I sent out an army of men, those who already worked for me, and professional investigators from London as well. Nothing. We never gave up hope, but I was forced to counsel my mother that we must expect the worst."

"I knew he was right . . . that we should never see the dear child again," Emily Alburton said, "but always I hoped. And then the miracle." She turned accusing eyes on each of the Hardcastles, finally resting them on the alleged Lucinda. "I was so beside myself with joy when we heard you had been found." Mrs. Alburton's face turned grim. "But when I met you, I saw nothing of my daughter in you. Nothing of my sisters, my son . . . or of his children. Once again, I was heartsick . . . and thoroughly confused."

"Fortunately," Jonathan Alburton said, "I am trustee for the sixty thousand pounds and have the right to withhold it until Lucinda's twenty-fifth birthday. Therefore, the inheritance is still intact, awaiting confirmation of my niece's identity."

"I do not suppose you have a portrait of Miss Challenor?" Damon inquired with bland innocence.

Jonathan Alburton held out an arm, and Jesse Wiggs presented him with a large painting, draped in blue velvet. "I fear not, Colonel, but I have a portrait of my sister Belinda when she was eighteen." He turned and looked directly at Katy. "I fear we spied on you yesterday in the Pump Room, my dear, so I know you will find this portrait of interest." He whipped aside the cloth.

Lady Oxley moaned, Eleanore shrieked.

"Knew it was too good to be true," said the alleged Miss Challenor with disgust. "Shoulda stayed with walk-ons at Drury Lane, I should."

"A nearly exact image of our Katy, do you not agree, Mama?" said the colonel, his eyes as full of mischievous triumph as a boy of ten.

"Enough, enough!" Oxley boomed. "Let us make an end to this farce. The chit's funds are but mixed with my own investments. The money's there. I shall make restitution, and you can scarce blame us for wishing to take advantage of old Alburton's bequest. Thought the girl was dead and gone, don't you know? Shame to let all that money go to waste."

"We are not yet done," declared the colonel over the baron's spate of excuses. "Our last witness, Wiggs, if you please."

The man of perhaps thirty years who walked through the door was of such obviously noble lineage, his clothing of the first stare, his arrogant stance second to none, that even the Hardcastle ladies, though overcome by humiliation, rose to their feet. As did Emily Alburton, shaking off her son's hand and rising from her chair. Katy, thoroughly awed, had been the first person on her feet. Her lips twitched, however, as she noted how thoroughly the newcomer was enjoying the moment, raising his quizzing glass for a leisurely inspection of each person in turn. His amber hair gleamed above a tawny eye grotesquely magnified by his glass. After this suitably dramatic pause, he dropped the glass, allowing it to swing slowly on its ribbon above the gray and silver brocade of his waistcoat.

Imperiously, he waved them all back into their chairs. He did not sit in the witness chair. "I am Montsale," he declared, standing tall. "Bourne Granville Hayden Challenor. His Grace, the Duke of Carewe, regrets he is in the gout and could not attend in person, but I trust I will be an adequate substitute."

Oh! Katy was not so far removed from the world that she did not know that the Marquess of Montsale—her cousin, the Marquess of Montsale—was Carewe's heir. He had come to Bath. *Because of her.*

"His Grace and I were uneasy with the alleged Miss Challenor," Montsale declared. "Quite frankly, it was not difficult for Colonel Farr to convince us we must take a look at his candidate for my cousin Lucinda." The golden god turned and bowed to Katy. "And, yes, cousin, I was lurking in the doorway of the Pump Room yesterday as well."

Impossible. The Marquess of Montsale could not possibly lurk. He would stand out in any crowd. He must have been peeking through a crack!

"I am here not only to confirm the family's belief in my cousin's identity, but to state that His Grace has arranged for transfer of her guardianship to himself." The marquess turned again to Katy, his voice remarkably gentle and reassuring for such a dynamic gentleman. "There is no need to fear, cousin. You will not be troubled by the Hardcastles ever again."

As mute as Lady Silence, Katy could only stare at her golden cousin, who—flanked by Damon and Jonathan Alburton—crossed the room and proceeded to deal with the Hardcastles. Their words flew over her head until a soft voice said, "My dear child, you cannot know how happy this makes me. Though you do not know me from Adam, I hope you will come to us for a lengthy visit before settling at Carewe Abbey. We discussed it, you see," Katy's grandmother continued, her faded blue eyes alight, "and since the duke is in the gout, it seemed a good time for you to become acquainted with the Alburton side of your family. Fortunately, the marquess and his father do not seem to be so high in the instep as the late bishop. So tomorrow you are to come to us. Can you be packed by noon, child? Dear Jonathan will send our coach for you."

Somehow Katy took her grandmother's delicate wrinkled hand in hers and said what she hoped were all the right things, but, truth to tell, for all the wonder of the moment—the result of a chain of events set off by herself the day she visited Mr. Trembley—her anger was spiraling upward, threatening to destroy this precious moment when she was taken back into the bosom of her family. When she discovered that, all along, there had been relatives willing to shelter her.

If only she had known.

If she had, she never would have met Damon.

The three warriors—Damon, her uncle, and her cousin—were still clustered in front of the Hardcastles, whose blustering voices had finally trailed into silence. Lady Moretaine, without a single sign that she recalled her companion's existence, was attending the byplay more avidly than any presentation at Drury Lane. Damon and his mother—the only family she had known since that blustery winter night when she was twelve—were sending her away. Would they even miss her?

Katy Snow, very prettily, once again thanked her grandmother for her kind invitation, assuring her she would be ready when the Alburton coach arrived on the morrow. She was even so daring as to kiss the elderly lady's cheek, leaving them both misty-eyed. And then she fled straight to her room, where she sat down hard on the edge of her high bed, clasped her hands beneath her chin—and quivered.

Time stood still—along with her mind. She should be in alt. Dancing on air. Instead, despite her genuine gratitude for Damon's astonishing manipulation of her life, she was devastated.

They wished to be rid of her.

Farr Park was her home. Yet without so much as a "by your leave," she was to be sent to live with strangers. Again.

Even though she was no longer a nobody from nowhere, Lady Moretaine and her son did not want her.

It could have been ten minutes or an hour when a pounding on her door pierced the skittering whirlwinds of her mind.

Katy ignored it.

The doorknob rattled. How fortunate she had locked it.

"Katy, Katy! Open this door at once!"

Damon!

"Katy . . . please. You ran off before I could speak with you."

The temptation to speak her mind was more than she could bear. Katy bounced off the bed, strode to the door, and turned the key with grim decisiveness. The colonel did not wait for her to open it, but burst through at the click of the lock. "Katy, I—"

"How dare you? How *dare* you?" she hissed. "At twelve years of age I made the most important decision of my life. It might have been a most uninformed decision, but it was all mine. I ran away and did what I had to do to survive. And managed very well, I thank you! And yet now—now that I am all of nineteen and a woman grown—you sneak behind my back, allow people to spy upon me without my knowledge. You turn my life topsy-turvy without so much as a *hint* of warning. You pack me off to perfect strangers, as if I were nothing more than a lost parcel. For shame, Colonel! I am not one of your troopers—"

"Katy!"

"No, no, it is my turn now. You have done quite enough." Arms akimbo, Katy stood nearly toe-to-toe with the colonel. Glaring. "Allow me to tell you that I am pleased to leave this house. I am pleased to go somewhere I am wanted. I am most wonderfully happy to have a grandmother, an uncle, cousins . . . even if one of them is as arrogant as he is handsome. And allow me to point out that he will outrank you, even if you should become Moretaine!" she added for good measure before being forced to pause to draw breath.

"May I speak now?"

Katy, huffing, nodded.

"I came here to ask you to marry me."

"Do not be absurd."

"Katy, I did this all for you. It was to be my special surprise." Katy's glare did not waver. "I have known for some time I could not live without you," Damon added.

"Now *that,*" said Katy Snow, "is truly most unfortunate. If you had shown me so much as an inkling of your affection—"

"You would have thought my intentions dishonorable. As I am sure you did on more than one occasion."

"As I am sure they were on more than one occasion."

"Cry peace, Katy." Damon held out his arms. "I want you for my wife."

Katy hugged her arms, suddenly aware of the chill of the room. "I need to find my heritage," she said at last. "And give my anger time to fade. I also need to take the time to decide if you will always ride roughshod over my life or whether you will love me as a man should love a woman. As a person of consequence in his life. Someone whose opinion he values—and for whom he will not rearrange her life without consultation."

"Touché," Damon murmured. "And how long will this contemplation take, my Lady Silence?"

Katy considered the matter with care. "Until after Drucilla's confinement," she announced. "If you are Moretaine, it is quite possible you will not care to marry the granddaughter of a wool merchant."

The colonel's lips twitched. "I daresay the Earl of Moretaine can bear to be connected to the Duke of Carewe and the Marquess of Montsale."

"Beast!"

"And just think what I could do with sixty thousand pounds," the colonel offered.

Katy launched herself at him, fists pounding on his chest, only to be caught up in an all-encompassing embrace. "Minx!" he chided softly, when he finally raised his lips from hers. "Come back to me, Katy, else I am lost, for I love you *à corps perdu.*"

"I should not say so," Katy confessed, biting her lower lip and peeping up at him with a decided sparkle in her green eyes, "but I have loved you since the moment I first saw you, staggering down the stairs of Farr Park."

And if Clover Stiles had not arrived at the moment to chivy Katy into dressing for dinner, everything Clover's active imagination had been conjuring while waiting in the corridor might well have come to pass.

Epilogue

When Drucilla, Countess of Moretaine, was delivered of a girl, it is said her shriek of rage could be heard all the way to Bath. The news was imparted to the former Katy Snow by a letter from the dowager countess. Her fingers shook as she opened it. Her grandmother Alburton, even her uncle and his wife, looked at her in concern as their dear Lucinda's face clearly expressed her dismay.

"It is a boy then?" Emily Alburton inquired.

"A girl."

"And you are not pleased?"

"I . . ." Lucinda smiled. Tightly. "Of course I am pleased. Colonel Farr will make a splendid earl.

"You do not *want* to be a countess?" asked Margaret, her sixteen-year-old cousin.

"The col—the earl and his mother may not think the match suitable."

"Nonsense," declared Jonathan Alburton in his customary hearty and decisive manner. "I daresay those are his wheels I hear upon the drive."

"Do not tease, Papa. That is unkind," chided the young Miss Alburton.

But the astute son of Matthias Alburton, the wool merchant, was not mistaken. The thud of four matched horses upon the drive was soon quite apparent to all. By the time the new Earl of Moretaine had pulled up his horses before the Alburton's gracious manor house, Katy was flying down the steps. The curricle's thin metal boost that had seemed so high in February flew beneath her feet as she launched herself into the air. "See," she breathed as Damon hugged her tight, "I am naught but a vulgar hoyden, just as you have always said. Are you sure, sure, sure?"

An accomplished whip, the Earl of Moretaine seemed to have no trouble juggling his reins and his darling waif, enabling him to deliver a most satisfactory kiss.

"Bring a special license, did you?" drawled Jonathan Alburton, who had joined them in the drive, along with all but the youngest members of the Alburton family. "Doesn't look as if you can wait for the banns to be called."

The colonel lifted his head long enough to say, "In my pocket," before returning to gaze at his beloved Lady Silence with all the besotted fervor of a man who has finally admitted the power of love. "I promise," he said, looking directly into her questioning green eyes, "I solemnly promise I will not forget you are my partner as well as my love. Will you have me, Katy? Now and forever?"

"Now and forever." Miss Lucinda Challenor demonstrated her willingness by shamelessly repeating their embrace as well as his words.

From a window, far above, a cheer rang out, as young Jeremy Alburton, age eight, expressed his approval. Cousin Lacy had nabbed an earl. *Hip, hip, hooray!*

About the Author

With ancestors from England, Wales, Scotland, Ireland, and France, **Blair Bancroft** feels right at home in nineteenth-century Britain. But it was only after a variety of other careers that she turned to writing about the Regency era. Blair has been a music teacher, professional singer, nonfiction editor, costume designer, and real estate agent, and she has still managed to travel extensively. The mother of three grown children, Blair lives in Florida. Her Web site is www.blairbancroft.com. She can be contacted at blairbancroft@aol.com.

"A LOVELY NEW VOICE IN THE GENRE...
A NAME FANS WILL WANT TO WATCH."
—*ROMANCE REVIEWS TODAY*

Blair Bancroft

The Lady and Cit

In order to properly own her beloved lands, Miss Aurelia Trevor needs a husband. Offering her hand to the infamous businessman Thomas Lanning promises him a seat in Parliament. But soon this marriage of convenience turns to one of love.

0-451-21432-3